FROM BLUE TO BLACK

JOEL LANE

FROM BLUE TO BLACK

Influx Press
London

Published by Influx Press
The Greenhouse
49 Green Lanes
London, N16 9BU
www.influxpress.com / @InfluxPress
All rights reserved.
© Joel Lane, 2000, 2022
Introduction copyright © Kerry Hadley-Pryce, 2022

This edition 2022.
Printed and bound in the UK by TJ Books.
First published in the UK in 2000 by Serpent's Tail.
Paperback ISBN: 9781914391033
Ebook ISBN: 9781914391040

Cover design: Vince Haig
Interior design: Vince Haig
Proofreader: Dan Coxon

For Kate Pearce –
never mind the Reds,
here's the blues

INTRODUCTION – KERRY HADLEY-PRYCE

Seven or eight years ago, I counted myself lucky to get hold
of a copy this novel. To read something like this for the first
time was – is – a visceral experience. Even then, my copy of
the novel was battered, with pages the colour of parchment,
or as if dipped in murky water, or affected by smoke. Now
it's even more battered, the tips of some pages folded over,
phrases underlined, annotations written in pencil here and
there and on the inside cover. I'm looking at that copy now
and thinking Nicholas Royle, Joel's friend and agent, would
not be impressed. But, you know, I think Joel would be fine
with it. I say this because it feels right that his writing should
be savoured, read slowly, teased out, studied. See, it's the use
of, shall we say, 'place' as a narrative element in this novel
that is so striking. I say 'place' with a wry smile, because
we're talking about Birmingham and the Black Country
here, the latter being somewhere many wrongly think of
as a suburb of the former. The confusion is not appreciated

by either. True, isn't it, that the likes of London and New York have tended to dominate much fiction? But though he was born in Exeter in 1963, most of Joel's life was spent in Birmingham, and for him, there was a West Midlands culture that was creative, inventive, and there was a folklore evoked by the railways and canals. Just as important to him, was a particular kind of peristaltic darkness about the region, which seeped into its music – the heavy metal sounds of Black Sabbath, then there's The Wonder Stuff, Ned's Atomic Dustbin and Pop Will East Itself, for instance – that echoes an industrial and solid, no-nonsenseness. You'll feel that sensation here in *From Blue to Black*. You might even think you're reading a novel about music. You might think that, but music's just part of the complex map of this novel where Joel's political discontent, great belief in the region, and his artistic (dark) visions meet to form a kind of Foucaultian heterotopia in which the focus is on the region's capability to transcend historical, cultural and moral acts.

True enough, as you'll see, the novel charts the aspirations of the members of a Birmingham rock band called Triangle, and the relationship between the protagonist, David, and the band's frontman, Karl. But this novel looks beyond that, with a particular psychogeographic underpinning, delving deeper into the darker 'noir' here at the truth and lies of life and relationships, and at the cost of things, politically and emotionally. The characters spend time walking – sometimes apparently aimlessly, sometimes not so much – through Digbeth and Erdington, Yardley and Kings Heath, but David's first glimpse of the Black Country is significant. He sees Smethwick through the window of a train and 'a high factory wall [that] had been sprayed with the jagged

SS logo and the message KEEP BRITAIN WHITE'. Then, 'At Stourbridge, the outer wall of the station was sprayed with ENOCH FOR PM'. It's this first sight of the Black Country landscape that creates the backdrop of unrest, and in itself is an overt political comment that sets you, reader, up for an unsteady experience. The 'dark visions' continue with characters David and Karl walking through Stourbridge town. Here, the mention of 'The sign CANAL STREET pointed to a narrow gap between two factory buildings' sees Karl transmute into a suspended state, in transition, between borders himself, looking into the past as if he has passed into another space within the place. And as Karl and David walk, a sense of transubstantiation takes place where the change in the backdrop operates as a change of substance and thinking by Karl. The narrative style here, of listing sensory descriptions moves the reader into that zone of heterotopia, opposing the ordinary with the extraordinary in a contradiction of sensations: 'One factory was open, the front rolled up to reveal a huge, gloomy interior with hanging electric lamps, grimy skylights, machines grinding and wheezing like decaying organs... "Nothing much has changed here," Karl said. "They try to build anything new, it falls apart. But the old shit remains. It's like a charm."'

The effect of contradiction, through the blend of fact (that is to say the existence of Canal Street in real life) and fiction continues as the two men walk, and the act of walking in that particular space within the place seems to initiate meditations, and reconstructed memories of Karl's experiences there.

Joel's fascination with a sense of 'edgeland', both in terms of characters who occupy the periphery of identities, and of untapped, transgressive landscapes, becomes clearer with the description of David and Karl's walking in the Black Country. They're repetitious descriptions of the industrial meeting the rural: '...the blackened factory landscape' alongside 'Overhanging trees... murky water... the whispering of the river across the strip of overgrown woodland.' But it's also the place where truth meets lies. This portrayal of place through an echolalic narrative that reflects and confirms the fusion of mental and physical space, together with factual topographical references to, for example, the canal, the scrap yard and the River Stour are supplemented by David's reaction to the psychological impact the place has on Karl. The darkness deepens even further through the simple sensory intensity of Karl's dialogue. He says, '"This place is strange, isn't it? Like a bit of wilderness. It's one of those points you'd use for reference when drawing a map – to set the contour lines or whatever."' And: '"This place is getting torn apart," he said. "Tower blocks, expressways, building over the past. I'm glad. I used to stand here and think nothing could ever change."' This repressed history of Karl's has been written over by him, though the readers – you – are yet to know the details. It forms a traumatic fascination with the dark side of his own experiences there, as well as the transtemporal link between him and David, and so to a connection with the you, the reader. Karl's nebulous sense of attachment and his resulting connection with the Black Country presents him as restlessly reimagining events, linking his psychical creative processes to the particular physical topography of 'wilderness' that is 'strange', forming a further link between him and that heavy metal music of the region. In fact, he says. '"That's why music is so vital to me. It's a way of being alone. Sending messages. Without that, we're all trapped in the dark. None of it means anything."'

Karl's dependence on music is, then, inextricably linked not just to the landscape of the Black Country, but to the things that happened to him there, forming a strange and unsettling psychological dependency. This essentially psychogeographic effect develops further because of the narrative description of Stourbridge as a bleak, ruined place with the potential to be dangerous. The flurry of intense description runs over seven pages in the novel, and results in a depiction of the Black Country – or specifically, Stourbridge, and more specifically, the canal and river there – as the embodiment of evil, a mix of misery and pain. The otherworldliness of the place, however, is really only revealed when the truth – or rather, what is given to be the truth – is told at the end of the novel.

The way in which space is conveyed in Joel's representation of Stourbridge is through the defining aspects of the contradictory or paradoxical combinations of life and death, love and loss, sanity and insanity, violence and desire, success and failure, and yes, truth and lies. A significant feature of the Black Country, in real life, is its refusal to be considered part of Birmingham – its refusal, actually, to be pinned down and precisely defined. Such contradictions form a vagueness that you might say Joel uses to show how characters, particularly Karl, battle in an effort to feed their creativity, and make sense of who they are or who they are reconstructing themselves to be. The experience of the Black Country, for Karl, is overwhelming. Vicariously, for David too.

I should say here – I should confess – that I am from that place in the West Midlands that Joel refers to in this novel: the Black Country. I should also say that I walk those streets, and that canal towpath every day, that I have a connection with the project involved in the renovation of the 'derelict house and the half-demolished workshop', that this morning, approaching from the riverside, the December 'air in front of me was webbed with fine cracks', and it struck me that what Joel Lane has done in this novel, possibly inadvertently, is to produce a strange love song to the Black Country with the darkest, most unsettling kind of music at its core.

I counted myself lucky to get hold of a copy of this novel and read it through for the first time years ago. Now, here it is, republished by Influx Press, and you're the lucky one.

Kerry Hadley-Pryce
Stourbridge
December, 2021

CHAPTER 1

feedback

Do the hours crawl
As you wait for the light?
Then call my name
In the long still night
— Gallon Drunk

It was the end of summer. A bloodshot moon hung above the tall houses in Salisbury Road, giving faint doubles to the shadows of trees. Across the road, the lights of a housing estate floated in empty air. I'd walked up to Moseley from the Bristol Road. A car backfired; a dog barked in response. Outside the off-licence on the Alcester Road, two drunks were being handled into a police van. One had blood all down the left side of his face like a birthmark. Up ahead, the external lamps of the Jug of Ale made its outline just visible.

Inside it was busy, but not full. The effect of brass chandeliers and varnished oak banisters clashed with the line of TV screens, all showing the same images, above the bar. 'Smells Like Teen Spirit' was playing on the jukebox. It was all you ever heard that summer. One of the walls was completely covered with little posters announcing past and future gigs in the upstairs room. And tonight's band, Triangle: three silhouetted faces in a black triangle like a halflit warning sign. The bar served Copperhead cider, which was good news. I took my pint upstairs, where the posters were older and the light thinner. They stamped my hand with a red symbol when I paid at the door.

The support band went by the name of Silent Majority. Four pallid youngsters in tank-tops, the kind you'd see providing atmosphere at any of the small city-centre venues. The vocalist's fringe was enough to get them signed to Creation Records. The melodic frame of each song was a keyboard figure, a pattern of light on the murky waves of guitar and percussion. The voice was in there somewhere, but either it was mixed too far down or the singer was waiting for his testicles to drop. He left the stage first, followed by the guitarist, leaving the keyboard player and the drummer to play out a solemn and vaguely unsettling coda. They didn't come back to watch Triangle play. Maybe they were shooting up in the toilets before riding their motorcycles out of town in search of further excitement. More likely, they had homework to do.

In the interval, I drank more red cider and reflected gloomily on the staleness of the provincial music scene. like those chain pubs that fabricated an Irish or Yankee or Somerset identity without ever deviating from the blueprint, new bands were judged purely by the ease with which they reminded you of something else. In every sense, karaoke was replacing live music. Australian cover bands were drawing bigger audiences in Britain than most real bands. What I loved about small-venue gigs was the sense of reality – of music being *made* rather than just performed. You accepted the flaws for the sake of those unexpected moments when it all came together. Imitation was distance: a screen, a code. It kept you on the outside. Why was that what people seemed to need?

By the time Triangle started playing I was fairly drunk. Predictably enough, there were three of them. The vocalist was a thin, dark-haired man with a faint Irish accent. He played guitar with a rawness that contrasted with the cold intensity of his voice. The bass player was as anonymous as all bass players. Each song ended with the drummer picking his way through the rubble of feedback. The singer's voice rose and fell nervously in the chaos, never quite breaking through. Several tracks used reverb to sound like the echoes of violence or applause. There was a song called 'Third Flight', about a fight in a tower block; and another about some kind of terrified fugue state – *The half-silvered window / That means I can't see you / The pane you watch me through / The pain you keep me in / The frozen point of view*. The crowd applauded uneasily. This was too strange for them.

Later in the set, the tracks became longer and more complete. A kind of love song had the singer staring into the darkness overhead: *There's a mask of silence in your face / It keeps me waiting in this place / Where the house is three bricks high / Between still and moving water / The grass is never dry*. The bass rose steadily behind the harsher chords of the lead guitar, finally engulfing it in a wave of close-knit sound. It was an effect borrowed from Joy Division's 'Dead Souls'; but here, there was something almost sexual about it. A sense of being taken over, not quite by force.

The set ended with 'The Answer', their only single, which I'd bought a few weeks earlier. On the Relent label. It was a slow, brooding track that never quite reached a focus on record. Live, its last verse went up in flames, burning into a jagged instrumental coda that owed more to atonality than volume. Karl played as if in a dream; he seemed calmer now, less on edge. That kind of finale always means more to the band than the audience. It ended suddenly, Triangle walking off with their guitars and sticks as though intending to play on in the next room. The applause was muted but lasting.

There was still time for a drink, though a lock-in was unlikely in a pub on the Alcester Road. The back of the room was clotted with smoke. It reminded me of the friend's bedsit where I'd lost my virginity to the sound of *Astral Weeks*. The audience was full of people I knew by sight, mostly from other gigs. There was a short girl with a halo of spiky black hair and eyeliner as heavy as dark glasses; she and her boyfriend, a stoop-shouldered mime artist with hair like rain, were in a thrash band I'd seen at least a year before. I didn't expect Triangle to show up in the bar; they were too precious, too non-Brummie, for that, local boys or not. Then I turned away from the bar, a full pint in my hand, and almost walked into Karl Austin.

He was a couple of inches taller than me, with a skullcap of black curly hair that looked impatient to grow into chaos. Close up, I could see the hollows carved into his cheeks, the coal-dust shadow along his jawline. He was somewhere below thirty and good-looking in an angular, Celtic way. A few feet behind him, the rest of Triangle were hastily necking Diamond White from glittering bottles. Karl raised a glass of some pale spirit to his mouth and swallowed hard. I bit my lip. 'Hi. That was quite a gig.'

Karl smiled. He had good teeth, but his smile was tilted as if ashamed of them. 'Ta. David Pelsall, isn't it? Glad you could make it.'

'Martin said you wanted to talk to me.' Martin was a local music journalist, film critic and mutual friend. He'd phoned me that weekend.

Karl's dark eyes grazed across mine. Then he pointed with his thumb towards the bass player. 'Steve here is fucking off to Bristol. New job. Martin told me you were between bands. I wondered…' He must have seen me with Blue Away on one of our better nights, I realised: when the booze was lighting us up instead of burning us out.

'Maybe,' I said. 'Yeah.' Triangle seemed a bit self-indulgent to me. But Karl had something, a real voice and a presence, however crowded out by ghosts. With a harder sound, they might be really disturbing. In any case, I was doing what I always do when praised: backing off. It's because I have an ego like a starving fox, and have to fight to stop it eating me from the inside.

Karl shrugged. Then he reached inside his black denim jacket and pulled out a tape. 'Listen. See what you think. If you're interested, give us a ring. The number's on the inlay card. Like, soon.' He placed the cassette box in my hand. It was a blank tape with a typewritten list of tracks.

'Cheers,' I said. 'Glad to have heard you play.' His fingers brushed my sleeve; I felt a brief rush of anticipation. As I downed my pint (only the third, but it was strong stuff), the corners of Triangle gathered together and returned to the outside world. The Goth pair from The Vacant Lot went with them. When I left the pub, alone, it was colder than it had been for months. Invisible rain smeared the lamplight and whispered like a drummer's brush on the roofs of cars. Reflected light hung thickly overhead, trapped between the clouds and the city, blanking out the stars.

The stretch of the Bristol Road between the University and Cannon Hill is fairly lonely at night. One end is the student ghetto: a cluster of second-hand bookshops, small record shops and Balti restaurants. The houses are mostly divided up into bedsits. The other end is a provisional red light district hemmed in by police and local vigilantes, an arrangement as mobile as the cars that set it up. In between, there's a mile of silence; trees lining the road like huge tattered feathers, shaking in the wind. The scale of it, the repetition, always made me feel lost.

It was past nine o'clock. Rain was scratching the discs of light around the streetlamps. The fallen leaves were black. Wearing headphones after dark is asking for trouble. But there was nobody around. I had the Triangle demo tape on my Walkman. It seemed to echo all around me: the hollow, insistent drums; the two conflicting guitars, one scratchy and one fluid. I was trying to follow the bassline, hear its role in the structure of each track. But Karl's voice kept distracting me. His vocals were too wired for the music. I started trying to rethink the band's sound, making it more abrasive and stark; not so textured. But how would he feel about that?

His voice in my head brought other things: his stark expression, the way his fingers curled round a guitar neck or a glass. The mixture of fear and excitement I'd seen in his face, then felt when he touched me. As if something of him could be transmitted by contact.

Just before the traffic lights on the edge of Cannon Hill, I saw a rain-blurred figure coming towards me slowly. Was he drunk, or was the wind so strong he could hardly push through it? As he got closer his face didn't seem to clarify. I thought he was going to walk straight into me, but I couldn't bring him into focus. Then his dark eyes locked on mine. For some reason I thought it was Karl, though his build was wrong. I stopped dead, fumbling for the Off button of my Walkman. Then somehow he passed me without getting any closer. You know how sometimes a gust of wind can bring the rain together so it makes a twisted shape and almost casts a shadow? It was like that. But rain doesn't have a face. I walked on as 'The Answer' plunged into chaos, the voice melting into feedback and atonal beats.

The tape ended in a faint hiss, a click. Overhead, trees broke up the lamplight into streaks. I thought of the band on stage: the stillness between tracks. It was cold out here, further from the buildings. I looked ahead, then back the way I'd come. In both directions, the road was empty.

─────────

We'd arranged to meet at Brindleyplace, a new development of the canal walkway off Broad Street. In early evening, with its image not yet fixed by electric light, it was a hollow bit of scenery. One side of the canal had been folded back into an arc of restaurants, cafés, and wine bars, each one themed: Chicago Exchange, Via Vita, Shogun Teppan-

Yaki, Café Rouge. The bridges across the water were also variously styled: cheap metallic pastiches of Italian, French and Chinese bridge designs I felt sure I'd seen in illustrated books. Old-fashioned lamps were suspended from the walls. The canal surface was dark, rippled and clean. Gusts of wind brushed highlights through it. When you looked up you could see the Hyatt Hotel with its distorted slate-grey reflection of Broad Street, as if the building itself were a canal.

I crossed a bridge and a deserted restaurant car park to reach the pub, which had entrances at two levels. Upstairs was a large-windowed circle with video games and a CD jukebox. Downstairs was a little darker and smokier. It was a Firkin pub, so the bar staff all had T-shirts with the message I'M A FIRKIN BAR STEWARD and other jokes too hilarious to be read safely on a full bladder. A short spiral staircase led down to the basement bar, where bands played on Friday nights. The brick framework around the bar was covered with gig notices and reviews from the sixties: The Animals, The Rolling Stones, The Grateful Dead.

Karl was already there. He bought me a vodka. In the halflight he looked like a charcoal sketch, the darkness of his hair and eyes marked crudely on his pale skin. 'How are you?' he said.

'Okay. Tired like. Some problems at work.' My manager was on holiday; the manager of the production department, a thin bully with a rather fragile sense of his own masculinity, had taken the opportunity to haul us over the coals about things he'd invented. The whole situation felt unreal. 'You?'

'Fine.' He looked edgy and hollow. 'You know, I saw you playing with Blue Away last year. You were the only good thing in it. Somehow, I'd never seen the bass player as being in control, not just an accessory. So you're not making a living from music?'

'Well, I tried. But the police moved me on.' The basement bar was slowly filling up; the support band would be on soon. A Nick Cave album was echoing through the smoky air, making the room seem larger than it was. 'Thanks for the demo tape. It's impressive. A bit frightening, when you're close to the sound. Like it's coming from somewhere else.' I didn't know how else to describe what had happened, the figure in the rain.

'It is, I think. Listen, I want to record an album. Those songs and some new ones. I think we've got a chance to ...' He pressed his knuckles against his mouth. 'To make a record that means something. We'll be gigging a little, just to get some attention. When Steve told me he was leaving, I thought of you. We need a harder edge. You agree?'

'Yeah, I do. But a bass player can't provide that. I mean, I'd like to be involved, but maybe you want another lead guitarist who can take over the playing while you sing. Your guitar playing's fine in principle, but...'

'Technically, I'm shit. Martin said you were honest. Tactless cunt was the phrase he used. Look, I need more practice, yes. But I know the sound I want. Virtuoso rock guitarists around here all want to be fucking Jimmy Page. I want musicians, not heroes.' He gave me a look of such pain that it was clear he didn't want to be the hero either. There was no point in trying to see through him, I realised. He wasn't transparent.

We carried on drinking steadily through the support band's mostly electronic set. They were shit, but we didn't resume our conversation until they had finished. People who talk during gigs are like the kind of people who talk during films. They should be dragged out into a shadowy hallway and garrotted, silently. Karl was drinking neat Bushmills; I was drinking Vladivar, for want of anything better. It was so warm in the crowded bar that the ice melted before you'd finished the glass.

During the interval, we talked about rehearsals and recording sessions. I had only fuzzy memories of studio work, rushed through on a minimal budget; it had paid my rent for a few months, but the serious contract never came. Karl didn't strike me as the commercial type, despite his talent. But it was hard to work and not get paid. I swallowed my doubts and let the atmosphere of the gig, with its echoes of the past and its largely teenage audience, do my imagining for me.

The Vacant Lot might have been playing the same set as a year before; it was hard to tell. The singer whispered and screamed in a claustrophobic voice, while the band thrashed out a dense, percussive storm. *The lines are dead, the screens are blank / You've only got yourself to thank.* She was very pale, her hair dyed black, her eyes a deep undersea blue. I couldn't guess her age. The drummer, her boyfriend, was in perfect accord with the sort of dark Gothic punk she was trying to create; but the two male guitarists buried everything under dull sheets of metal. At the end, she stood with her eyes closed and let the other three wrap themselves around her silence. There was no encore.

It was only ten-thirty. Half the audience stayed to drink; and after a few minutes, The Vacant Lot joined us. While the drummer was at the bar, Diane walked up to me and Karl. 'Hello, darling.' She kissed Karl briefly on the mouth. Offstage, her voice was pure Brummie. 'Who's this lovely young man?'

'That's my new bass player,' Karl said, putting the faintest emphasis on the word *my*. 'He was in Blue Away. But they, er...'

Diane smiled at me. She had perfect but rather broad teeth. 'What, a *blues* musician, Karl? Is your new album going to turn into *Jazz Odyssey*?'

'Is yours going to turn into *Smell the Glove*?' We all found this intensely funny. Alcohol does that sometimes. Diane wished him good luck before turning back to the bar, where the long-haired youth was waiting with two ominously dark pints. Karl drained a double whiskey in one slow gulp, shuddered, then said 'Let's go.'

Outside, the buildings looked much older than before. The moon was so bright, the clouds seemed to pass behind it. We walked along the renovated canal towpath under the pale lanterns. The water seemed on the point of reflecting something. Above us, drunken youths in white shirts laughed and argued with a kind of exhausted violence, like brass trumpets. 'I used to go out with Diane,' Karl said. 'We're still close. She's too good for that band. But she wants noise. The sound of conflict. Discord. It's what we all want. You agree?'

'Well, maybe. They're still crap, though.' We were walking under the main bridge, taxis swarming up Broad Street above our heads. Down here, everything was still and quiet. I could see a jetty full of inert barges and narrowboats; a tall factory building with an advert for Bobby Brown's nightclub painted on its wall. 'Who are you involved with these days?'

He turned, fixing me with his bleak eyes. 'I don't know. No one really, but…' He shook his head. 'Never mind. What about you, David?' If he'd talked to Martin, he probably knew everything about me. Martin was like that. But I told him about Adrian, the graphic designer I'd been living with until early summer, who'd left me for an arrogant bridge-playing American. What still ached, like a dislocation that hadn't quite gone back into place, was the months of trying to believe his promises. The bad faith, the plastic displays of honesty, the despair, the empty bottles… it's a really tedious story. 'I should have known better at the start. You can tell a man's soul from his record collection. Adrian was into Genesis. And Mike Oldfield.'

'Fucking hell.' Karl was genuinely shocked. 'At least you won't be reminded of him whenever you go to the pub. Did he come from a small town?' I nodded, surprised. 'It used to be like that in Stourbridge when I was growing up. People in love with their childhood, some whimsical English dream.' He put his hand on my shoulder. We were standing under another bridge, the canal beyond us shadowed by industrial buildings, the water no longer visible. 'Are you cold?' I realised I was shivering. He embraced me gently. I could smell whiskey on his breath, other people's smoke on his cotton shirt.

'Karl.' I felt the damp stone behind my back. 'Don't do this to be kind to me.'

His grip shifted, his hands stroking my back and shoulders. A faint smell of rot clung to the wall, like the smell of a wooden pavilion or a forest after rain. 'I'm not,' he said. 'I'm doing this because I want to. I'll stop if you want.' I said nothing. After a few seconds he put his hands on my neck and kissed me. Our mouths locked together. His tongue probed, asking questions.

Broad Street was packed: an unstable, directionless mass of youngsters in search of taxis or nightclubs or a fight. Karl and I made our way with practised caution towards the city centre, stepping around fresh wounds of vomit. Black cabs were clustered in the roadway; between them, the crowd broke up into twos and threes. We decided to try New Street Station instead. In the subway we stole a quick kiss like teenagers, though neither of us was into nostalgia. Romance fucks your taste. Navigation Street was littered with chip wrappers and half-eaten kebabs, beggars searching through the round waste bins. Teenage girls sat on the wall above the railway line, yellow light reflecting from their pale stomachs and thighs. A cluster of Birmingham City fans outside the Gents were failing to keep right on to the end of the song. The toilet was closed for the night, but a few of them didn't seem to have noticed. There was a long queue at the taxi-rank. Still, it was a queue.

Dawn light soaked through the red curtains of my studio flat. Karl's sleeping face was darker, flecked with ash. He opened his eyes and reached for me. I could still taste whiskey in his mouth. My hands traced the shape of his lean body under my own, testing his reality. We'd both been too drunk to make love the night before, and sobering up had brought a painfully tense excitement. Karl whispered in my ear. I turned him round, half on his side, and reached for the packet of condoms. When I entered him he spread his arms, as if preparing to fly. I gripped his wrists and pressed my mouth against the back of his neck. Our legs curled and kicked under the blue duvet with its pattern of roses. Suddenly, Karl froze. 'Are you okay?' He was breathing slowly, reluctantly. His whole body was tense. I withdrew from him. He pulled his arms against his chest and curled into a foetal position. 'Karl, what's wrong?'

His face, twisting on his neck towards me, was blank. 'Nothing,' he said. 'It doesn't matter.' He pulled me onto him and lifted his knees, his back arching as we embraced.

'Go on.' He stared into my eyes, the panic screened by desire. 'It's okay now.' I never tried to screw him from behind again.

———

Hours later, we stumbled through the shower and the reclaiming of our muddled clothes before admitting daylight into the room. I cooked toast and scrambled eggs while Karl browsed through my collection of records and tapes, muttering approval or disgust at each discovery. 'David. Put this on.' It was Felt's *The Splendour of Fear*. Maurice Deebank's taut guitar playing shone like a thread of mercury in the dusty flat. We talked about music, Triangle, our day jobs. Karl was restless. 'Let's go for a walk. It's too good a day to spend indoors.' I wondered if he was trying to put some distance between us and the night. But he seemed quite at ease in my company, as if sleeping with me were part of a band rehearsal.

Outside, a faintly golden sun flickered through a gauze of cloud, like a reflection in still water. We walked through

Cannon Hill Park and up Salisbury Road, where the trees were caught in a slow-motion fire. Sex and lack of sleep made my senses mysteriously acute: I saw every thread and current of the slow light, smelt the traffic and the dead leaves, heard the bruised voices of pigeons like accident victims waking up. The world seemed about to reveal itself to me. On the Alcester Road, Karl gripped my arm. 'David, I'd better go.' A bus was turning the corner a hundred yards away, framed by rusting trees. 'I've got to go home and change,' he said. 'I'm going to see my daughter.'

accessories

And we tried so hard
And we looked so good
And we lived our lives in black
— The Jesus and Mary Chain

What do you get if you cross a drummer with a musician? A bass player. The music world is full of dismally tuneless vocalists and patchy, ego-ridden guitarists. Yet it's the rhythm section who get blamed for everything. We're the dead weight, the fellow travellers, the accessories. We're only in the band because our dad let the band rehearse in his garage. We're boring on stage and useless in bed. We guzzle the rider and mistake our own dandruff for cocaine. Low notes, low-slung belts, lowlife.

The bassline rarely dominates a track, but it's often a foundation. Listen to the early New Order songs: the way

Peter Hook's stark, hollow chords build up a feeling of tension and menace, pushing the other instruments from the back. Or the way Simon Gallup makes The Cure's fragile song structures whole, and the way it all turns to dust without him. The bass guitar earths a track the way sex earths a love affair: without it, the other elements don't work. I don't mind being faceless. Much.

That autumn, Karl wanted us to focus on writing and rehearsing new material. We'd do a few gigs in the New Year, to road-test the tracks before we recorded the album. Triangle's contract with Relent Records wasn't exactly a living wage. Karl had this idea that the music needed to express how the band lived, what we felt about our lives. His relationship with me was a part of that; so getting to know each other was tied up with being in Triangle. In retrospect, that was manipulative. But aren't most love affairs a means to an end? I don't think Karl expected either the band or the relationship to go as far as they did, or he'd have kept them apart.

We started rehearsing in a place called Canal Studios, near the big cemetery in Yardley. It was surrounded by light industry and cheap furniture shops. Karl and I often walked back through the graveyard, which was full of Celtic crosses, angels and saints. One toppled figure had fallen headfirst in the mud, like a soldier in a trench. Opposite the studios, the narrow river crossed a canal. A giant ribbed sewage pipe ran beneath the bridge, a few feet above the still water. Somehow, a local youth had climbed onto it to spray DAZ 4 JANE close up. At the end of the bridge was a sycamore with a black leaf blight, like drops of tar or cigarette burns. For some reason, Karl always stopped there for a cigarette before we went on to my flat in Moseley or his in Erdington. The view along the canal exposed the backs of disused factories: broken glass, rusted wire netting, dreamlike silhouettes of machinery.

I carried on with my job at the Medical Centre, checking their frozen stock of blood and antisera. All the samples were kept in three cold rooms: giant locked refrigerators with strip lights and grey metal shelving. There were thousands of tiny bottles containing freeze-dried matter, sorted into polythene bags and stored in red plastic crates. Several times a day, I'd put on a thermal jacket and go in with an empty crate and a shopping list of samples. By the end of each session, the chill was a blurred ache in my hands and feet. I used to imagine finding a bag of freeze-dried human fingers, and being chased through the dim storerooms by a psychotic surgeon with a pair of pliers.

Karl worked as assistant manager of a TV and audio shop in Erdington. An odd job for such a nocturnal person; but he liked to keep his evenings free, and lived on a perpetual sleep deficit. Besides, he was good with machines. Occasionally I'd come round to the shop to meet him if he was working late; but most of my impressions of Erdington came from late nights or hungover mornings in his company. It's a lonely district, an old suburb isolated by the industrial wasteland of North Birmingham. Karl's flat was part of a Victorian house in a quiet street near Spaghetti Junction. We used to walk out there at night from the district centre, over a bridge and past the Gothic silhouette of the Highcroft asylum with its high spiked railings. You could hear foxes barking, sometimes, from the patches of wasteground between the buildings. The street where Karl lived was two lines of thin houses pressed together; it ended in a brick factory wall.

His flat took up the first floor. It was sparsely furnished, cluttered with books and records. The bedroom window overlooked a tangled back garden where broken glass caught fragments of light. The flat was cold and slightly damp. Karl told me he'd moved there in a hurry when his marriage broke up, around the time of the Gulf War. They weren't divorced. He never said much about why they split up, but it seemed to have to do with him wanting to be alone. Words like *gay* didn't seem to apply to Karl. He was just Karl. His friendship was so intense it included sex; but in all the time we were together, I always thought of him as a single man. His loneliness was something permanent, unchanging, but lovers of either sex helped him to live with it. I found that reassuring at first: I'd had enough of playing happy families.

There's a venue in Kings Heath, a room above a pub, where I played with Blue Away a few times. The walls were painted in thick black and white gloss paint: singers and bands from the last three decades. The faces were always gaunt, cheekbones edged with darkness, eyebrows flooding the eyes with shadow. Their mouths were sardonic creases. The artist had caught them in some doorway or alley of their lives, where they had stopped playing but were unable to shake off the intensity of being on stage. That was how Karl looked.

Triangle didn't have a manager at that time. Kieran, the guy from Relent Records who'd produced 'The Answer', helped out with recording. Our journalist friend, Martin, sometimes helped to set up gigs or interviews. But mostly, we were on our own. The three of us met up about twice a week to practise, write or just drink and make plans. Ian Priest, the drummer, had been working with Karl on and off for a couple of years. He was a stocky, not unattractive youth with cropped hair and round glasses; he always wore black, even when it was warm. He worked part-time at the Triangle cinema, a little arts cinema that was attached to Aston University. That was where he and Karl had met. Ian lived in Kings Heath with his sarcastic Northern girlfriend, Rachel, and a large collection of videos. He was obsessed with UFOs and occultism; after a few pints, he invariably got into some deep argument about how percussion carried messages from the spirit world, or how shamans used rhythm to induce visionary trances.

To begin with, I concentrated on working my own bass into the tracks on Karl's demo tape. Ian's drum technique was sharp but opportunistic, lacking in rhythm. He was a devotee of the single dramatic moment: the hard roll or cymbal clash, injecting fury into a track at a vital point. It tied in well with the more extreme aspects of Karl's guitar playing. I was happy to let them dictate the endings, while I focused on the beginnings. Playing with a blues band had made me painfully aware of structure. As Keith Richards said, you can't have rock without roll. But the rhythm needs to be *hard*. It needs gravity. Like fucking: you have to work at it, use timing to make it mean something. MTV is the pornography of rock. All riffs and chorus, no structure. And no meaning.

With new songs, I kept trying to make Karl build up more slowly. 'Let the music do the work. If you throw in everything at once, it gets confusing. Use time to spread it out.' He never trusted that idea. Of course, he knew that I was trying to simplify the arrangements because his guitar playing wasn't up to the more difficult bits. I told him his voice was more important. His lyrics deserved not to be buried under layers of sonic rubble. I wasn't flattering him, either. He wrote 'Stranger Key' that autumn, and I couldn't get the words out of my head. *You're killing the stranger because he reminds you / That you don't belong any more / But he's followed you home / He's standing behind you / He's there in the dark of your door / And the edge of the voice that you broke / Is sharp at your throat / Like a joke.* On stage, Ian used to laugh into a mic at that point; the audience couldn't see him. In the studio, we taped the three of us laughing and distorted the sound until it was more like a clarinet. The effect was unsettling somehow.

Another song from that time, 'His Mouth', became the most talked-about Triangle recording. I wasn't sure what I felt about it. It didn't seem to be about me, though Karl let me drag a wavering bassline through it and only used his own guitar for brief decoration, foam on the waves. I always felt there was something vaguely religious, an echo of Karl's upbringing, in its dark recounting of sexual passion. *He brushed his hand across my neck / As I knelt between his legs.* I was always moved by the ending, with its blend of desire and sadness: *Can't swallow this / Can't spit it out / Tonight his name is in my mouth.* It reminded me of fierce one-night stands from my younger days, when sex seemed to be a language that reduced all others to silence. *Your thin body over mine / Filling me with cold clear light.* A few times, when we played 'His Mouth' live, Ian and I worked in a few bars of New Order's 'Temptation'; Karl responded by raising a finger behind his back.

Karl and I had this ritual when we slept together that

whoever was providing the bed would play a track, and we'd listen to it before undressing. My early selections included New Order, Felt, The Jam, Nico, Marc Almond and The Jesus and Mary Chain. The opening chords of 'Happy When It Rains' are the most effective sonic foreplay I've yet discovered. Karl played me songs by Nick Cave, Scott Walker, The Pogues, My Bloody Valentine, Hüsker Dü and Kitchens of Distinction. The latter's 'Prize' was his favourite track of all time: a song about a gay couple getting drunk and falling out. The mood escalates from sullen mistrust to bitter rage: *So do I get a prize / For remembering his name?* The music takes the violence of the last words and drags it down into a whirlpool, tearing at itself, finding release only in exhaustion.

The tone of any relationship is set by what happens in bed. With male couples, one particular mode of sex tends to take over, to become the dominant key. Most often it's oral sex, though I've had quite successful relationships based on mutual masturbation. From the beginning, Karl and I usually fucked. When we didn't, we pretended we were going to, then rubbed off against each other. It gave a certain harsh intensity to our lovemaking – like an electrical storm, the tension discharged through static.

Usually Karl took me, his tense face pressed against mine, his arms folded like a straitjacket across my chest. *Are you okay?* he would whisper, his lips brushing my ear. I learned to be still and passive, caressing him only when it was over. It never took him long to come, even when he was drunk. Sometimes we'd wait until the morning. Whenever I took him, he put the bedside light on and curled up on his back, watching me steadily, his eyes filled

23

with night. Karl's lovemaking was a burst of uncontrolled passion; mine was a steady, rhythmic escalation. We only had unprotected sex once.

Karl's wife, Elaine, lived in Oldbury with their four-year-old daughter Theresa. He went to visit them about once a month. He and I didn't spend all our free time together. Karl insisted that living in each other's pockets would split us up. And we both had reasons to be cautious. When we got together, it usually started as band stuff: studio dates, practising, whatever. And we went to see other bands, of course. As many as we could. It helped being into bands that wouldn't play Wembley Stadium. And there were still a few medium-sized venues in Birmingham at that time: the Hummingbird, the Institute, the Powerhouse. The indie-rock fans were surprisingly young, even when the bands had been around a while. Occasionally some hollow-eyed youth would recognise Karl: *You'm in a band. Troy Engel.*

Those first few months, we saw some remarkable gigs. The Fall at the Hummingbird, seething with ecstatic rage. Ian McCulloch at Birmingham University, still achingly beautiful, wearing his sense of failure like a hairshirt. The Charlottes, bringing poise and passion to the shadowlands of Goth. And My Bloody Valentine, weaving Celtic mysticism into thrash metal. That gig started and finished late, and some of the younger fans had passed out by the end. They blasted through 'You Made Me Realise' as an encore, playing that middle chord for ten minutes at least. On stage, the two vocalists stood apart: an image of divided sexual need, their voices mapping out passion and separation. We dutifully went to see every other shoegazing band of the time – Slowdive, Ride, Chapterhouse – but none of them came near the visionary erotic charge of MBV.

We saw local bands, too, from the sardonic beauty of The Cantels to the blunt rage of punk karaoke band The Bostin' Stranglers. And we would have seen the Manics at the Digbeth Barrel Organ, but the gig was cancelled because Richey Edwards was being treated for self-inflicted wounds. When their first album came out, Karl adored 'Motorcycle Emptiness'. He said it was a song about how being powerless could give you visions. He loved 'Repeat' as well, and wished he'd written it first.

Our favourite club was also a concert venue: Edwards No. 8, in John Bright Street. They alternated Goth/Indie and Metal/Alternative nights on Fridays. A damaged globe of lights flickered on the street corner. It was a vampire heaven, that place: an inverted crypt with black-painted walls and cheap doubles of vodka. There was a quiet bar at the top where you could sit and talk; the chairs soon ran out, and couples or groups clustered on the floor, music throbbing through the walls as if you were in a heavily soundtracked film. Both dance floors were crowded and anarchic, with youngsters in an alcoholic or drug-induced frenzy goading each other's emotions. The dancing could easily slip into foreplay or violence. Beyond the main bar, in the shadows, pairs were slumped against the wall like dying spiders. There were gay couples as well, male and female; nobody was bothered, and it was hard to tell the difference.

The Goth nights were best: the dark, bass-heavy music suited the venue, and the people were sexier and more intelligent. Projected swirls of deep colour swept across the walls, bits of pattern attaching to people's heads as they went past. Even The Sisters of Mercy made sense in this context. It was a place midway between reality and dream. A couple of times, we ended up taking some young lad back with us. I don't think Karl intended it; he just had trouble saying no. It appealed to the voyeur in both of us, to watch each other with someone. And to share that curious, bittersweet mixture of sudden infatuation and fear, the way we shared our experience of bands and records. Later, I regretted it.

The metal nights at the same club were scarier. It was better not to drink too much, and to be careful who you looked at. The music was dry, hard, relentless; Pearl Jam and Nirvana were the only moments of humanity in a measured industrial onslaught. It corresponded to an angrier side of Karl's nature, and he sometimes dragged me along for an hour or two of oblivion. There were fights around the dance floor; glass broke, and dark-suited bouncers shot through the crowd like missiles. The toilets were a no man's land of scattered piss and vomit. On the night bus, Karl would mutter about atonal music and the visionary power of chaos. His eyes looked past me, down into some broken corner of his mind.

———————

Christmas was quiet and frustrating. Seeing old friends in Birmingham, then going to stay with my mother in Exeter, reminded me of a past I wanted to escape from. The unexpectedly mild weather made me feel still more out of place, as if the season only existed in pictures. Karl was away with his parents in Coventry. He was spending a couple of days with his wife and daughter in Oldbury as well; he didn't talk much about them. 'You wouldn't like Oldbury/ he told me. 'Parts of it are okay, but as a whole … well, that's what it is.' Later, a little awkwardly, he told me he'd be staying the weekend with them. I didn't ask him what that meant. Honesty's not always a good thing.

To make matters worse, something odd happened the next time I saw him. We'd arranged that I'd come round for the evening, the day before New Year's Eve. I phoned to check before setting out; Karl told me, in a rather defensive voice, that two old friends from Stourbridge had turned up unexpectedly. 'Come anyway,' he said. 'I want to see you.' He'd given me a tape of Stina Nordenstam's *Memories of a Color* for Christmas; I played it on my Walkman as the bus climbed through the grey ribbons of Spaghetti Junction and past the white gravestones that ringed Erdington. Her voice was cold but tender, framed by bleak arrangements. It reminded me of Nico. The weather was less mild now; highlights of frost shimmered in the yellow streetlight.

Karl introduced me to Stefan and James. They looked about thirty, dressed in black, with tightly cropped hair and emergent beer-guts. The four of us sat in the shadowy living-room with very little to say, drinking beer and half-listening to a recent Triangle rehearsal tape. Karl sat with his guitar propped against his legs, fiddling with the keys or strumming inaudibly. It wasn't connected. I wondered if Stefan and James were a couple; but they didn't sit together or refer much to each other. They talked to Karl about Triangle, and about the growing success of Stourbridge bands The Wonder Stuff and Pop Will Eat Itself, of whom they seemed more jealous than Karl was. The rest of the conversation had to do with people I didn't know. They seemed to regard me as an extra, though Karl had pointedly introduced me to them as his bass player and lover (in that order).

The evening dragged on; more beer was drunk, and Stefan's Black Country accent thickened to something tangible. James's voice was softer, more rural. I wasn't listening. Let them think I was some kind of hanger-on, entering the band arse first. I knew Karl didn't imagine that. He was uneasy that evening, but I somehow felt it wasn't me he was uneasy about. Nobody mentioned food. Feeling vaguely pissed off and a bit confused, I poured myself a large vodka and browsed through Karl's bookshelves. Brendan Behan, Jean Genet, James Baldwin, Richard Allen, lots of second-hand crime thrillers. A hardback copy of *The Ice Monkey* by M. John Harrison, inscribed *To Karl – with love from Diane XXX*. Behind me, three cigarettes glowed red in the dim light of Karl's floor lamp.

Eventually, James muttered something about getting hungry. 'I'm afraid I can't really feed you,' Karl said. 'Me and David were going out.' They took the hint and left, promising to come and see Triangle in the New Year. As the car started up, Karl walked through the living-room door towards me, then stopped. 'I'm sorry, David,' he said. Half his face was brightly lit, the other half invisible. I embraced him and felt how tense he was, wired up and exhausted at the same time. His mouth tasted of smoke. I thought he'd explain to me later, but he didn't.

The night after that, New Year's Eve, Ian and Rachel were going to join us for a drink. And a smoke. It was a cold, bright day; the pavements were slippery with frost. Karl and I had been working on a new track, a kind of drifting repetitive sequence that eventually became 'Fugue'. At that time, its lack of a focus had become a kind of image: a song about someone who'd gone missing. But the lyrics wouldn't come. I was getting irritated by Karl's mysterious approach. 'Either give it a melody of some kind or write some words,' I said. 'You can't record ghosts on a four-track.' Ian and Rachel turning up gave us an excuse to drop it. Rachel was wearing a new, bright red jacket.

After we'd shared a bottle of wine, Karl started rolling a joint on a Stranglers album cover. He crumbled a rich, dark lump of hash into some torn-up Marlboro cigarettes and skinned the resulting mixture as a thin stick. We were sitting in the living-room on chairs and the black corduroy sofa, huddled around the gas fire. For some reason I decided to light a few candles. Karl inhaled raggedly, then passed the hazy red eye to Ian. We all took turns to look through it. Another bottle of red wine was passed round; and then a third. Some chocolate Hobnobs were eaten. Karl turned up the stereo until it filled the room: *Murmur, Love Is Hell, The Top*, then Coltrane's *Blue Train* (which I'd bought him for Christmas). I don't remember what else.

Conversation drifted like smoke across the gaps between tracks. Ian and Rachel were lost in each other's eyes, but didn't embrace – perhaps because they'd have been embarrassed to see me and Karl do the same. Romance was the last thing on my mind. I rarely smoked, because lack of experience with tobacco meant that I had trouble inhaling; repeated efforts on this occasion had reduced me to a state midway between slow asphyxia and spaced-out psychosis. The biscuits tasted of decay. I tried to calm myself by focusing on the sleeve notes to *Blue Train*; it didn't work. I recognised the words as belonging to the English language, but I couldn't read them.

'Of course, Jim Morrison was a shaman.' Ian was in flight, his characteristic excitement overlaid with a strange calm. 'The spirits were with him on stage, you can hear it. He was really into Native American magic and all that. To him, the landscape of America wasn't cities and freeways, it was animal and tribal, umm, territories like. He was the holy man of the tribe.'

'Was that why he couldn't hold his booze?' That was Rachel. The candlelight picked out embers in her auburn hair. 'He was the whiskey priest of the global village.'

'*Bollocks*,' Karl whispered. Rachel got on his nerves. The record finished, and he replaced it with 'Dead Souls' from Joy Division's *Still* album. The eerie call-and-response of guitars through the first two minutes of the track reduced everyone to silence. I could have sworn the candles shivered. Rachel stubbed out the remnant of the last thin spliff in one of Karl's little ceramic ashtrays. It must have been long past midnight. I looked at my watch, but the hands were too similar. The crystal intensity of 'Dead Souls' gave way to the drunken, abbreviated cover of 'Sister Ray', which seemed a cue to wind up the gathering. Rather than spend the night on Karl's sofa, Ian and Rachel decided to get a taxi. Karl and I walked them out to the all-night cab office on Slade Road.

A bitten moon stared through a frame of branches. Cars passed silently, heading for the city centre. Somewhere among the trees, a fox barked: a strange choking noise, as if it had trouble breathing. I couldn't feel the cold. Surprisingly, we didn't have to wait long for a cab. As it drove off, Ian waving goodbye through the window, Karl linked his arm with mine. 'Fancy a short walk?'

Halfway between Erdington centre and Spaghetti Junction, a side road goes uphill between two small lakes to a stretched- out housing estate. Both lakes are surrounded by trees. Away from the streetlights, the moon seemed much brighter. Moving lightly, as if dancing, Karl led me through to the far side of the bigger lake. Fragments of the moon littered its surface. On the bank, a willow tree washed its hair in the still water. Something moved close by, impossible to make out. I was still confused. As we neared a lamp, both Karl and I cast double shadows, as if we were following each other. The grey mass of the housing estate hung above us, reducing the lakes to a picture on a concrete wall.

Karl kept glancing over his shoulder; but there was no one in sight. He was shivering. I put my arm around his waist, and he turned and kissed me hard on the mouth. We stood there for a few minutes, saying nothing. Then Karl led me back down to Slade Road. Our footsteps echoed from the buildings on either side. Because it's above the city centre, Erdington doesn't have the vague ceiling of reflected light you get in most of Birmingham at night. We seemed very exposed. Karl walked quickly, staring straight ahead. His arm was tense; I had to let go of him. There didn't seem anything I could say.

When we got back to the flat, the candles were still burning. Karl stepped away from me. He seized a piece of paper and a biro and stood there writing in his own shadow. A minute later, he put the pen down and looked at me as if he'd only just noticed I was there. He was trembling as we embraced. 'Are you cold?' I said. He touched my cheek, then stepped into the bedroom. I went to blow out the candles, holding the piece of paper up to the light so I could see what he'd written: *Do you want to look for me? Do you want to find me? Were you here ahead of me? Are you there behind me?* By now I could read the words; but I couldn't see what they meant. Of course, it eventually became the chorus of 'Fugue'.

The bedroom was ice-cold. I drew the curtains and shut the door. Karl was stretched out on the bed, still dressed. I couldn't wake him, and eventually I half-undressed him and pulled the duvet over us both. Lying in the dark, I heard the fox barking throatily out there between the houses. At least it knew how to communicate, whether or not anyone was listening.

CHAPTER 3

hooks

They stood in the dark
Swayed by the wind of a voice
— Triangle

The Barrel Organ pub in Digbeth no longer exists. In 1993, it was given a costly makeover and became the Dubliner: an Irish theme pub with fake showbands and other accessories. Back at the start of 1992, the Barrel Organ was the venue for my first gig with Triangle. It was a rough place, full of brittle-haired punks and skinheads drinking cider from plastic glasses. Rumour had it that the National Front's Birmingham HQ was just up the road, above an antiques shop. A few yards down the road was an all-night café that was a known haunt of rent boys.

It was a Friday night. We were sitting in the little backstage enclosure, listening to our support band: a thrash outfit called Quay. Halfway through a track, their lead guitarist had somehow disconnected his guitar. The vocalist, trying to compensate, had played his own vocal line as a riff, and the drummer had stopped dead for several seconds before improvising frantically. A dense rumble of feedback stalled the band completely. The audience response was merciless: a wave of jeering, then a slow handclap that carried the lyric *Fuck-off-fuck-off*. Karl glanced at me. 'They'll take no sodding prisoners.' He was drinking a can of Special Brew from the rider. Suddenly, he put it down. 'Shit this.'

He was shaking. I stopped trying to tune my Rockwood and went across to him. 'Are you alright?' His face was very pale, damp with sweat. 'Don't get the fear now, Karl. It's your gig. We're right behind you.' I touched his arm, and he flinched. Then he grabbed my hand and closed his teeth around the base of the thumb. His hair was cropped short, a mass of wiry hooks like Velcro. The bite seemed to release his panic, though he didn't let me go until Quay stumbled backstage, their amplifiers still howling feedback to mask the lack of applause. Someone had thrown a pint of lager over the vocalist, Darren; his red shirt was stuck to his torso like a fresh bloodstain.

The three of us went out together, in darkness. The audience were hardly visible. Ian beat out the time signature, and we crashed into 'Third Flight' as a pale blue spotlight flickered above us like a police car. I'd helped Karl to tighten up all the instrumental arrangements, link them to a hard beat rather than an ocean of ethereal sonic effects. Karl was still jittery, playing too fast in a stop/start manner that turned the song's feeling of menace into violent panic. *Third flight / Coming back for more / Goodnight / Heard you kiss the floor / Blood footprints on the stairs / Blood footprints on the stone.* We paused for a count of three, then blasted out a discordant storm. The audience were drenched in cold blue light. I could see the front row moshing viciously, their eyes blank. Karl's black hair was highlighted with sweat. His voice was nervous, a little higher than usual. It didn't matter. Triangle were his real voice.

The next track was one we never recorded: 'Worm in the Bottle'. This was mostly an instrumental in the vein of the Velvet Underground's 'Heroin', built around a repeated D chord. Karl's guitar shuddered into a fragile solo, then fell away, leaving me and Ian to rumble ominously in the dark while Karl sang *I can move the world / I can paint the sky / But I can't stand up.* Finally, Ian went into a violent drum solo that lasted for five or six bars, then stopped dead. Karl tipped the microphone towards his mouth like a glass. I could hear people at the back shouting for 'The Answer'. *Give us a chance*, I thought. Diane and her boyfriend were at the front, struggling to remain upright.

Then we did 'Still and Moving Water', the one that had struck me that night at the Jug of Ale. I concentrated on the rising bassline, and didn't really listen to Karl's lyrics. The audience probably couldn't hear them anyway. Strange how you can follow the words at a gig if you've heard the recorded version, but not if you haven't. The lead and bass guitar must have meshed particularly well, because I had the feeling of some other instrument coming through: a kind of shadow, made up of reverb and the echoes in the tiny venue. Something whispered through us like the wind in a forest. Karl must have heard it too, because he glanced at me and then backstage before snarling into the mic: *The grass is never dry / Your children never cry.*

It was probably a mistake to play 'Fugue' next, since that was another strange one, and we hadn't got the sound right at that time. Without all the effects we used in the studio, it came across as a sub-Primal Scream ambient thing with a few creepy waves of distortion. Karl's vocal was subdued, almost as if he didn't want to provoke whatever phantom had breathed on the last number. A few of the audience drifted to the bar. Ian did three quick beats to wind the song down. Applause was half-hearted.

For the first time that night, Karl introduced a song. 'This is called "His Mouth". One. Two. Three. Four.' He muttered the last words through clenched teeth, before playing a loud and distorted version of the bassline and then grasping the mic in both hands to sing: *I drank the whiskey from his mouth / He drank his seed from mine*. That song was always harder-edged, more brutal live than on record. In between verses, Karl's guitar scythed wildly across my bassline, cutting it up with hostile mimicry. I didn't know what he was so angry about. As the song ended, he walked across to me and gripped my shoulder. Gently, as if to thank me. Someone in the crowd yelled *Fuckin' queers!* Karl counted in the next song: 'Stranger Key'. At the end of the track, he put the microphone into a small glass and stamped on it. A security man waved at him and made a chopping gesture: *Cut that out*. But they didn't stop us.

The next track was another one we never recorded: our cover of Scott Walker's 'Big Louise'. Without the violins, obviously. We did it as an R&B song, with the lyrics almost snarled over a slow, shuddering beat. It's a bitter song, about a transsexual robbed of her dreams. Karl's guitar joined mine for a few bars at the end, before a delayed second chorus.

He was blazing now, his voice clear and intense. As the last note faded, the same heckler as before shouted *Bollocks!* Karl stepped forward, a can of Special Brew in one hand. 'This is for Mr Bollocks. *Shut your fucking mouth.*'

Ian tapped out the signature and we plunged into a raw, percussive version of 'The Answer'. This was another track where I had to concentrate on playing Steve's bassline accurately. But I knew Karl had changed the second verse to make it blacker, more accusing: *When they ran out of coal / They burned flesh / They wanted Enoch for king / ... Their Holy Communion was beer / When I was born they asked me / What the fuck you doin' here?* We kept the energy under control until the last verse, when all three of us threw our passions into the instruments. The cold blue light came back, pulsing steadily. I played the same riff over and over; Karl tore jagged strips of noise from his Fender; Ian played drums with one hand and cymbals with the other. We had a drum machine playing as well, and the feedback levels were going up and down like a fever.

I glanced up at the audience. They were surging back and forth, their faces blue and expressionless like extras in *Dawn of the Dead*. A plastic glass flew up, spraying light. Then Karl played the first of his deep signal chords. On the third, we all stopped dead. The feedback and drum machine went on for a few seconds before the sound engineer pulled the plug. We left the stage in darkness, stumbling over wires and amps. The applause that followed us sounded impossibly distant, like traffic in a tunnel underground.

Backstage, Karl was too high to do anything but drink. Breathing could wait. Even Ian, who didn't get excited about anything unless it contained the word 'Roswell', was unable to keep still. He sat with a drumstick in one hand and a can in the other, listening to how the sound made by hitting the can changed as the level of Special Brew went down. I felt drained. Like a schoolboy after an exam, I kept replaying bits of the gig in my head, criticising flaws, gloating over successes. The more I drank, the clearer it all seemed. Then a question occurred to me. 'Where did you get that fucking glass from?' There'd only been plastic glasses in the gig area of the pub.

Karl smiled. 'Home.' We went on drinking until we ran out of lager. The bar was shut, of course. A few people joined us backstage: Diane and Gary the drummer; Rachel, who helped Ian get his drums home; Martin, who'd helped set this gig up for us. The Barrel Organ fined us thirty quid for the glass-smashing incident; Karl was inclined to argue, but Martin persuaded him to leave it. I vaguely remember Karl and me getting a cab back to my place. We must have drunk some vodka, because there was an empty bottle and two glasses on the table when we woke up.

It was noon on Saturday. Karl's eyes opened, turning from pale to dark. 'Not a bad gig, eh?' I nodded, aware of a great silence in the room. I could hear Karl's breathing, my own, the traffic outside. So what was this wind of silence blowing past my face?

I put my arms around Karl and we kissed deeply. His mouth tasted of Special Brew. So did mine, presumably. His hand gripped my cock and rubbed. I kissed his hair, tasting salt and alcohol in the dense forest of hooks that covered his narrow crown. Then he sucked me, and I stretched under him as if truly waking up. Minutes later, we came in each other's mouths and lay tangled on the dark floral duvet.

My limbs felt suddenly unfamiliar. I wanted to get up and make coffee and toast, but the slow wash of endorphins through my body left me floating in a haze of tenderness. The only real thing I could hold onto, in that room or the world, was Karl.

That's what alcohol does to you.

———————

Triangle's Barrel Organ gig was reviewed in *Brum Beat*, a local free magazine given out at record shops and cinemas. The reviewer, Helen Fell, seemed a little distant from the heavy metal/grunge hegemony of local music journalism:

> Triangles are spiky, angular things. They don't roll over. True to their name, Birmingham band Triangle are not unduly eager to please. Their recent debut single 'The Answer' suggested a loud but harmless shoegazing band in love with feedback. Live, they seem far more dangerous. Their new bass player thinks he's in The Jam, pushing things along with aggressive briskness. Irish vocalist Karl Austin is a mass of contradictions. He plays the hard man on stage, breaking glass underfoot and staring out an unlucky heckler. But his lyrics deal with gay love and the damage done by male violence. Perhaps deliberately, the band walk a fine line between melody and noise. They are that increasingly rare commodity, an indie band with something to say. If they don't get killed off by stroppy hecklers or the West Midlands Serious Crime Squad, they could go a long way beyond Digbeth – and in the process, knock the likes of Ride and Spiritualized into a three-cornered hat.

Our next gig was supporting The Great Outdoors, a local band whose vocalist ran a record shop in the city centre. That was at the pub where I'd seen The Vacant Lot – Karl always referred to it as the Fuck and Firkin. Support gigs were useful for us at that time, because our live set wasn't fully worked out. Rehearsal just wasn't the same: there was no fear to play against. After a brief set, Karl and I relived our first date by watching The Great Outdoors together and drinking whiskey. Their music was fluent, graceful with an underlying toughness. It made me think of Spaghetti Junction: the giant shadows, the harsh poetry of stone. We were both very drunk. Afterwards, Karl took me down to the canal bridge where we'd first kissed. It was a Wednesday night; there was no one around. This time we did more than kiss.

As the winter gradually shook off its tension and started to breathe, Triangle played a succession of local gigs: the Jug of Ale, the Varsity Tavern, JB's in Dudley, the Mitre in Stourbridge, somewhere dreadful in Wolverhampton. Martin seemed to drift into being our manager, since the guy at Relent Records didn't want the job. He contacted a number of music papers, getting us mentioned and eventually reviewed. He was good at dealing with venues, sounding urbane and reasonable where Karl would have been nervous and argumentative. He could be a pain too. We all took the piss out of each other, but he did it to hurt.

I remember one night when we were tuning up in the dressing-room, our nerves as tight as our guitar strings, and Martin popped his balding head around the door to tell us he'd sent the Triangle demo tape to Alan McGee at Creation Records. Had he heard back? we wanted to know. 'Yes.' Had

McGee listened to it? 'Yes.' What did he think? 'Queer mix.' Catching the look on Karl's face, Martin beat a hasty retreat.

All this gigging, of course, tended to make us drink a lot more. It's inevitable: you finish a gig and your brain's on fire with adrenaline, but it's too late to go to a pub. What can you do to get back down to earth except drink until the world is silent again? And because everything slows down when you're drunk, it can help you stay in control. The drinking spread to the nights in between gigs, when we relived the excitement or tried to find the right mood for creating songs. I used to wake up with my head so scoured by alcohol that the music filled it like some great revelation, as if it were the first music I'd ever heard. My face was stiff in the mornings, like a mask with stubble growing through it. Karl's only hangover cure was to smoke heavily, which didn't do much for me. I found passive smoking erotic in the right circumstances, enjoyed having smoke kissed into my mouth or blown gently over my eyes; but on those cold mornings it just seemed another poison, something to be washed away.

It got to me on stage sometimes. A faint sense of nausea, mingled with something sexual, like the smell of rotting wood. I'd be watching Karl launch into a bitter vocal and suddenly the air would be thick with torn-up shadows. Dark ripples of something passing behind the light. I always thought of rain. Layers of rain that stripped the colour from everything. I don't know if Karl or Ian ever felt the same thing. I'd have been embarrassed to discuss it, as if I were admitting to some kind of DTs.

The other thing that was happening that spring was the countdown to the 1992 General Election. All three of us in

Triangle had been Labour Party members since before we knew each other. I helped Karl to deliver leaflets a few weekends in Erdington, once getting my fingers bitten by a guard dog. I was paranoid about septicaemia, and couldn't play the bass for a few days until the bite healed. The owners of guard dogs seemed to keep them indoors on perpetual red alert, fed on a diet of Pro-Plus tablets and food substitutes rich in E numbers. They also put up printed signs from some local shop, saying things like BREAK IN – MAKE HIS DAY or SURVIVORS WILL BE PROSECUTED. These reminders of territory made leafleting far less enjoyable, but gave it a kind of uneasy edge that we both appreciated. We looked forward to a Labour victory the way an insomniac looks forward to a night's unbroken sleep.

In this climate of alcohol and expectation, music became the only reality. Karl was obsessed by two records he'd bought in the New Year, playing me one or the other almost every night I spent at his increasingly chaotic flat. One was Bob Mould's solo album *Black Sheets of Rain*: a stark, brooding landscape of rage and jealousy that left us both awestruck, like children after their first glimpse of adult violence. Karl taped it for Ian, who was knocked out by its echoey, shuddering drums – 'Like a soundtrack to the actual track, not part of it, like something outside.'

The other record was Scott Walker's *Climate of Hunter*, which Karl had picked up second-hand on one of his visits to Stourbridge. It was a set of songs about being on the run – both physically and mentally. The music combined pounding heartbeat percussion with sparse, fragile guitar. The lyrics were fragmented, repetitive, with odd phrases splintering off from the melody: murder and exile, drowning and blood.

Karl said it was the most frightening album he'd heard since *Unknown Pleasures*. Certainly it reminded you of Martin Hannett's agoraphobic production. But I found the lyrics too hard to swallow. It was exactly Karl's wavelength, of course.

The only time I really felt what Scott Walker's lyrics were getting at was one rainy morning in Karl's flat. My mind was blank and cold from the previous night's drinking. I wanted to make love, but Karl wasn't in the mood. We sat apart on his black sofa and listened to the album, turned up loud. In the grainy curtained light, Karl's face was little more than a silhouette. My eyes stung and I rubbed them, wondering whether or not I was crying. I suddenly knew that the songs were literal descriptions of a reality lit up by some kind of mental breakdown. The thought was so unsettling that I couldn't speak for a while afterwards. Karl interpreted it as a sulk, and ignored me. Then he tried to help, but I couldn't explain what was wrong; though I returned his embrace in the same automatic way that I'd accept the contact of a stranger.

Another time, he played me 'The Electrician': a song that Scott wrote for the last Walker Brothers album. It was about a torturer in South America, pulling switches to make people beg for death. The song ended in a mood of sombre beauty, with distorted piano chords and soft guitar leading into a lullaby of pain. I'd never heard anything so disturbing in my life. He played it twice, then put the record away. We never discussed it.

———

One weekend in March, when Karl was away visiting Elaine and Theresa, I decided to go out on the town. I wasn't sure how the scene would look to me now I had a lover: more or less enticing? Most of the gay venues were clustered around Hurst Street, on the edge of the Chinese quarter. I'd spent a lot of time here after the breakup with Adrian, but almost none since meeting Karl. The streets were shiny with rain, the air sour with petrol fumes. The Nightingale Club had vaguely mock-oriental red awnings, perhaps in the hope of being mistaken for a restaurant. The interior was no longer officially camp: they'd redecorated it in black wood-chip wallpaper, with black leather seating. The effect was deadpan and cold. Blue-white lighting jittered above the dance floor. The music was three or four years out of date. I started drinking quickly – not because I wanted to be drunk, but because the habit was too strong to break.

To combat a growing sense of disorientation, I flicked through the free magazines on the table by the cloakroom. There were two: the serious gay community magazine and the frivolous gay lifestyle magazine. The irony was that the 'serious' paper never had anything new or interesting to say, whereas the 'fun' paper contained a wealth of satire and insight. As well as male nudes. An article on drugs observed: *Gay men tend to use drugs to accessorise sex, not to improve it.* The "serious' paper could never have allowed such an acute comment. They would have said: *Drug abuse is a growing problem in the lesbian and gay community.* And even that would have had someone writing in to complain.

After eleven, the club began to fill up with the usual half-drunk, restless crowd. I recognised quite a few of them. The regulars tended to be people who weren't comfortable anywhere else, and who staked out their own little territories in the quiet upstairs bar, the sound-blasted inner bar or the restaurant area. There was Fey Ray, a boy with blond highlights and a tired smile who wore a very short T-shirt. And David, a tall semi-TV who looked capable of hospitalising any queer-basher who got in his way. Or anyone else who got in his way, come to that. And there was Robert, already very drunk, a thin youth with dark hair and bitter eyes. He looked as young now as when I'd taken him home three years before. I counted six people I'd slept with. At one time, before Adrian, I could have counted twenty in this place.

Since they'd started admitting women – actual women, that is, and most of them gay – the leather queens had stopped coming here. But there was still quite a range of ages. And more than before, I noticed, people who didn't belong to a type – who weren't drag queens or *faux* rent boys or skinheads or bull-dykes or Goths. Presumably they were students. I drifted for a while, drinking bottles of Diamond White and window-shopping, though I didn't need a window any more. Even as a fantasy, the idea of two-timing Karl was losing its appeal. I watched men in shorts and vests jinking to Madonna's 'Vogue' on the dance floor, big patches of which shone like ice in moonlight. The sight was arousing and depressing at the same time, like a boxing match. *Nothing to it.*

By now, couples were silhouetted against the walls, caught in the stasis of foreplay. The area around the dance floor was packed solid; the cold smell of amyl nitrite cut through the warmth of human bodies. I escaped to the upstairs bar, where MOR crooners took the place of electronic beats. From a distance, I recognised the nervous gestures and bleached quiff of my friend Dominic. He was with a bald, fat man who looked like a monk in a comic. I bought a vodka before joining them. Dominic greeted me with vaguely ironic surprise: 'Hello, David. Haven't seen you in *months*. This is Peter.' The monk smirked at me. Dominic always seemed to go for older men, despite his often-stated contempt for them.

'So where have you been?' he asked. 'I haven't seen you anywhere.' I told him I'd been busy with Triangle. 'That's the strange thing about you,' Dominic said. 'I don't know any other gay men who are into rock. It's either opera or musicals. Rock is just so uncouth.' He caught Peter's eye and smiled. 'I've never met this Karl, either. And I know *everyone*. Or is he one of those boring people who says he hates the scene?'

'He doesn't hate it. He's just not into it.' I had to stop and think for a few moments. 'If he has a scene it's music, really. And… well, he's not entirely gay, either. He goes out with women. I'm the only serious boyfriend he's had. I think.' It sounded more difficult here than it did in the outside world. I didn't know how to explain that.

Dominic raised his eyes to the ceiling. Peter smirked again, then leant forward to say: 'Being a little bit gay is like being a little bit pregnant.' Just then, another friend of Dominic's came up and started chatting to him. Peter's face went blank; he studied his drink like Van Morrison studying Yeats. Perhaps he didn't realise that Dominic's flirting was instinctive, not calculated. When the friend moved on, Peter raised a small hand to Dominic's shoulder and ruffled his hair.

Across the bar, I could see a papier-mâché figure just inside the doorway: a clumsily sculpted Greek god with an erect cock that someone had broken, so that it flew at half-mast. Peter went to the bar. Dominic put his mouth close to my ear and muttered, 'I've been seeing that one for three weeks. Once he's taped all his Streisand albums for me, he's history.' I couldn't work out if he meant it; self-parody was so deeply ingrained in him by now. He'd been a young protege of Adrian's; and whereas Adrian disguised his cynicism by appearing to take an idealistic stance on everything, Dominic was a pretty decent person under the bitchy facade. But as time went by, the mask became thicker and the face harder to see.

By now, the second bar was uncomfortably crowded. I finished my second vodka at a rate only possible when already drunk. When I said goodbye, Peter gripped my arm. 'Let me give you a piece of advice,' he said. 'As an older queen. Ditch that closet you're seeing and find someone who knows what he wants.' I gave him a tight smile by way of thanks. The dance floor was a blur of dry ice and strobe lighting. I could hardly see the dancers. The music had progressed from happy handbag to some kind of hardcore dance music, like punk speeded up. Alone, I slipped onto the floor and let the turbulent rhythms carry me through the storm. Close up, I could see men's white T-shirts glowing mauve in the UV light. They floated around me like candles on a river. The electronic beat pulsed faster and faster until it was a single unbroken note, beyond words or music.

That last week before the General Election, we ended up playing two gigs. The Friday night one was planned as a chance to try out some new songs we'd written, before going into the studio in Digbeth to work on the album. Karl wanted to try a slower, quieter approach, with less emphasis on hard edges. He was getting tired of hearing Nirvana soundalikes everywhere. We were booked to play at the Hibernian in Stirchley, one of the greyest districts anywhere in Birmingham.

Then, suddenly, we were playing on the Thursday too. One of our favourite current bands, The Family Cat, were touring with Dedicated labelmates Hard Wayne in tow. With three dates left to play, the support band had found themselves minus a vocalist; he was in hospital with appendicitis. The Family Cat were forced to rely on the venues to provide support. The manager of Edwards No. 8 in Birmingham was a friend of Martin's. Naturally the three of us were all free to play that night: we'd all been going to the gig.

Backstage, The Family Cat were as friendly – and as nervously alert – as their namesake. We shared a quick drink with them: *To a change of Government*. Then we filed out of the dressing-room, around the speakers and up the steps to the yellow-lit stage. The audience filled the entire space, going back around the bar to the murky depths where couples hid on the club nights. 'Hi,' Karl said. 'We're Triangle.' A few people cheered: friends of ours, no doubt. We started with a shuddering, reverb-heavy version of 'Stranger Key', including a sample of breaking glass; then 'Third Flight', with the pause/blast effect exaggerated into something that literally had the audience falling back; then 'His Mouth' with Karl hunched over the microphone, caught in a narrow white spotlight. We'd decided to stick to the best bits of our usual set, leaving out the more difficult songs and the new stuff we'd been working on. The venue's powerful sound system and thin corridor of space worked in our favour. After the applause, complete silence led into each new track.

Before the last song, Karl paused to tune his guitar. 'Thanks for listening,' he said. His voice was tired. 'Last time I was here, a Megadeth fan stamped on my head. You can still see the blood on this shirt, if you look closely.' It was a black cotton shirt with red threads. 'Why can't people have a good time without causing pain? I don't know the answer.' He beat out the time signature with his foot, and 'The Answer' took off in a siren-wail of guitar. We kept it reasonably short, since our half-hour was almost up.

After a couple of backstage drinks and a quick change of clothes, we slipped out into the audience to watch The Family Cat. They played an intense set, combining darkly poignant lyrics with fiercely dynamic guitar playing. A beautiful new song, 'Amazing Hangover', described the loneliness of sailors and miners: people trapped in the shell of a dying industry. It reminded me of an obscure folk song my parents used to sing to me when I was very young – something about bank vaults stuffed with silver that the miners sweated for. 'Colour Me Grey' was a groan of bleak regret for opportunities wasted in a time of conformity. 'Steamroller' was a pounding, furious surge of tongue-in-cheek romantic bravado, like The Clash playing Springsteen's 'Rosalita' after several bottles of Thunderbird. Karl and I stood with our arms round each other's shoulders, listening like small children. Someone close by recognised us. 'Hey, you were great.' After their set, we rejoined The Family Cat backstage and got severely wrecked.

That gig was reviewed in the *NME*. They don't usually mention support bands, but the review began:

> In their current bid for popular acclaim, the Cat are keeping some weird company. Tonight's support comes from the atonal Triangle, who are rapidly becoming a cult band in the West Midlands despite having short hair and being quite good. Their singer seems perpetually about to ask the audience who they're looking at, while the other

two corners amplify his chilling angst and then hammer
it into silence. Class revenge, they seem to be saying, is a
dish best eaten cold.

The next evening, still hung over, we played the Hibernian
in front of sixty or so people. It was a fair-sized venue,
with the ghosts of drunken hoedowns and ceilidhs waving
spectral bottles at us. We opened with 'Fugue', then 'Still and
Moving Water', then a slow instrumental that eventually
became part of 'Road Into Fire'. And then we played 'Curfew
Town' for the first time: a fatalistic narrative about insane
teenagers, with Ian brushing the drums and me playing a
low riff like an underwater bell. *There were colours around him
/ That changed when he lifted his head / There were songs in the
air / That took up all the words that he said.* Part-way through,
a cropped-haired lout in the audience started chanting *You-
are- shit! You-are-shit!* I glanced at Karl; he bit his lip and kept
playing. The applause sounded uneven, like static on a badly
tuned radio. A voice bellowed through it: *Wankers!*

Karl shook his head and counted in 'Stranger Key'. We
began it on a subdued note, as we'd planned; but some kind of
interference distorted the guitar, and Karl had to play harder
to drown it. A half-full glass flew over our heads, spraying us
with a fringe of beer, then smashed against the wall. But the
song's violent coda seemed to calm the audience down, as if
vicarious rage could drain whatever they made themselves
feel. We followed up with 'Third Flight', an onslaught of torn-
metal riffs breaking apart the core of rhythm. At the peak,
Karl raised his hand and we all stopped dead.

Propelled onward by a mate, the crew-cut drunk was
making his way up onto the stage. His face was nodding

between his raised fists, like a parody of a boxer. Karl put down his guitar and stepped forward quickly. I followed, as much to hold Karl back as to protect him. But a security man got there first. He gripped the *faux* squaddie in a painful armlock and pushed his mate viciously back into the crowd, then marched his captive through the back exit. We heard a struggle, a thump, a high-pitched yell of pain.

Karl took up his guitar and snapped at me and Ian: 'The Answer'. It wasn't next on the set list, but I could see his point. We stretched it out for ten minutes or so, Karl's wailing guitar underscored by my aggressively solid bass and Ian's frantic drums. Then we played a new song called 'For the Distance'. It sounded far bleaker here than in rehearsal. I think the lower frequencies were echoing somewhere else in the building. Although Karl's lead guitar was fragile and partly improvised, thinning the sound, his vocal was raw with loneliness. We'd written this song together; I'd come up with a slow blues track, and Karl had overlaid it with fragments of melody and strange, deadpan lyrics. The closing lines were half-spoken: *The train runs empty down the track / Fades with the night / From blue to black / Wave goodbye to the future / It's never coming back.* We left the stage in darkness.

The half-lit dressing-room contained Martin's bearded smile and a crate of cheap wine. We ignored the former. Through the closed stage door, we could hear a few voices calling for an encore. We were thinking about it when the voices were drowned by U2's 'Where the Streets Have No Name'. Presumably the lights had gone up. Through the opposite door came the Hibernian's manager, wearing a tweed jacket older than the furnishings. With the air of a busy man who has meetings to get to, he signed a cheque and handed it to Martin. Then he turned to Karl. 'I don't know what that was supposed to be, lads, but it certainly wasn't entertainment. I thought you were a rock band. Don't bother coming back, okay?' Then he was gone. We shared a bottle of wine. It was too sweet. Leaving the rest undrunk, we packed up our instruments and fucked off. Outside the pub, an ageing drunk was lying unconscious on the pavement. A security man was talking into a mobile phone. A group of youths, on their way to the bright lights of Stirchley, jumped over the still figure as if he were a ditch.

CHAPTER 4

saxon salvage

You saw your life as a series of complicated dance steps
Impossible to learn, it had to come naturally
— Tindersticks

The weekend after the General Election, we were supposed to start work in the studio. But Ian had a migraine and couldn't play. It turned out that Relent Records could use the studio time for another band's new single, so Karl took the opportunity to cancel both sessions. He and I spent a hungover, bitter weekend together at his flat. Music was not uppermost in our minds. On Sunday morning, Karl screwed me with a desperate passion that made him seem helpless. The sounds in his throat were echoes from a long way away. After breakfast, I offered to help him tidy the flat. He told me to fuck off. Then he paced around the living-room for a while, straightening pictures and ornaments; I sat on the couch and watched his shadow throw itself against the walls. Eventually he sat down next to me and stared into my eyes. I could see the fine red cracks, the irises almost as dark as the pupils. 'Come on,' he said, 'let's go somewhere.'

We'd played a gig in Stourbridge two months before; but we'd been travelling in a van, after dark, and I hadn't seen much of the place. This time, we took the train from Snow Hill. The sun flickered through gaps in the pale clouds, giving some images a cold watery glow. In Smethwick, a high factory wall had been sprayed with the jagged SS logo and the message KEEP BRITAIN WHITE. In Lye, a sculpture of rusted car bodies towered above the sign SAXON SALVAGE. The landscape started to break up: industrial estates and rows of terraced houses mixed with fields, woodland, rubbish tips and wasteground. It was quiet on the train, this being a few years before the cult of the mobile phone transformed trains into horizontal office blocks. Even the group of men sitting across the carriage from us, playing an interminable card game, spoke only in monosyllables. One had a copy of the *Sunday Times*, its front-page howling with triumph. The train's slow, insistent bassline divided the journey into bars.

At Stourbridge, the outer wall of the station was sprayed with ENOCH FOR PM. Karl laughed. 'That's been there since Thatcher went. You know Powell was MP for Wolverhampton South-West? He was a real cult figure around here when I was growing up. I was in junior school when he made his "river foaming with blood" speech. Powell apologists like Thatcher claim he was quoted out of context. He was. You have to look at the whole speech to see what a manipulative, vicious little prick he really was. It gave a glow of heroism to every beating, every brick through a window, every turd through a letterbox. Now Powell's senile, everyone's treating him like some elder statesman, a wise old man. I'd hang him from a lamp-post. I always used to think he had syphilis, because his brain was rotted.' We were walking past a line of black spiked railings, trees on the other side. Karl set the pace. I couldn't see why he'd brought me here if the place infuriated him so much.

We had lunch and a pint at the Rock Station pub, which had photographs on the half-lit walls – Mick Jagger, Axl Rose, Robert Smith – and a painting of an oncoming train behind the small platform where bands played. 'We 'aven't seen you in ages,' the barmaid said. 'How's that band of yours?' Karl introduced me as his bass player. 'Is he any good?' she asked, winking at me. From somewhere behind us, Pearl Jam's 'Why Go' spilt its hollow rage. Karl and I walked on into the town centre, which seemed to consist largely of take-aways and charity shops. He pointed to a second-hand record shop with old posters in its windows: 'That's where I bought all my Scott Walker albums. And loads of other stuff. Rock, blues, folk even. You want to go back to the origins, this is a good place to start.'

All of the shops were shut, of course. Karl led me in a circle around the town centre, looking for something. 'Christ, have they closed it off? No, here it is.' The sign CANAL STREET pointed to a narrow gap between two factory buildings. A concrete drive with gravel scattered across it. Two rows of small warehouses and factories, some of them derelict: windows smashed and bricked up from within. A desiccated sign identified the contents of a windowless building: COLD ROLLED STRIP STOCK. One factory was open, the front rolled up to reveal a huge, gloomy interior with hanging electric lamps, grimy skylights, machines grinding and wheezing like decaying organs. At the side, an extension jutted out that hadn't been built too well: cracks and brick-sized gaps spread in a lazy grin across the bottom of the wall, where KEEP CLEAR was painted in red.

'Nothing much has changed here,' Karl said. 'They try to build anything new, it falls apart. But the old shit remains. It's like a charm.' Despite the machines, the air seemed colder here than in the streets. We walked on to the canalside, where a few men were fishing in water that held a storm of weeds. As the canal turned right at a lock, we passed the ruined outline of a house. Karl stared at it for a few seconds, then walked on. 'I'm not ready to go there,' he said. 'Come on.' Gnats in the air made his face seem to tremble.

The canal water was so still that it reflected the mass of ivy on the bank. A bronzed dragonfly, maybe six inches long, hovered above our heads. 'This was on my way home from school,' Karl said. 'Some of us used to come here and fish with worms. It was a great spot for fights, 'cause the loser usually ended up in the water. You'd be surprised how warm it could get. Like a massive storage heater with walls made out of shit.' I raised my eyebrows. He nodded. 'Four times. I don't recommend it.' The canal ended in a cloudy, stinking collar and a few stone steps up onto the bridge.

Rain was drying on the pavement; sunlight flickered on the roofs of cars. Stourbridge was cut in pieces by expressways that ran to a different kind of time. Karl looked back at the canal; he hadn't finished showing me what was there. But we walked on, past a car park where children performed desperate stunts on battered skateboards. 'My parents came here in the fifties from Ireland,' he said. 'The

Black Country's full of Irish families. I think they found the isolation, the strangeness, a sort of comfort. They weren't city people. And there was work then. My dad's an engineer. That garage up there was the first place I worked. Repairing cars, fitting spare parts. You see down there?' He pointed to a narrow shopfront cluttered with guitars and drum kits. 'Bought my first guitar there, twelve years ago. A Hondo.'

He speeded up. 'Look at this.' A crescent of renovated cottages ended at the mouth of a light industry estate: a dozen or so workshops clustered together. Steam clouded the air. I could hear the sounds of hammering and sawing, rusty gears, chains clashing, somebody's voice lost in the mix. To one side, a scrapyard called SALVAGE CITY was piled high with various steel components painted in different colours. 'We used to live just round the corner from here. I don't feel like going to the house. My dad got a job in Coventry a few years ago, so they moved. I don't know if they ever come back here. If they've got memories that won't lie still.'

'Karl.' He looked at me. 'What's the matter?' Silently, he led me back the way we had come. As we rejoined the canal towpath, a few yards below street level, his hand brushed mine. Somehow I felt he didn't just want to *show* me what was here. He wanted me to be with him because he couldn't have come here alone. 'Are you okay?' He shrugged. I gave up asking questions. On the metal grid across an overflow conduit, we stepped over the headless bodies of two blackbirds surrounded by hardening shreds of feathers. In my head, I could hear some crackly old blues number: Robert Johnson or Howling Wolf. The accidental percussion of worn- out vinyl. The Mississippi delta. Origins. Starting points.

Whether it was insects or the thickening clouds overhead, the air above the dense undergrowth seemed to vibrate as we stared through the trees along the muddy towpath. Beyond the frame of the demolished house was a squat building with its windows and doorways bricked up; then a workshop of some kind with its front wall destroyed, exposing a brick furnace and barred, glassless windows at the back. A tarpaulin nailed over the roof-timbers had mostly rotted away. The ground was spotted with clusters of pale fungi like a recurring dream. I had the sense of something invisible close by, moving silently past. Then Karl led me on towards the green wall of shrubbery at the back of the field, and I realised what it was.

The river. It was slower and wider here than in the town, a skinned mass of dark muscle and yellow fat. The trees lining the bank were heavily cloaked with green ivy; even the young saplings that poked up out of the nettles were coated in moss. There was a rich smell of rot and growth, something powerfully sexual. I put my arm around Karl's waist; he twisted and pressed his mouth against mine. His face was blank. I felt the imprint of his cock through his tight jeans, reached down to trace its outline. Then he pulled away. 'Not here.' We left the damaged buildings behind and followed a hardly traceable path into the trees between the canal and the river. A thin stream trickled down from one to the other, whispering like a child's ghost. There was hardly any direct light coming through the patchwork of leaves overhead.

Where the stream ended, a huge oak tree leaned towards the riverbank from a mound of earth held together by knotted roots. A thin severed branch hung from a length of blue nylon twine over the stream; it didn't look strong enough for anyone but a small child. The tree's bark was rusty with disease, its lower leaves bleached. The tilted, deeply furrowed trunk was split into two muscular limbs, spreading out through the tattered undergrowth. Where the limbs met was a blackish knot, like a scrotal sack, with a small rain-hollow just below. Karl stepped onto the base of the dying tree, then climbed to its groin and sat there. He gestured at me to join him. I fitted myself on the trunk next to him, my arm around his tense shoulders. The air was cool; it smelt of fungus and rotting wood. The tree felt cold and unyielding.

'I was born in Stourbridge,' Karl said. 'My childhood was really peaceful. It seemed such an innocent place, the mixture of forest and factories. When I went to secondary school, things got more difficult. Suddenly the accent I'd picked up from my parents meant I wasn't a local person any more. I had to belong somewhere else. You know, there's nothing at all natural about prejudice. Children learn it from adults. And when you reach puberty, you start to hate yourself and your life, and someone outside has to take the blame. Plus, it was a bad time to be Irish in this country. Especially after the pub bombings. It was like every Irish person was to blame, not just the six innocent men who were jailed. So I wasn't just an ignorant Mick with the intelligence of a boiled potato, I was a psychopath and my family were terrorists. My dad actually got questioned by the police a few times: who he knew, who'd been in town lately, that kind of shit. Mr Penn the games teacher used to ask me, *Is that a bomb in your pocket or are you just pleased to see me?* He was a shit. Used to hang around the showers to check out our state of development.

'So, yeah, I got picked on for being Irish. And skinny. But it was more verbal than physical bullying – at least when I'd proved I could fight. I got blood on my fists a few times. There was only one bully who wouldn't let up, and I couldn't make him stop. His name was Dean. Him and his giggling retard friends used to follow me around, chanting *No surrender to the IRA.* I fought him twice – he hammered me both times, and after that there was no stopping him. He made my life a misery for two years. I used to come down this way to avoid him. But sometimes, I'd miscalculate and they'd be here, waiting. Once he knocked me straight into the canal, threw my books in after me. Another time, he threw a tyre chain at my legs and I went flying, hit my head on the wall. They left me there. When I came round, it was dark. Only an hour later, but dark and freezing, and I thought it was midnight in the underworld.

'That was when he had his mates with him. When he was hitting me, standing over me, I could see him getting a hard- on. Sometimes he came. I don't know if they noticed. And that wasn't all.' Karl stopped. His face was locked. I shivered and held him close, but he didn't seem to notice. Beyond the dark river, the sun was out of sight; but it caught a few shreds of cloud and torched them like paper. 'This place is strange, isn't it? Like a bit of wilderness. It's one of those points you'd use for reference when drawing a map – to set the contour lines or whatever.'

'Karl, what were you going to say?'

'I found this place by accident. Dean didn't know about it, nobody did. Those derelict buildings were houses and workshops then, and it was harder to get through. I used to climb up here and watch the sun go down, feeling like the last human being on Earth. One day when I was thirteen, Dean followed me here. On his own, minus the back-up. He'd been picking on me for about a month – not long compared to what happened after, but long enough for the sight of him to make me feel sick with tension. He said he just wanted to talk. But instead of saying anything, he pushed me against the tree, this tree, and put his hand on my crotch. Suddenly I remembered him looking at me in the showers. I hadn't realised what he wanted. Anyway, that first time, we tossed each other off. And he kissed me, which felt more intimate than anything. I still can't believe that.' Karl leant forward, his arms folded across his chest. He was very tense.

'The next time I saw him, he was with one of his mates. They trapped me under the railway bridge, by the station. Dean punched me in the mouth, split my lip. He called me Paddy. *You fucking Paddy, fucking potato-digging cunt.* I didn't know what to do. Thought he'd kill me if I told his mates what had happened between us. A few days later, I came here and he was waiting for me. Alone. I told him to fuck off. But he didn't. We went further this time – blow jobs, fingering. We didn't get on to fucking for quite a while. All the time, he was keeping up the attacks, the insults, in front of the other kids. Sometimes he'd hurt me – knock me down – spit on me. His mates would kick me, whatever. But he never beat me when the two of us were alone. When he hurt me then, it was different. He used to take me from behind, against a tree or on the ground, kissing me as we came together.' Karl paused. He was breathing hard. His face was a shadow.

'I thought I was going mad. Well, I was. My first lover. He told me I was his girlfriend.' Karl laughed emptily, a dry sound. 'Dean was shorter than me, but heavier. Solid. He had spiky blond hair and blue eyes that looked emotionless till you saw the misery behind them, how lost he really was. We were kids. I just didn't want to lose him. I shut my world down until it was just here, me and him, and a few other places where we did it; and nothing else was real. I never told anyone, until it was over. It was like the beatings and the... affair were part of the same secret. I never liked the violence, David; I never wanted it, but in the end it became part of what excited me. It took me over. Maybe that was easier than believing the pain.' He began to weep silently. I embraced him and felt helpless. In the back of my mind I could still hear the twelve-bar blues of the train wheels, comfortable and alien.

After a minute or so, Karl stopped shaking and wiped his face. 'How did it end?' I asked. He looked away. All around us, leaves had become silhouettes, the spaces between them filling up with smoke. Karl seemed to be listening for something. An image rose suddenly from the back of my mind: Rob's face in the cloudy light of the Nightingale Club. Rob was one of my first boyfriends, a camp teenager whose hunger for experience had both scared and excited me. After we split up, he got into the leather ethos, had a number one crop and became overweight. Once I saw him in the Nightingale, standing absolutely still by the wall in the pool room. I went up and said hello; he didn't glance at me, let alone speak. A bead of sweat trickled down the side of his forehead. His boyfriend, Danny, took me aside and explained: 'Rob's not allowed to speak to anyone until his master gives him permission. His master's over there like, getting a drink.' He looked at the bar, where three middle-aged leather queens were holding pints of lager. The glasses sweated like Rob's blank face.

'The flexible world of work,' Karl said at last. 'Dean's father got promoted and transferred to Leeds. The family went with him. Typically for Dean, he never said goodbye. It would have ended anyway. You can't go on being the school bully at fifteen. I had friends by then. James and Stefan, you met them. They were the only people I told about Dean. It took me years to get over him. I would still have been attracted to men... but I would have found it easier. And I never told Elaine. Not about the bullying part. That's history anyway. I'm not into pain. So you can put the nipple clamps away.' I laughed and stroked his hair. My back was beginning to ache. 'When you've known violence ... in that way, you can't live as if you didn't know it, as if it wasn't there. Do you understand?' He stared at me. I couldn't see his eyes. We kissed, shifting our balance in an embrace and almost slipping out of the tree's crotch.

'We'd better make a move,' Karl said. He was shivering. We negotiated a path through the trees, following the stream up to the metal walkway that covered the overflow. The canal reflected nothing. 'I could find my way around here in the dark,' Karl said. 'But I'm glad you're with me.' I could hear the murmur of traffic, not far away.

We crossed Canal Street and walked past the back of a factory; broken glass crunched under our feet. Then Karl stopped. 'Are you okay?' he whispered.

'Yes,' I replied. There was nothing more I could say. How could I help what was beyond my reach?

He kissed me fiercely. 'This place is getting torn apart,' he said. 'Tower blocks, expressways. Building over the past. I'm glad. I used to stand here and think nothing could ever change. That's why music is so vital to me. It's a way of not being alone. Sending messages. Without that, we're all trapped in the dark, none of it means anything. You know?' I gripped his hand.

It was still early evening. The last weekend of daylight saving time. We walked up a new expressway towards the station. 'I think Rock Station's got a band on tonight,' Karl said. 'Fancy a few pints of cider and some bad heavy metal?' An old, blackened iron bridge carried the railway line across the narrowing road. Three Conservative Party election signs were still hanging from the metal trellis. Karl stopped, looking up at them. 'You wonder why a victim can fall for a bully, and go on taking abuse without trying to stop it? I bet those fuckers know the answer.' We walked on under the bridge, the lifeless sound of cars echoing louder and louder around us.

reverb

It's your second nature
Don't fool around till that's gone
— Felt

Several things happened in May. I lost my job. Karl had an affair – apart from me, that is. And Triangle recorded their debut album, *Hard Shadows*. The demise of Relent Records actually happened in April, but nobody told us about it. Their offices were taken over by Furnace Records, a new company with heavier financial backing. In retrospect, that was an important step for us. At the time, it was an unwelcome intrusion of the outside world into our narrow territory.

Alan Winter, the head of Furnace Records, was a Jewish ex-punk with spiky hair and round glasses that made him look like an angrier Ben Elton. He seemed unable to decide whether to be camp or butch, and so flickered nervously from one to the other. We got on well with him, but he always seemed wary of

Triangle as an entity – as if the darkness of Karl's songs was somehow a threat. The same couldn't be said of Pete Stone, our new producer. He was Welsh, unshaven and very technically minded; he'd once worked with John Cale. Bands on stage meant nothing to him, but he was obsessed by the power of the studio – 'an echo-chamber of the collective unconscious' as he put it after a few glasses of Southern Comfort. Naturally, he and Ian got on like a pagan shrine on fire.

The lease on Canal Studios having expired, Alan set us up with a recording studio in Digbeth. It was a scary place, even for three fit young men with violent tendencies. Digbeth High Street is lined with Irish pubs, ranging from the contrived and spurious to the shabby, depressive real thing where the vibe of exile was as pervasive as the smell of malt. But hardly anyone lives in Digbeth: it's a run-down industrial district whose factories and scrapyards have all seen better days. Houses, pubs and even a few churches are used to store machine parts and scaffolding. Old railway lines criss-cross above the streets.

Our studio was about a mile from the number 50 bus stop. Our only neighbours were a glass recycling plant and a railway salvage yard, both of them closed half the week. It was as private as the studio in the Welsh hills where the Stone Roses were rumoured to be hiding out. Summer only meant that we had more daylight hours: Digbeth remained stark and monochrome, a bit like Triangle's music.

After an afternoon or evening in the studio, we often went to the Cannonball, a jazz pub near the High Street that occasionally had musicians playing. The dark walls were lit by old photographs, and piano solos crept from the hidden speakers. The pub was at the corner of Upper and Lower Trinity Street, and when you came out you could see why:

a blackened viaduct crossed over both roads, with three narrow arches visible above each.

Another Digbeth pub we liked was the Railway Inn, whose back room was a popular hardcore venue. The Vacant Lot played there sometimes. It was painted all in black, with crinkled roofing tiles above the stage and the bar. The side walls were covered with framed photos from the sixties: Hendrix, B. B. King, The Animals, The Who. There were cheap gigs there most nights; beforehand, it was a great place for band meetings.

After one of these evenings of recording and drinking, I made a technical error at work. It might have happened other times, I don't know. But a blood testing kit came back from a French hospital with the complaint that a freeze-dried sample had been mislabelled. At least they hadn't used it and made some terrible mistake. There was no lawsuit, but we lost their custom. Real life is more like a gig than a take. My manager established that I'd both made the error and failed to get my assistant to check the kit. I didn't tell them I'd been groggy with the aftermath of Smirnoff Blue; it wouldn't have helped. I got a month's notice, less a few days' outstanding holiday. The humiliation of working out my notice doing the most basic tasks, with every step being double-checked by my manager, fed into some of my bass playing on the album. My style became hard and minimalist. So did my conversation.

As a result of our gig with The Family Cat, a local fanzine called *Empty Frets* offered to interview Triangle. We met the interviewer, a Birmingham Polytechnic student called Janis, at the Fighting Cocks pub in Moseley. Karl did most of the talking. 'Our songs are about how the three of us feel about our lives,' he said. 'It's in the music, that feeling, not just the words. I've been writing songs all my life, but I could never hear the right sound in my head. Now, working with David and Ian, I can hear something coming through the songs like a voice, an echo. It's all there.'

'Is it important for there to be three players in the band?' Janis asked. Her hair was dyed in red and black stripes. 'To be Triangle, I mean?'

'I'm not sure,' I said. 'When we're recording, we mix in other things. I wouldn't mind having keyboards, maybe a clarinet. In the studio, at least.'

Karl shook his head. 'We wouldn't be Triangle then.'

'Yes we would.' He gave me an icy stare. I shrugged and bit my lip. She asked Karl some questions about his lyrics, his background. In response to the inevitable question about his sexuality, he said he'd been married but now had a boyfriend – me. Janis looked at me as if for the first time.

'David, you used to play in a blues band,' she said. 'Isn't that a fairly macho kind of music? Misogynistic, even?'

'Like Bessie Smith? Or Nina Simone?' The interview was not going well. 'Look… what's in the music is one thing. What's in the people who play it is another.'

'I'm not sure you can separate them,' Karl said. 'But there's like a dialectic. Different people can turn the music around. And different music can turn people around.'

Janis sipped her rum and Coke thoughtfully. Then she looked up at Ian. 'How do you fit into the picture?'

'I play the drums.'

When the interview appeared in the June 1992 issue of *Empty Frets*, it was accompanied by a photocopy of an onstage band photo. Our faces looked uneven, shadowy, the mouths stretched open. But that was only the effect of a cheap Xerox. Janis kept in touch, phoned Karl up to ask if he and I would like to meet her for a drink in Saltley. I was depressed about losing my job, so I made an excuse and let him go alone. The other times, I wasn't asked.

I was at Karl's flat one evening when she rang. He didn't say much, but his muttered comment *David's here* and the choked intimacy of his voice told me enough. I got him drunk, which was never difficult, and asked him what was happening. He seemed relieved to tell me, as if it were one less secret to carry. 'We're in each other's pockets too much,' he said. 'It's a safety valve for me. A balance.' I shut my eyes and heard him sigh. 'I'm sorry. David, look. Look at me.' He was standing by the window, backlit by the tawny sunset. I felt as though his back were turned.

Arguments always provoke a strange mixture of desire and hopelessness in me. I reached out and felt his shoulder underneath the collar. 'Don't take me for granted,' I said. Memories of Adrian crowded my head. I felt like a session musician. His shirt tightened across the back of my hand. 'Don't assume that I'll be here, no matter what.'

'You don't own me, David.'

'You don't fucking own me, either. This isn't about monogamy. It's about trust.' From force of habit, my hand slipped down his chest, brushed a nipple. He was breathing hard.

'Okay, listen. Janis is a friend. My affair with her could stop at any time. If you really want it to, it could stop now. But these things *happen*. If you want to stay with me... It doesn't mean I take you for granted. It'd be very bad for me to lose you.' We kissed briefly; then he stared at me. His eyes were black hollows. 'Am I forgiven?'

'Don't go fucking Catholic on me. It's okay. I mean... it's all right. Just.' He had no idea what it cost me to say that. When I shut my eyes, I could see Adrian's smug face. But Karl wasn't the same. He gripped me hard, as if the idea that I might need him had shaken him. Outside, the streetlamps came on. We went to bed and fucked each other slowly. As we lay together in a shadow of combined sweat, I wondered if Karl might be having an affair to test my loyalty – or his own.

A couple of times after that, he told me he was meeting Janis. They stopped seeing each other a few weeks later, though Karl didn't tell me until we were touring in late summer and I asked him if Janis was going to come with us.

'She might come to one of the gigs,' he said. 'But we're not in touch any more. That finished back in June.' I thought, *You might have told me.* But then, I'd hardly have wanted him to cry on my shoulder. He never told me why they broke up either, which made me think it had to do with me – or with the band. It came to the same thing.

———————

The first tracks we recorded were 'Curfew Town' and 'Still and Moving Water'. From the start, we had trouble recreating the intensity of live performance. Karl wanted the band to record complete takes; but Pete kept saying it was better to work on each element in turn. 'You don't mix the paints when they're already on the canvas. It'll come together, don't worry. Put it this way: the record already

exists, it's in the air. We have to find it. It's a bit like a séance.'
As if taking that idea literally, he put lots of reverb on Ian's
drumming and Karl's guitar until the sound was almost lost
in its own echoes.

At that time, using strange effects was pretty much
compulsory for any indie-rock band that wanted to be
taken seriously. It was a way of not being innocent, not
being a wee anorak child. All the bands who'd started on
Creation or 4AD with a naive waiflike sound were making
surreal, drugged-up records with a carefully contrived
feel of disintegration. Karl was a sucker for that kind of
thing – he liked The Cocteau Twins, whose records always
reminded me of William Morris wallpaper designs – and
seemed happy to let his vocals get drowned in waves of
distortion. I had to keep saying: 'If they can't hear the
words, why bother writing decent lyrics?'

The other big thing at that time was the murky sound
of the American hardcore 'underground'. Thanks to
bands like Hüsker Dü, Pixies and Nirvana, a lot of fairly
abrasive stuff was becoming really commercial. Most of it
was conventional pop delivered in a churning, bass-heavy
style with a lot of discord. For English rock bands, it was
a reminder that music could hurt. The American media
couldn't handle it as music, couldn't take it in: they had to
turn it into a 'scene' so that they could dismiss it, the way
the English media did with punk. Every sound was defined
by its following. Even in 'serious' rock journalism, every
sound was a kind of *core:* hardcore, slowcore, speedcore,
sadcore. What next? Is Michael Bolton blandcore? Is
Madonna egocore? When you fixate on a word, it stops
meaning anything.

What Karl seemed to take from grunge – especially from Bob Mould and Hüsker Dü – was the sense of vocalist and band being somehow in conflict. I'd heard that in their gig at the Jug of Ale: Triangle didn't accompany Karl, it framed him. In an odd way, that sense of being walled in helped him to put more feeling into his vocals. Too many early nineties records were about sounds and effects, not songs – all those precious confections that were only the sound of a claustrophobic studio, not a claustrophobic world. Through the combined unhealthy influences of post-punk, hardcore and alcohol, Karl developed an approach to playing that isolated him from the band. That was part of how it worked, and how Pete wanted it to work; but there were other things involved.

When Pete and Karl reconstructed 'Still and Moving Water' from its components, it still lacked the power of the demo version; but there was something else, a feeling of quiet menace, like the disorientation I'd experienced a few times on stage. The instruments were separate, alone, but there was a flickering between them. I don't know how to explain it. 'Curfew Town' was pale, not quite alive. 'It needs something more,' Pete said. A few days later, Karl gave him a tape with a few minutes of noise on it. The sound of a factory: machines hammering, gears clashing. It wasn't a good recording, but that helped it to fit behind the track as background. We could never have played it.

We spent as much of the next fortnight in the studio as possible. I got a part-time job working in the basement (the 'alternative' section) of Tempest Records, through a friend who worked there. Karl took some time off from the shop. Ian came in as often as he could; we filled in his parts with a drum machine sometimes, then got him to record over it. Next, we put together the four tracks that worked best on stage. To compensate for the slowing-down of other tracks, we did 'Third Flight' as a head-on assault; but then Pete stripped it down to its essentials, made it cold and distant. Karl decided he quite liked that: 'It sounds more painful, you know?' Because we weren't getting on very well, Karl and I didn't work together on 'His Mouth': we recorded separate tracks, and Pete fitted them together a bit awkwardly. In the quieter bits, Karl's guitar cast a jagged light over the bass. Pete got a session musician to record the melody line on tenor saxophone, then added a few bars of that to the start and end of the track at a level that was just audible.

For 'Stranger Key', probably Karl's best song, we spent days getting just the right blend of melody and discord. My repetitive bassline was mixed down, with Karl's guitar stretched across the top and his voice filling the gap. There was some kind of interference on the tape – maybe sounds from outside, though none of us heard anything at the time – and we had to ditch some of the best takes. Ian did some rapid, high-pitched cymbal playing at the start that sounded like a lot of thin glasses shattering at once.

'The Answer' was even better, less effects-dominated than the single version and more aggressive. Pete wanted to blur its edges with lots of spooky overdubs, but I told him not to. Then, when we heard the master tape, it was drenched in feedback that Pete swore he hadn't added. Some of it sounded like distorted echoes of the vocals. We kept it in, but mixed it down so you needed good speakers to hear it. Karl's vocal was tight, controlled, menacing. By now I'd stopped hearing the lyrics; they were just part of the track.

Sometimes we'd come out of the studio mid-evening and the sunset would turn Digbeth into a Victorian furnace. The light blazed through glassless windows and flashed from heaps of rusting car bodies. Near the studio was a café where we sometimes ate in the daytime, alongside silent factory workers and lorry drivers. There was a salvage yard where someone had sprayed the words SOCIALISM OR BARBARISM on the far wall; and beyond that, the old station with its thick Victorian columns. At the far end of the road, a boxing club advertised itself with the image of a hard and undamaged male face.

Karl wrote 'Nowhere to Go' one evening in the studio. It was about a prisoner on parole, staying in Digbeth and slowly falling apart. You never found out what he'd done, and whether his pursuit was real or imagined. The imagery seemed a bit over the top, but Karl's quiet delivery made the paranoia convincing: *The cracks in the pavement / Show me where to walk / Presbyterian guard dogs / Warn me not to talk.* He played as little as possible on that track, letting me and Ian frame his voice in a dark, military beat. The other new song that he wrote for the album, 'Road Into Fire', was completely different: a gentle, almost folkish lyric about a journey through the land of the dead. He based the melody on an instrumental we'd performed a few times. I made the bassline as harsh as possible, like thunder. The song's ending always gave me a cold feeling: *Leave the fire behind you / Climb the broken stairs / To where your lover waits for you / With a baby in her arms / And ashes in her hair.*

'Fugue' had never worked for us live – another case of a song needing more than the three of us could play.

Pete distorted Karl's vocal track into a hollow groan, then wove bits of it in between phrases of the music. He used a drum machine to shadow Ian's tight drumming. Finally, he got Karl and me to write a delicate keyboard track; then he brought Matt Pearce, the keyboard player from Silent Majority, into the studio to record it. The end result was genuinely disorientating, since none of us could work out who had played what. We never performed that song again.

There were three tracks we recorded that didn't get used. One of them, 'A Yard of Skin', would have been on the second album. The last track we recorded on *Hard Shadows* was 'For the Distance', which had the simplest arrangement of them all. Karl's voice sounds so flat and exhausted on that song because we used his final take, at 2 a.m. after too many cigarettes and cans of strong lager. Pete dubbed a train whistle over the last few seconds. We only had one more recording session booked; somehow, we knew the job was finished.

Karl came back to my flat and slept so deeply I had to let his coffee go cold in the morning – and again at lunchtime. He surfaced in the afternoon, slow and red-eyed; after some blank dialogue, he left to go and see Janis. I was vaguely relieved: his emptiness was scaring me. I didn't want to pin his shadow to my wall.

Two other events from that time stick in my head. The first is a party at Nathan and Steve's, ten days after the General Election. They were a young couple, friends of Dominic's, living near town on the edge of the jewellery quarter. These were mostly people I'd got to know through Adrian, and Karl had only met one or two of them. It was already dark when we got to the party. Their flat was on the second floor of a small private block, but we could hear the music on the street. Dannii Minogue. Although the frontage of the building was a tasteful ash-toned brick, the spiral staircase was whitewashed and manky like any housing estate interior.

This is it. The walls of Nathan and Steve's flat were covered with framed prints from Athena or HMV: Monroe, Madonna, Mark Wahlberg, Minogue Senior. The light came from pink bulbs in modernist fibre-glass lamps on the tables. In the flawless kitchen, silver cans of Grolsch and bottles of dry white wine perspired brightly on the. Formica shelf. Black plastic bowls of nuts, Twiglets or pretzels were placed on every appropriate surface. It looked as though they had just moved in, though they'd been living there for a couple of years.

That afternoon. Triangle had been in the studio recording 'Third Flight'. Karl had been on great form, injecting a harsh urgency into his singing and guitar playing that Ian and I were working hard to match. In between takes, he'd been scribbling down lyrics and chord sequences for a new track. The music had focused him. This evening, despite a shave and a red silk shirt that made him look vaguely Italian, he was under a shadow. People smiled at him, but his lack of response put them off. There was a distant look in his eyes – not the endearing lost look of an innocent, but the confusion of a fighter whose opponent has suddenly vanished. I led him into the kitchen, where he seized a half-bottle of Vladivar and a tumbler.

Dominic had brought his friend Sally, a red-haired woman in her early twenties who was drinking and talking rapidly. 'What are we doing here?' she said to a girl wearing a flattened beret. 'What has anyone got to celebrate? It's just consumer bullshit—' she waved a jagged hand at the kitchen unit '— and lifestyle crap, keeping the bourgeoisie contented while the oppression tightens. What do these *queens* care about women *anyway*? They're celebrating the whole culture of men as heroes and women as accessories... I can't work, I can't go out at night, I can't even walk down the street without being insulted. What do these bastards care?' She broke off to light a cigarette; her fingers were trembling.

In the living-room, Dominic was talking to a recently qualified therapist called Gary – who was probably the only person there whom Dominic would *not* talk to about his love life. Gary asked me how the band were doing; I told him about the album and how, after the initial sense of flatness, the recording process was taking on a scary excitement of its own. Dominic stopped nibbling pretzels and commented: 'You said before that Karl doesn't like the gay scene. Is that because it doesn't go with his image as a rock musician?' This was a jab aimed at Gary, who twitched and said: 'I wouldn't think that had much to do with it. Every guy wants to be in a rock band.'

'Well, *I* don't,' Dominic arched. 'I'd like to be a great, *great* songwriter like Stephen Sondheim...'

'Or Andrew Lloyd-Webber?' said Gary.

'Well, he must be doing something right. Or why would Elaine Page record his songs?'

In the kitchen, Sally and her bereted companion were still cataloguing their oppression to each other over a shared pack of Marlboro. Their anger had reached such a pitch that no one else would go near them. I thought about the election. How feminists, like socialists, were living in a space narrowed by defeat. Most of them tried to hold on and wait for a chance to do more than believe. But others would rather choke than breathe tainted air. So they fought everything around them, accepting pain as evidence of the struggle. The moment of crisis froze into a way of life. I could see it, but I couldn't feel it.

Karl had gone. I found him in the bedroom, where several people were huddled against the wall. The bed was covered with coats. Karl and one of Dominic's exes were finishing off the half-bottle of Vladivar and sharing a battered pack of Embassy. There was a pattern here that I felt excluded from. The ex was near forty, but tall and fit (in both senses). Not one of Karl's types, I hoped. The wine had a faintly chemical bouquet. *Château des Fausses flames with added antifreeze. Breaks the ice at parties.* I headed for the toilet, where half a dozen people were waiting impatiently. 'Mark's in there with that TV producer from Nottingham,' Steve explained. 'Been twenty minutes now. They're probably editing the footage.'

Time passed. I found another room where people were dancing; an Erasure album jittered from speakers around a bare floor. A red light-bulb glowed through a Chinese paper lantern, a moon of blood. Karl was standing by the wall, mouthing a bottle of Budweiser. I pulled him onto the floor and we danced together, awkwardly, walled in by moving shadows. I could smell the vodka on his breath. His dark mouth fastened on mine; then he kissed my neck, hard, his teeth denting the skin. He drew back and smiled at me. I knew what he was thinking. He might not like this party very much, but where else could we dance together like this? His depression was lifting.

We found some more alcohol and settled in a corner of the bedroom. 'These people are so fucked,' he muttered to me. 'Little princes with their Bette Midler albums and their bathrooms full of cosmetics and their petty little careers. They're so full of shit, if you fucked them they'd change shape. Except that William, the tall guy. He's not full of shit. He's just empty.'

I was about to ask him what he meant when I heard glass breaking and voices shouting in the next room. Something thudded against the wall. Then I heard Sally's voice, calling. 'Dominic! Help me!' The pile of coats on the bed rose like a swamp creature and fell apart, revealing the dishevelled forms of Dominic and another boy. I lipread the word *fuck* on Dominic's pale face.

In the kitchen, several broken glasses had scattered their jewellery across the pale blue lino. Two men were holding Sally's arms as she twisted to get at someone who had backed against the wall. It was Gary. 'Fucking woman-hating pig,' she snapped at him. 'So scared of women you have to fuck boys.' Gary shook his head, too angry to speak. Then Steve charged into the room, crushing glass underfoot. 'Come on,' he said to her. 'Time to go.' As Sally broke away from the other men's grip, Steve grabbed her left arm with both hands. Her black shawl flapped loose, like a torn cobweb. Confused, I followed them into the hallway.

Steve was in a towering rage. He pulled the flat door open and shoved the terrified Sally down the spiral staircase, yelling 'Get out! Get out!' Whenever she tried to stand still, he pushed her arms and shoulders violently; the only way she could stay upright was to keep moving back. Finally, he threw open the door to the street. With a breathless cry, Sally backed through the doorway. I followed with some vague intention of helping her find a cab, checking she was okay. But then, Karl stepped quietly past me and took hold of Steve before he could slam the door.

Karl twisted Steve around, ripping the top buttons off his shirt, and slammed him against the wall. 'I didn't know you were into beating up women,' he said. His voice was low and icy. Karl wasn't that strong, but he was taller than Steve. I'd never seen him angry like this before, and didn't want to again.

Steve glanced at him drunkenly. 'She's mad,' he said. 'She's a fucking lunatic.'

'So you're helping by nearly breaking her neck? You could see she was pissed. You're a fucking bully. And a coward.'

'You can fuck off too, Mick. Who the fuck brought you?'

Steve lurched towards Karl, punching his ribs. Karl didn't move. I could hear Sally crying, some distance away from the open door. Steve blundered into Karl, swinging another punch. It hit the side of Karl's face. Suddenly, Karl exploded. He punched Steve hard in the stomach, then stepped back and drove a fist up into Steve's mouth. Another three or four silent blows, and Steve collapsed heavily in the doorway. His face was sheathed with blood. Karl stepped out into the street; I followed him, closing the door behind me. Sally was standing in the roadway, open-mouthed, her face dead white. There was no colour anywhere on the street, just pale lights and dense blocks of shadow.

I walked up to her. 'Are you okay?' She nodded, staring. 'What happened?' I asked.

'What happened? I was assaulted. You saw. That pig threw me down the stairs. I'm going to phone the police, now.' She looked in both directions; there was no telephone box. 'I'm not leaving.' The curtains of Nathan and Steve's flat were still closed. I could hear music pounding from the second floor, high notes riding the waves of bass. Red wine surged in my throat, and I had to shut my eyes. When I opened them, Karl was standing between us. He put a hand on each of our shoulders.

'Let's get away from here,' he said. 'Before he comes after us. Or they find him.' We formed a V in the roadway, heading for Snow Hill. It wasn't long after midnight; people were still queuing up outside the clubs, and black cabs formed most of the traffic. Each of us, alone, might well have collapsed; but together, we kept going. Karl no longer seemed capable of violence. He hardly seemed to know where he was. I concentrated on the rhythm of walking.

'It makes me so angry,' Sally protested as we came to a taxi rank outside the glassy Post & Mail building. 'The way those queens pretend they adore women, when the only women they can stand are the stupid bitches who adore *them*. They're all a lot of fucking pricks.' She laughed uneasily. 'I'm not homophobic, you know. I just don't appreciate men who hate women.'

'What happened back there?' I asked.

Sally looked blankly at me, then shook her head. 'It was just that guy being a prick. I don't remember what I said. He was going on about… something. I don't know.'

By now, I was finding it impossible to keep track of who represented what, or what anything meant. But it was late. Tomorrow it would be easier. I didn't like men who used violence against women. And I didn't like having my inability to take action in a crisis proved to me once again. Sally's taxi drove away; she huddled in the back, becoming invisible. Karl stood still. 'Let's go home,' he said. 'We're recording tomorrow.' In the cab, going back to Karl's place, we didn't touch.

A week or so later, one of the recording sessions broke down. It was one of the tracks we didn't use, an icy little number about an insomniac going for a walk in the middle of the night and finding the streets full of zombie-like people. Ian and I tried to give it a driving beat, but Karl kept trying to break down the structure – to inject panic and confusion. It was an approach that worked better in the songs for the second album; but here, before we'd even recorded 'Fugue', it seemed like a blind alley.

After hours of nothing coming together, I suggested that Karl might try using a vocoder to get the effect of disorientation he was talking about. Karl looked at me as if I were trying to sell him double glazing. 'Can you stop thinking like a machine for just one fucking minute? Everything's technique with you, isn't it?'

'It has to be,' I snapped.

Karl stared at me furiously; I stared back at him. Not many people could do that. Then he laughed, unstrapped his guitar and put it gently on the floor. 'Pub,' he said, and was out the door before Pete could try to stop him. Ian muttered something about Rachel, curry night and getting home.

Outside, the sun was setting; black shadows were tilted like the bars of a cage. I found Karl at the back of the Forge Tavern, drinking whiskey and staring at a wall covered with framed industrial photographs. 'Have you noticed how strange fire looks in black and white? So pure, like the smoke's just a shadow. No heat. No sweat.' He drained his glass, biting the ice. 'Will you get me another?'

We sat and talked for a while. It was a difficult conversation. He was apologetic about the argument, the recording session, Janis and even Elaine; but I couldn't get him to say what was bugging him. 'The songs aren't there,' he said. 'They don't feel right. Or maybe the tracks are fine, and it's just me that's wrong. What do *you* think?' I didn't try to answer. We talked about how the words fitted into the music; Karl was still insecure about his guitar playing, and I was in no mood for cuddling his ego. Neither of us could afford to keep buying whiskey in pubs, but we had cash. Debt was becoming our local.

I'm not sure quite what made him walk out of the pub without telling me. Perhaps nothing at all. I came back from the toilet and he was gone. A few minutes later, confused and angry, I went to look for him. Somehow I knew he wasn't on the bus home.

Night had fallen. The streetlamps in Digbeth were quite far apart, but the sky was heavily stained with reflected light. I walked at random, looking out for a solitary figure. A tall man crossed the road ahead of me, but then bent his white head over the pile of rags he was guarding. A dog threw itself violently against a locked gate, leading a pack of echoes. Then I saw him, on the other side of an empty car park, walking away. I recognised his stooping, uneven walk; the way his b lack hair seemed to remove his face.

I followed him for a hundred yards or so, around a couple of corners, drawing closer but not wanting to shout in case he ran. Did he know I was stalking him? Did he want me to? At last, he came to a railway bridge and paused. As I approached him from behind, a train passed overhead; it had small red lights attached to its wagons. Karl turned, and suddenly it wasn't him. Not even like him. A younger man, stocky, blond. He looked straight at me. Panicking, I asked: 'Got a light?'   .

'Yeah.' He reached in his jacket pocket, pulled out a small plastic lighter.

I pretended to search my shirt and trouser pockets. 'Fuck. Left my cigarettes in the car. Sorry to bother you—'

He smiled. 'Don't want a light at all, do you? I know what you want. This.' Stepping back into the shadow of the bridge, he began to unbuckle his jeans.

Pavlov was wrong. I shook my head and ran, turning corners at random, finding my way through some weird instinct to the bottom of Fazeley Street, close to the studio. There was another railway bridge there, with stiff worms of lime crawling from its roof. From here, it was a mile or so downhill to Digbeth High Street and the number 50 bus route. Instead, I carried on up the hill. Security lights flashed over yards filled with broken scaffolding, car bodies, nothing at all. Then I was at the narrow building Furnace Records had leased as a studio. No lights were on. The faint rhythm of the music could have been a night shift in the factory next door.

I let myself in and climbed the stairs in darkness. The music grew louder. It was 'Stranger Key', without the vocal track. My hands and ears guided me to the studio door. It was open. I reached for the light-switch, but didn't press it.

The music pounded and surged around us, an enclosure

without walls. I could see a point of red light on the tape deck. The track reached its conclusion and juddered to a halt, without the slow fade we added later on. Against the level whine of the machine, I heard Karl's breathing. He was standing by the wall, close to me. 'Karl,' I said. 'It's me.' He reached out, drew me to him. Our mouths clasped together like empty hands.

CHAPTER 6

static

Your dreams are spread on the road
Petrol mixed with rain
One match and it's all gone
— Triangle

Alan Winter loved the album. He took the three of us and Rachel out to dinner – a Chinese restaurant in St Paul's Square, not far from the Furnace Records building. Hockley is a district composed entirely of backstreets. With his shabby charcoal-grey suit and permanent stubble, Alan fitted its vaguely criminal ambience so well that he could have been hiding there. Perhaps he was. We ate at a revolving table with little dishes scattered across it. 'This record's frightening,' he said. 'It's so romantic, and so violent. Like fist fucking on a gondola.' Karl touched my knee under the table, leaned over and whispered *Later*. A lot of red wine was drunk, a lot of rubbish talked about urban blues and urban ghosts. It was that kind of evening.

Over coffee, Alan began to sketch out plans for a new contract, a tour, more recording sessions. He knew we wouldn't sign anything there and then. But his seduction technique was immaculate: sell us the idea when drunk, and we'd find it harder to reject when sober. If things went as well as he said they would, we probably wouldn't stay with Furnace Records for long. But I knew Karl liked the idea of helping to build up a small label. The immediate plan was a short tour to promote the album and practise the new songs, then a proper nationwide tour when the album came out in October. Meanwhile, Alan said, we could rush out a single and get it some evening radio play. But which track?

Here, of course, we couldn't agree. Karl suggested 'Third Flight', because it always worked live. I thought 'Stranger Key' was more distinctive, more likely to get noticed. Rachel suggested 'His Mouth', because 'it's beautiful and strange, like having your genitals tattooed'. Ian blinked sleepily, muttered '"Fugue"... when you've heard it, you can't get it out of your head,' then went back to his dream of cosmic percussion. Alan said 'Road Into Fire', and gave us three good reasons why it would work as a single. I can't remember what they were, but they were persuasive. At least we were happy about playing it live.

Near midnight, we staggered out into the warm summer rain. St Paul's Square was like an underground cave, all blurred lights and dripping stone. Rachel held up her hands. 'The stars are melting.'

Karl put his arm round me. 'Let's walk home,' he said confidently. 'It isn't far at all... Where the fuck are we?'

'St Paul's Square.'

'By our standards, maybe. But those were very harsh times.'

The five of us shambled up to Hockley Hill, wrapped in a wet blanket of darkness. Ian and Rachel caught a black cab; Alan caught another, waving goodbye to us from the murky window. Karl and I went on to the Hockley flyover: a swooping arc of stone, like a still image of something in flight. Rain dripped from its edges onto the pale, broken concrete where we walked.

We went back into the studio for an afternoon to record 'Silence Broken Down', the instrumental on the B-side of 'Road Into Fire'. Alan rewarded us with our own tour bus: a sleek, compact vehicle, almost new, with a body the colour of butterscotch and smoked windows like sunglasses for an alien. Inside, there were three long seats behind the driver's cabin – enough for maybe nine skinny people, or three sleeping bags. It had central locking, and closed up as hermetically as an Egyptian tomb. It was quiet, inconspicuous, but quite evidently a band's tour vehicle. That the previous owners had left a few black cigarette burns in the grey seat covers, like dead insect eyes, didn't bother us very much.

Karl quit his job at the TV and audio shop; I was only doing casual work in any case. Ian and Rachel had some money saved; and she had always earned more than him, so the band's transition to 'professional' status wasn't too difficult for them. I don't know if I envied them the apparent stability of their relationship. Probably not: I couldn't have stood having that much to lose.

'Road Into Fire' did much better than 'The Answer'.

Mark Radcliffe played it a few times on his late-evening show and commented: 'If you've ever tried to get through Spaghetti Junction the night the Birmingham chapter of the Hell's Angels are having their annual get-together... you'll probably be dead, not listening to this.' *Melody Maker* called it 'a weird midnight travelogue, like the soundtrack to some postindustrial road movie.' *NME* paid it a backhanded compliment: 'Triangle's new single is a four-minute rewrite of *The Odyssey* and sounds curiously like Morrissey fronting the Jesus and Mary Chain. If that sounds to you like a formula for greatness, then you are a sad little indie tosser and Triangle will be the new love of your non-life.' That delighted us, since the *NME*'s core readership are like the clients of a dominatrix: they feel validated by abuse.

A local station called Radio Scratching, run by two middle-aged hippies in Erdington, played 'Road Into Fire' solidly for a month. Karl and I went to their rather shabby studio to do a graveyard shift interview. We told them – and any listeners there might have been – about *Hard Shadows* and our tour plans. Later still, we bonded with Pete and Mark over a bottle of Jack Daniels. They were a couple, their macho bluster a typical Brummie irony that regular listeners understood. They were also deep-dyed blues fanatics – electric more than acoustic, steel more than cotton. Mark knew Simon McKie from Blue Away; he was in Bristol now, playing guitar on various people's records and smoking too much hash in a hopeless attempt to stop drinking.

Simon was Blue Away's vocalist, lead guitarist and chief songwriter. A tall man with big hands and wavy black hair, capable of injecting pace and venom into the most languid track – or, alternatively, slowing everything down to the point of silence. He wasn't a great singer, but his guitar was his real voice – howling and moaning like a tenor saxophone with a broken bottle in its throat. I had idolised him, but got no closer than the limited intimacy of music and booze. Apart from one night, when he'd stayed at my flat and I'd blown him twice. He'd even reciprocated, sensitive enough to do more than play the man. At that time he was between girlfriends – not a state that lasted long with Simon. I hadn't said much to Karl about him. There's a line of Simon's I always loved: *It was in the past / Before it even happened.*

Karl was nervous about touring. He didn't like the idea of travelling from gig to gig with no life in between, 'like the whole world's just a backstage. There's nowhere to hide if it goes wrong.' It was like a widescreen version of stage fright, and it shadowed the rest of his time with the band. I began to see why he'd waited so long before getting into the music business. He was afraid of being possessed – by record companies, by audiences, by music itself. Ian seemed entirely matter-of-fact about touring, despite Rachel's claim that he got jetlag if he travelled further than Halesowen. I focused on my playing and other practical things, trying not to think beyond what was visible.

That phase of preparation seemed oddly static. The days were bright and humid, building up to a storm that never came. The nights were too warm for either sleeping or sex, which left only one alternative: well-chilled alcohol. In the evenings, at least the cinemas were cool. Ian got me and Karl tickets for several films at the Triangle – including *Stalker* and *The Crying Game*, which we both thought were among the best films we'd ever seen. Stress can heighten your enjoyment of things – films and music in particular. You watch and listen more closely, not sure how much is really there and how much is in your imagination. That moment of going over is as close to the truth as you'll ever get. Whatever comes after.

———————

Two days before the tour, I phoned Karl at three in the morning. He answered almost at once. 'Hello?'

'Karl, it's me. You're a madman.'

The sound of shifting bedclothes. 'What's the matter, David?'

'I couldn't sleep. It's too hot. So I got up and looked at the map. Thinking about the tour, the seven dates. Bristol. Reading. Cambridge. Nottingham. Sheffield. Preston. Stoke.'

'Do you know what time it is?'

'I kept thinking, *why Preston*? There's nothing there but dead factories and miserable pubs. Then I saw it. The seven venues. It's a triangle, with Birmingham at the centre.'

'Or Stourbridge. Yes. It was Ian's idea, not mine.'

'Why didn't you tell me?'

'We thought you might be a bit superstitious about it.'

'Like fuck. I couldn't give a toss.' My hangover was kicking in early. 'I don't even care that we're going round the triangle anticlockwise. It's just the stupidity of it, Karl. The sheer fucking—'

Who's that? I heard someone say, quite close to the receiver. A female voice. More shifting of bedclothes.

'Look David, I don't feel like chatting just now. It's late, and I've got things to sort out. I'll talk to you tomorrow. Okay?' The receiver clicked, and I was listening to static.

The Vacant Lot came with us as the support band. They had their own vehicle, a black-painted transit van with an expressionless version of the Smiley face on the back. The face broke open to reveal a smoke-stained, metallic interior with cushions, instruments and bottles scattered in comfortable disarray. Andy, the drummer, had wired up the car stereo to an additional speaker in the back; with the door closed and 'Wherever I May Roam' shaking the dimly lit walls, it was like being inside the head of a misunderstood teenager.

Our road crew was pretty minimal: two young guys from Furnace Records, called Jim and Alex. With Martin, that made eleven in all. Jim, who had red hair and the face of a happy squirrel, was a genius at handling guitars. Alex, a massive guy with long black hair, took care of lighting and sound. Those two, Karl and Andy made up a natural team for discussion of technical matters. Or even, in a crisis, for actually sorting out problems. I'd never shared Karl's interest in the theory of sound transmission and reproduction; during this tour, it seemed to go beyond the anal into the small intestine. It was a part of his struggle against stage fright.

In retrospect, that was when Karl and Martin started to fall out. On the way to the first gig, the Bristol Fleece and Firkin, Martin told us he'd got us all single rooms at the hotel. I'm feeling generous.'

Karl and I looked at each other. 'You might have told us,' Karl said.

'Why?'

'Because we don't want single rooms. We want to be together, you cunt.'

'They won't like that. Another time, maybe you and David could get a twin room. You could push the beds together.'

As it turned out, Karl had a double bed and it was easy for us to sleep together. We fucked in the morning and came downstairs too late for breakfast, feeling vaguely awkward. Although touring forced us to be together almost all the time, the nights and early mornings were our only chance to be *alone* together. We used those times to rediscover what we felt, creating a fragment of home in the backstage world. It helped Karl to recover from the manic state of performance, or from the bleak emptiness that sometimes followed it. I was glad to help – not because of any master/servant crap, but because I could see how much he needed it.

During the journeys, he tended to huddle in a back seat with his lyrics notebook or a crime novel. He'd brought a dozen or so Cornell Woolrich novels, all in black-covered paperback editions from the seventies. One night, drunk, he read me a few pages from a story about a killer on the run from the police. His attempts to cover up his crime had only resulted in his becoming a wanted man, since he imagined everyone who saw him was a witness and had to be silenced. After four more unnecessary killings, he was shot by a cop and knew he was dying. Bleeding under his jacket, but unwilling to get help, he got into a taxi and asked the driver to take him around the park. The driver set off and switched on the radio. *It made the pain a little easier to bear, like music always does.*

After gigs, or on non-gig evenings, Karl drank like a madman. He seemed to be reaching for silence, trying to shut out the music in his head – even if it meant shutting out everything else. But no matter how wrecked he was, he could always walk, always function at a mechanical level. The rhythm was in place, but the vocal track was fucked. One particularly chaotic night – in Reading, I think – I lost him in a crowded nightclub. After twenty minutes, I found him near the entrance. He was leaning against the wall, twitching in a way that was part dance and part naked anxiety. 'Hello,' he greeted me casually. 'Are you getting around?'

'Actually, Karl, I was looking for you. Are you all right?'

'David, are you getting a round?' He gestured towards the bar. 'It's okay, I'll get one.' His gaze was bloodshot but steady. 'Straight vodka, lots of ice?'

A few of those late nights, when Karl had withdrawn into the shuttered privacy of his own head, I ended up talking to Diane. She was a quiet, self-contained person; her singing depended on concentrated effort rather than spontaneous rage. I found her dry, ironic wit something of a relief after Karl's moody intensity and Ian's unconvincing attempts to be mystical. 'I'm not comfortable with all this divine inspiration stuff,' she told me. 'If you think what's in your head comes from angels, or demons, or Earth spirits, or whatever, you're just trying to avoid knowing that you've made it. You're working even when you dream. Writing songs is just another kind of work, not a magical communion.'

Karl, in particular, worried her: 'He's got no balance. It's like he's about to fall over. He holds onto people to balance himself, then lurches away from them, expects them still to be there when he falls back. He's got no sense of self. He needs people, but he doesn't need them. Like that line in the Cantels song: *She wants then she doesn't want me / I don't know what she means.* That's why we split up really. That, and the fact that he gave me syphilis. But I'm sure he's told you about that.'

Live, The Vacant Lot were more convincing than before. Diane's sense of atmosphere was winning out over the crass HM dynamics of the two guitarists. Matt, the lead guitarist, was more willing to let her carry the song, his riffs backing her voice like blows provoking cries. Before each set, and in between songs, Diane was quiet and very still. The words broke from her as she stared into the darkness, apparently surprised by her own voice. *You watched your children / So you said / They saw the eyes / In the back of your head.* I could see why Karl had been so attracted to her. She had depth without inconsistency: she was the same all the way down.

Triangle performed well enough. There were some technical problems: feedback from tired amps and interference from backing tracks, making Karl wish bitterly that we were famous enough to do an MTV *Unplugged* show. Most of the venues we played, the back wall was so close the sound was mostly echoes. Being away from Birmingham made us realise who our fans were: the people who bought a T-shirt at one gig, then came to another gig wearing it. Not surprisingly, 'Road Into Fire' always seemed to go down well. I began to hear it as a song about touring, and about how Karl felt on stage. *They'll travel with you on the road / Their voices, their faces, their hands / Just to tell you you're alone.* Because it was a quiet song without the aggression of 'Third Flight' or 'Curfew Town', he seemed a bit lost in it. Although it was great to have the album finished – as if the songs were already being played behind us, and all we had to do was let them through – it seemed to make Karl feel more distant from the band. It was as though he was afraid of the music. The performances became dislocated, things that should have come together seeming more like call and response.

Martin was worried about the sound. 'It's too bleak. You're not coming through to the audience. Nobody wants to leave a gig feeling cold and empty inside.' But Diane, whose instincts were less commercial, was more impressed. 'I don't like you as a hero,' she said to Karl. I'd rather listen to The Fall than U2. It's good to be reminded that things are complex.' Our audiences were enthusiastic, but small. We were playing rock clubs, sometimes in rooms above pubs; a hundred people at most. Martin said that going for smaller venues wouldn't help, since the crowd usually came with the venue. 'You have to make yourself visible.'

The audiences seemed younger than in Birmingham. We were feeling our age, of course; Karl was twenty-eight, Ian and I were twenty-six. Now that Triangle was beginning to take off, we began to realise how much time we'd wasted. How fast things moved on. Fans talked to us about new bands we'd scarcely heard of: Marion, Strangelove, Tindersticks. New blood, waiting for contracts to be signed in.

I remember one moment when lost time seemed to harden around us. We'd arrived in Nottingham late, after The Vacant Lot's transit van had suffered engine failure while crawling along the baked M1. We were hung over, tired, and wearing as little as possible. There were already a few fans outside the locked doors of Nottingham Rock City. As we parked, a young couple waved to us from the shade of the doorway. They were maybe eighteen; despite the heat, they were wearing furry black cardigans that matched their electric hair. Karl glanced at them and touched my hand. 'We're getting old,' he said. I felt a loss of innocence, a tingling shock of envy.

The best gig of that tour was the last one: the Stage at Hanley, in Stoke. We arrived in time to check in at a small Greek-owned hotel and go out for a pizza. Hanley was crowded with old buildings, many of them abandoned or in demolition. The roads were tilted and narrow, with traffic bombing around corners. Near the venue, we saw a poster for Triangle among many others on the bricked-up windows of a church. The clock on its stunted tower was stuck at one minute to three.

While The Vacant Lot went through their soundcheck at the Stage, we quit the dressing-room for the more reassuring shadows of the pub next door. The Stage Door was an old theatre pub, with hundreds of yellowed cigarette cards showing forties and fifties film actors displayed in cases on the walls. The only link with the club next door was the jukebox, which had so much metal you could have used an electromagnet to make it jive. Ian selected five Metallica tracks, including 'The Unforgiven' and 'Friend of Misery' – the latter probably a dig at Karl, who'd been silent all evening. He'd been in a weird mood earlier, getting Martin to play The Pogues and Christy Moore on the tape deck – and that Sinead O'Connor song about leaving England to stop her child growing up like the English.

Travelling's not the ideal way to prepare for a gig. The

band becomes your world: you can't relate to anything else, and you can't be alone. It's easy to lose the sense of what was firing you in the first place. You get obsessed with technique and equipment, like lovers who've forgotten the romance. Karl's way of holding onto the music was to hide in himself. It seemed to work for him, though it pissed off the rest of us.

Ironically, the Stage had an unusually small stage for a club venue. About two feet behind the drum kit was a breeze-block wall with three extractor fans, through which you could see out into a grim backstreet. The soundcheck indicated that the bass and drums would echo mercilessly, as if the whole room was a speaker. This was fine by us. As the club slowly filled up with thin, drowsy-looking kids in Ride and Primal Scream T-shirts, we bought some drinks and sat at the back. There were a few faces I recognised from previous gigs, but no one noticed us. According to Martin, you always got fair-sized audiences here. What else was there to do?

The Vacant Lot played a subdued, rather downbeat set that exploded into rage, then spiralled down into melancholy. Andy's drums crashed through the dark like thunder; a hiss of feedback blurred the silences like rain. 'The Lines Are Dead' was crowded with electronic sound effects, threatening to break down the song. In 'Gift', a new song they'd been rehearsing on stage, the guitar howled savagely between verses that were backed only by slow drumming. *It was a gift, its voice was black / I tried and tried to give it back / It was a gift, it came from you / It had a face I never knew.* They were getting more like Triangle all the time. But they weren't borrowing our melodies or riffs: it was the whole approach, the coldness, the vibe of fear, that seemed to have infected them. It was like watching cast iron turn to broken glass.

As the lights came up, we scuttled hastily to the dressing- room and wrote out our set list. Karl decided he wanted to start with 'Curfew Town' instead of 'Third Flight', because it seemed more appropriate to a town like Hanley. We'd keep 'Third Flight' in reserve, to play if the audience got bored and started talking; if the gig went well, we'd keep it for the encore. That sorted, we stood uneasily and watched The Vacant Lot getting drunk. After their uncharacteristically moody set, they hastily reverted to type and started improvising obscene versions of Triangle lyrics, accompanied by a mock blow job routine inspired by David Bowie and Mick Ronson. While Matt and Jerry collapsed in post-coital rapture on the dressing-room floor, Diane and Andy swapped kisses smeared with Southern Comfort.

Karl, whose stage fright seemed to have come and gone ahead of time, applauded wearily. 'Don't they look sweet,' he muttered to me, 'like a double-neck guitar?' Diane flipped him the bird. Resignedly, Karl gripped the neck of an open whiskey bottle and took a fierce swig. He shuddered as it went down, then looked at me with eyes full of dark fire. 'You ready?' He'd say the same thing to me in bed, sometimes.

Edging into place on the narrow stage, we stood there backlit for a few seconds. The white light blinked and reddened. T-shirted kids were packed at the front: a pent-up moshpit waiting to be switched on. Ian struck the dry opening beats of 'Curfew Town'. Karl's guitar muttered and cleared its throat, then began to sing. His voice followed the melody, raw and melancholic. A hand touched the back of my neck; it was only the vibration from the speakers. The audience swayed uneasily. *We lay down in the dark / And counted the stars in our blood / The windows were broken / The children were crying to God.* As the song ended, a hiss of static drowned the applause.

Next, we played a brooding version of 'Stranger Key'. Karl stood very still, focusing all his rage on some invisible figure just in front of him. The sound was dense; it felt louder than it was. Despite all the work on melody we'd done in the studio, I could feel the band's hidden violence about to break loose. Karl sang like he was pursued by demons; his playing was more uneven than usual, but it didn't matter. Ian and I kept up the structure, a hard wall of rhythm on which Karl could stand to curse the sky. As we shuddered to a halt, I saw him wipe the sweat off his face. The crowd were surging forward, leaving the back of the club empty.

To let Karl rest his throat, we played 'Silence Broken Down' fast and hard. Ian and Karl did a strange effect like a gun firing and glass shattering. A boy got up onto the stage and jittered in the pale light, then threw himself backward onto the front row. They caught him and passed him back, safe. It didn't always work like that. Sometimes they'd let you fall. Without pausing, we went on into 'The Answer'. During its slow buildup, there wasn't a sound from the audience. The lights flickered, red and green. Karl's back twisted as his head dipped below his shoulders, reminding me of a teenager trying to box. *Take me with you when you go / But you'll never have the answer / 'Cos you'll never want to know.* It was a fragile moment, but it triggered the ascent to a storm of riffs. The moshpit went crazy, surfing and struggling like a monster trying to tear itself apart. Chords were drowned in a fury too dark to be called white noise. We flew with it for a couple of minutes; then stopped dead.

Next was a stark, panicky version of 'Nowhere To Go', Karl walking in a spotlight like he was under surveillance. He played a few sharp chords at the end: pulses of energy, too high-pitched to echo. Then 'His Mouth' was slow and dreamy, the washes of guitar more gentle than ever before. An unintended but quite effective surge of feedback distorted the bassline halfway through; Karl tensed but didn't lose the thread. His voice was wavering like its own shadow. Blue lights flickered, died, came back.

As Karl changed his guitar, I could hear voices talking in the audience. The mass of bodies at the front was breaking up into knots. I signalled to Karl that we should play 'Third Flight', but he shook his head. 'Here's a song about going home,' he said. 'You think it'll be different. But nothing ever changes.' We plunged into 'Still and Moving Water', a song which needed careful handling. But Karl went at it like Nick Cave, howling the words and sacrificing melody to rhythm. The call-and-response of the lead and bass guitar, usually a careful rise to passion, became a dirty and desperate fuck. We should play 'His Mouth' like this, I realised. Christ, we should *fuck* like this. Karl broke a string, tried to play on – then gripped the mic in both hands and shouted *Still water's running shallow* – then improvised a verse to follow it: *But blood is running deep / However long I lay there / You would never sleep.* He left out the last chorus and dropped to a crouch, gulping beer from the small bottle behind his pedal rack.

We closed with 'For the Distance'. After the violence of the last track, it sounded faint and displaced. The blue slowly faded to black as Alex brought the sound level on each mic down to within a breath of silence. Only Ian's drums went on, a dry heartbeat. Then nothing. 'Cheers.

Goodnight.' As we stumbled through the narrow corridor to the dressing- room, Karl muttered: 'Now we'll show those fuckers how to drink.'

The Vacant Lot were slumped in a corner, looking dozy and furtive. Matt was crumpling a piece of tinfoil in one fist. A bottle of Southern Comfort stood on the table. Karl opened it and poured half its contents into three tumblers; we drained them while the applause slowly faded. Maybe they didn't *want* an encore, I thought suddenly. It was nearly eleven; the bar would close in a few minutes. You couldn't blame them. As the whiskey made my lips, fingers and balls tingle, I heard the crowd begin to stamp their feet. Their voices floated like the sound of cars in a tunnel, not quite distinct and not quite together. Ian picked up his drumsticks; but Karl sat immobile, staring at his empty glass. He was fucked.

Silence descended. Then Karl looked at me. 'Go on,' he said. 'I'll follow you.' Ian and I walked back onto the dark stage, glimpsing a huddle of faces blank with expectation. We couldn't start 'Third Flight' without Karl's guitar. To our relief, he stepped between us after a few inert seconds and waited for Ian's time signature before ripping the silence in half. We built up tension with jittery riffs and fragments of echoed noise, slowly filling in the gaps between Karl's lyrics. Then we let the sound fade, took a deep breath and counted to three. The jagged pulse shook the crowd like a train braking. Arms flailed in the strobe light. The faces I could see looked dazed and worried. These were indie kids, wee anorak children; they weren't expecting this.

What they were expecting, probably, was 'Road Into Fire': a hard bassline and a tender lyric, going through horror on the way to redemption. The studio version was a bit too 'epic' and U2-ish for my liking; but it was a good note to end on. Karl was slurring his words slightly, and our timing was a bit off, which gave the song an oddly vulnerable feel. Not Hell, but limbo. *Be careful out there.* It was over. No need for instrument-smashing or other childish gestures. We couldn't afford that anyway.

Backstage, The Vacant Lot had eaten most of our food; but they hadn't touched our booze. In case they were thinking about it, Karl had given them a map of Stoke-on-Trent with all the hospitals marked in red. Within a few minutes, we had everyone who'd been on the tour gathered in the dressing-room, plus a few unfamiliar faces. Jim had three youngsters from the audience with him: a boy and two girls, all dressed in black. Martin was accompanied by a tall, thin man wearing glasses, who he promptly introduced to us: 'This is Mike West.'

Karl frowned. 'To follow that star?' We knew who he was: an ex-guitarist from Scotland who'd recently joined the *NME* staff, writing scathing reviews of bands the magazine usually praised. Karl shifted his glass to his right hand and raised his left to shake. 'Hi there.' West stammered something about having been knocked out by the gig. His voice was heavily accented. Martin pressed a drink into his hand.

By midnight, we were all gathered in the hotel bar. Two men from the Stage – a DJ and a sound engineer – had joined us. Andy and Diane were asleep, huddled together on a sofa like children. Karl was drinking Bushmills in a slow, controlled way that seemed unstoppable. Jim was making determined play for one of the two girls, who was making a point of mentioning her boyfriend at every opportunity. She was very drunk, which Jim (a bit naively) seemed to regard as a green light. Her two friends – a couple with soft, lilting accents and fiercely lo-fi sympathies – were calmly watching over her. I wished I'd been a tenth as clued-up about music at their age.

The last hour or so of that night is a blur, though I'm not sure whether it was my mind or the reality that was blurred. The DJ invited us all to a party at his house the following night; we all promised to go, though we'd planned to be back in Birmingham by lunchtime. Martin carried on buying rounds on his hotel tab, insisting that Furnace Records was paying. We had a competition to find a slogan for Furnace Records, based on a song: *Hotter than July. Melting pot. A night on fire. Hotter than a crotch. Fuel for your love. The queen and the solder.* And so on. Mike's stammer healed with alcohol and growing confidence; he talked about his experiences of touring with the blues singer Jackie Leven, including a number of hilariously bleak drinking anecdotes. 'He'll tell the same stuff to his audience. Typical Scot. The Scots make confessions about drinking, the Irish make confessions about sex. They all booze and fuck just the same, but the guilt focus is different. A different compass point, like.' Meanwhile, secure in Anglo-Saxon freedom from guilt, Jim had got the dark-haired girl on her own and was gently whispering to her. Eventually, their faces moved so close together their only option was to kiss. They seemed to be holding each other up. The other two teenagers decided to head for home and take their friend with them. She was quite willing to be parted from Jim, who slumped grimly in the armchair and tuned an imaginary guitar. More whiskey materialised. The night took on the colour and consistency of amber.

———————

The next morning, Karl and I discovered we still had glasses in our hands. We used them to drink water. Lots of it. We'd crashed out in our twin room, clothed except for shoes. It was too late for breakfast; I finished a packet of Hobnobs and Karl finished a packet of cigarettes. The day swam gradually into focus, like an elusive frequency on the tour bus radio at night. Karl's face hardened from shadow to stubble. We stared at each other and vowed solemnly never to drink like that again – a ritual which, by now, had become purely ironic.

Then Martin rang to say that Neil, the DJ, would let us crash at his place if we wanted to stick around for the party. 'It won't be another heavy night. He's not into boozing.' We all gathered in the lounge, avoiding mirrors and bright lights. The Vacant Lot were keen to stay, but Ian wanted to go home. 'You'll like Neil,' Martin said. 'He's into Shamanic music, bass and drums, the rhythm of the cosmos. All that crap.'

Ian stiffened. 'Don't try to patronise me, okay? I'll stay, but only because I can't be fucked to get the train.' After some ill-humoured discussion, five people – Ian, Jim, Alex, Matt and Jerry – decided to go home in The Vacant Lot's transit van. The rest of us piled our bags and instruments into the Scarab and drove to Neil's house in Northwood, a couple of miles from the hotel. It was quite like Karl's house. Stoke generally seemed to be quite like North Birmingham or the Black Country. But the traces of industry were more recent, wounds rather than scars.

Karl and I wandered off for the afternoon. It was going to rain; the air felt warm and prickly, like a cardigan. Sunlight painted the clouds. Beyond the terraced streets, we could see the backdrop of green hills. From a distance, the elaborate Victorian frontages of the factories and civic halls looked impressive; but close up, you could see the sprayed messages and the chicken-wire over blackened glass. One street was decorated with signs and graffiti mourning a local boy called Skinny. The messages spread from a factory wall to a derelict theatre with its windows boarded up and its roof protected by coils of razor-wire. 'Like a shrine,' Karl said. 'A theatre turned inside-out. The stage is out here.'

It was a too-much-perspective kind of day. The short tour had left us exhausted but unsatisfied, waiting for the album to take our relationship with the audiences beyond a one-night stand. Unless we took steps to make the money last, we'd be broke by the end of the year. Martin was pissing us all off. Karl's drinking worried me; so did my own. The emotions we'd torn out of ourselves in the studio and on stage would be less easy to live with back in the streets of Birmingham. And here was Stoke, beautiful and destroyed, to remind us that whatever you thought was precious would go when the bailiffs came. Whether they could sell it or not. We drifted from Northwood to Hanley and back. Karl scribbled lyrics in his red notebook; I considered my chances of getting Ian McCulloch to ditch Lorraine and travel with me through an industrial wilderness. We stayed out of the pubs, at least.

The party started in Neil's gravel-strewn back yard, watching the sunset blacken the skyline with crimson and violet flame. Neil cooked a huge tray of chicken and rice. He was a quiet little man with bleached dreadlocks and pale blue eyes. His house was strangely minimal: not much anywhere but futons, cushions and speakers. We drank bottled beer and listened to the increasingly weird combination of R&B, hardcore techno and spacerock that shuddered in fits and starts from wherever his sound system was hidden. By the time it was dark outside, the music was too loud and intense to do anything but dance.

Other people arrived, mostly kids. The party spread through the entire house. Only the upstairs rooms were without speakers, though sound twisted from both ends of the hallway. Paper lampshades glowed flesh-pink or electric blue. Skinny teenage boys mimed shutting themselves up, swallowing pills. Couples writhed in the twilight zone between dancing and foreplay. Everything was on the way to becoming something else.

Karl had disappeared. Diane and Andy went upstairs to sample the contents of a foil packet they'd just bought. I was pretty much a drugs virgin, booze and dope excepted. It seemed to take so much out of people, and I wasn't sure I had much to give. Whatever. As well as beer, Neil had some vodka in the kitchen; I filled a wine-glass with it and slipped out the back door, where a few people were sprawled on the cool stone. A thin lad was leaning against the wall, his bony hands twitching in rhythm. He tugged at my sleeve as I passed. 'Hello, stranger. Are you new around here?'

'Yes, but I don't need directions to your place.'

'You don't know what you're missing.' Under his bleached eyebrows, his eyes were dark with questions. 'What brings you here? Are you staying with Neil?' I explained about Triangle and the gig. He laughed in an oddly deadpan way. 'That's fucking sad. Live music is so fucking dead, sweetheart. Nobody needs people to climb up on a stage and sing. What's the point?'

I thought of Triangle on stage, how much better we were live than in the studio. And The Fall. And the Bunnymen. 'Live music's different,' I said. 'It's something real. People still need performance. Doing it, seeing it. Like theatre.'

'Theatre? What the fuck's that? Like plays on stage? You're not telling me that still happens?' He slipped a long hand into my back pocket, fingers pressing. 'If you're so into performance, how about it?'

I made my face go blank. 'Are you a fucking queer or something?' He backed away in silence, nearly falling over in his haste to get out of my sight. I almost felt guilty.

Back inside the house, Neil and Martin were deep in some private conversation. Neil gestured towards me and whispered something to Martin, who laughed. I decided to refill my glass with vodka; but while I was looking for the bottle, the music slowed down and the kitchen began to shudder. The walls broke out in a cold sweat. I sat down in a corner, ready to cover my head if the building collapsed. Jagged electronic riffs blazed across the inside of my closed eyes. To settle myself, I listened. This music had more bass in it than house or techno: a deep blue-black pulse that held you down and stroked you into pain. It might be the next phase of dance music, but it sounded older.

Not that I was much of a dance enthusiast. At that time, the music press had just broken off its three-year affair with house and the rave scene. Three years of every other form of black music being completely ignored, while failed rock journalists like Jack Barron sneered at the 'retards' who hadn't yet connected with 'the new music revolution'. Who hadn't yet realised that wearing a baseball cap back to front and weaving around on E chanting 'ba ba *dee*, ba ba da, ba ba *dee*, ba ba da' was going to bring capitalism crashing to its knees.

When I opened my eyes, the walls were stable again. Never underestimate sulking as a displacement activity: it's helped me to hold onto my sanity since early childhood. I stood up and watched people drifting past in search of things I couldn't see. They all seemed vaguely familiar, like people I'd seen at gigs but never met. A hand gripped my shoulder. 'Y'ull roight, chuck?' It was Neil, imitating a Brummie accent.

'Fine, yeah. Just tired.'

His eyes were china-blue, amused, sympathetic. 'Do you want something to help you keep going?' He fished in the pocket of his red shirt, drew out a white pill. 'You need to relax, David. Your boyfriend's upstairs, getting stoned. I've seen him. Let the train go on running. You can travel without it. You can fly.' He was mad, I realised. I took the pill from his hand, swallowed it.

A few minutes later, Neil and I were dancing in one of the downstairs rooms. I felt much lighter and freer than before. He wove towards me, and I backed into the wall. Our belt buckles clashed. For a second, our cocks brushed together through denim. I shivered, breathing darkness. This was as good and as problem-free as it was likely to get. I smiled at Neil and headed back towards the staircase. He tugged at my sleeve. 'Wait.' We floated along a sluggish canal of faces. He ducked into the kitchen, came back with two bottles of water. 'Take these. And come back for more. Don't dry out.'

On the staircase, people were lying at impossible angles. My vision lurched like a hand-held camera. Somehow my mind was detached from my body and senses, able to read the sheet music for chaos. I wasn't fooling myself that two men touching me up within half an hour was due to my being Adonis. It was the effect of E, or a certain kind of it. I thought of the night I'd picked up a boy at the Nightingale who was tripping on a very sexual wavelength. A *love dove*, he called it. Which was how he seemed in my bed, pale arms spread out above me as he spurted over my chest, crying out *I'm flying, I'm flying*. The next morning, his hangover seemed to clothe his entire body in pain.

Music was still twisting like smoke through the upper hallway. In the first room I tried, no one was moving. The only light came from the red eyes of spliffs, though hash wasn't all I could smell. Diane was there, head tilted back, mouth open as if she was about to sing. In the next room, I could see nothing at all. From the sounds in there, a number of people were either drowning or making love. The air smelt cold, but felt warm. Then a shape reared up from the darkness and came towards me, hardening into a shadow with a pale head. It was Karl. He was fully clothed. We stood in the doorway, confused. 'Let's get out of here,' he said.

Moonlight gave the streetlamps a paler echo, turning narrow alleys into canals. In a car park framed by a cut-down brick wall, new and wrecked cars shared space. Karl and I wandered into a disused yard whose surface was patched with gravel, tarmac and grass. At the top end, there was a derelict bungalow with empty doorframes. Its interior was whitewashed. We stood there as if posing for a video, and kissed. Our lips were dry and cracked. We drank some water. All around us, these dark-smeared back-to-backs with oddly tiled doorways.

Karl was more relaxed than I'd ever seen him, even when asleep. His fierce energy had drained away, leaving him passively aware, like a child. 'I can't get over how beautiful this is.' Neither could I. The moonlight guided us from the maze of backstreets to a vast and wonderfully uncrowded cemetery park. Gravestones were placed at convenient vantage points on hillocks or in the shade of trees, as if the dead needed space to picnic or privacy to embrace.

As the foliage became thicker and the ground more uneven, Karl slipped an arm around my waist. 'It feels so safe here,' he murmured. 'Like we're not in the world. We could do anything, say anything, and not have to pay for it. I could tell you.'

'Tell me what?' He didn't reply. The moon slipped behind a cloud. It was cold here. I could smell rotting wood and fungus; it reminded me of the dark room at the party. 'What were you doing in that room?'

'Hiding.' We paused, at the edge of the wood. A series of thin, discoloured houses stood in the crease of a railway embankment. I could smell the acid smoke from a bonfire.

It had to be close by, since a grey streak was coiling in the sodium light ahead. My mouth was dry, but I had no water left. The orange light tasted of ashes. It wasn't a lamp. The house at the end of the embankment was burning.

As we stepped out of the shade of the trees, the light flared gold and crimson. I was too drugged to feel the heat from the wavering flames. In fact, I was still cold. The sounds of the fire – wood cracking, paint turning to light, cinders breaking open in the air – seemed to reach me through a dense barrier of silence.

The house was derelict, I realised, like the others. There was no glass in its windows. I could see the moon through its blazing roof. There was a balcony on the first floor, with some kind of ironwork: a rose, painted black. I looked down and saw railings around its basement. What was this house doing here? Without knowing why, I began to shake. A cloud of smoke drifted across my face; it was freezing, like mist off the sea.

Karl gripped my arm. 'Come on.' He glanced at me, then stared helplessly at the burning building. I could tell that he recognised it too. 'Come on, David.' He turned away, tugging at me. I couldn't move.

'There might be someone—' In the backlit porch, ashes rose like a bouquet of black flowers. Something moved behind them. A flake of ash touched my face, stuck, and melted. I felt Karl let go of me. Blinking smoke from my numb eyes, I turned and ran blindly after him. The red light faded around us, became a vague paleness like the edge of a shadow.

When we came back through the cemetery to the empty streets, the sky overhead was glowing faintly. Only with the dawn. We passed the disused yard and the car park, and found the street where Neil lived. But without the pulse of his sound system to guide us, we couldn't tell his house apart from the others. They all looked the same. I stumbled, and Karl put a hand across my chest to keep me upright. 'It's okay,' he muttered, holding me. 'It's okay. There was no one there. No one to be saved.'

without a face

I was searching for freedom
But I found only bars
The small hours never end
— Blue Away

A fortnight later, we caught the ferry to Ireland. Karl had friends in the Dublin music scene, and had fixed up a gig to get Triangle out of the dry, sour atmosphere of Birmingham in August. 'It rains in Ireland,' he said by way of incentive. The ferry was steeped in booze, a ship in a bottle. If you were drunk enough, it seemed not to be moving. Rachel was with us, but The Vacant Lot were off to the Only Card Worth Winning festival in Wolverhampton. The four of us sat on the deck with cans of Special Brew, watching the water shatter the morning light and drain it into deep bruises of shadow. Karl was scribbling in his notebook, biting his lip, tapping out rhythms on the grey struts of the table. The ship's engine throbbed its dull, hollow bassline at the edge between sound and feeling.

Mike West's review of the Hanley gig had appeared in the *NME* five days later:

> Triangle are a Birmingham trio on the dark side of the tracks. With an album due for release soon by Furnace Records, they are chilling audiences with their steely music and bitter, haunted songs. They alternate between loud and quiet numbers, an immaculate rhythm backing singer Karl's Irish-accented, snarling delivery. He sings about violent towns, strangers, victims, blood and sperm. Their current single 'Road Into Fire' is a bleak, desperate finale. Instead of imitating the trappings of folk music like The Waterboys, Triangle take the dark themes of traditional folk music and re-invent them as a twisted urban blues. They'll be in your town, your face and your dreams before long. Be very afraid.

The *Melody Maker*'s Gary Allen, who saw us in Bristol, was less impressed:

> Triangle are an insular and negative band. They wear their influences – the Velvets, the Bunnymen, the Smiths – like a heavy coat. Tonight's set was long on angst and sonic dry ice, but woefully short on entertainment. Perhaps it's symbolic of how out of touch indie-rock has become. Where the new dance music is all about sharing, trad rock bands like Triangle just try to make the listener feel alone. If you're feeling weighed down by existential misery, cheap cider and student loans, you're probably still better off with the Manics. Or even the Samaritans.

We liked the bit about 'sonic dry ice'. On the ferry, we

were too insular to talk football with the beered-up Man United fans just up the deck from us; but we were enjoying ourselves. Even Karl was in a good mood, talking about bands he'd seen in Dublin and Belfast on past trips. 'Even the kids playing fiddle and accordion in pubs go at it like Stiff Little Fingers. The intensity is stunning. The hunger for music.' On the road together for the first time – even if it was a road of water – Ian and Rachel clung together like teenagers on their first date, breathing an air saturated with the taste of kisses. Their eyes gathered scraps of light from the waves. Karl and I knew better than to kiss in public; but we leaned together, using drunkenness as an excuse for contact. It's a trick you'll see in any pub.

The good vibe was a little soured at Customs, where the band were detained and checked for over an hour. They went through our bags and instrument cases as if looking for a speck of dust on an army parade. Then we were separated and closely searched. The booze made me clumsy, and I felt like I was in one of those dreams where you lose your clothes or can't find the toilet on a crowded train. I don't know if they were looking for drugs, or something else. None of us spoke on the coach to Dublin.

We'd left the Scarab in Birmingham and brought our guitars, Ian having been promised the use of another band's drumkit. The wet streets glowed like strips of magnesium. Our hotel was just off the O'Connell Bridge, facing the river. Beggars sat or crouched at either end of the bridge; one held up a mug as if it contained poison he was almost ready to drink.

The hotel was old-fashioned without being grand; oversized oil paintings lent it the air of a museum. Ian and Rachel were on the second floor; Karl and I were on the third. A twin room. We tuned our guitars and practised a couple of new songs, then drank some coffee and had a quiet snog. Rain scratched at the window. Karl drifted into sleep, and I watched his face become childlike and peaceful in the grip of darkness. When he woke up, we made love and took a shower together, then went out for a walk. What had happened in Stoke was still bothering us, but we couldn't discuss it.

More rain had fallen while we were in the hotel; shop canopies were still dripping, and ghosts of the river flickered in the dark gutters. We passed along Burgh Quay, which made me think of Philip Chevron's song 'Under Clery's Clock'. *Burgh Quay at night / In this dark and stinking place / Urges I can't fight / With a boy without a face.* A bridge reduced the water to a slab of darkness. 'So where's the clock?' I asked.

Karl smiled. 'It's not actually here.' We retraced our steps, past hoardings layered with posters for gigs. One small blue poster announced that Hidden Bruises, Triangle and The Black Stone were playing tonight at the Mean Fiddler. Back in O'Connell Street, Karl pointed to a department store with scrolled neo-classical carvings around its windows. The clock hung above the white pillars at its entrance. A bus marked *En Lár* was standing a few yards uphill. Behind us was the stone figure of an Irish hero, his hands reaching up to direct the traffic. Karl stepped forward to read the inscription below the statue, but stopped. Near its feet, there was a dry patch on the dark pavement: the outline of a human figure, curled up on its side like a reversed shadow. An image printed by the rain.

Later, I realised that someone must have passed out in the street and remained there through the shower, then got up or been carried away. Karl and I had a drink in O'Neill's, a warren of a pub where you could hide from anything. Irish measures of spirits were so large there was no need to buy doubles. Then another pub, where a teenaged folk band – fiddle, bass, flute and drums – played a slow set of instrumental ballads. Karl listened closely, but then turned to me and said: 'I don't like folk music. It's too homely. Too well- brought-up.' As we returned to the hotel, the streets were packed with rush-hour traffic and pedestrians. There were beggars everywhere, few of them making any spoken appeal to the passers-by. All around us, I thought I could hear a great rushing sound, as if we were inside the river. We both had some sobering up to do before the gig.

We met Ian and Rachel in the hotel bar at six, and went out for some fish and chips at a nearby restaurant. They'd had a row about something and were now making up, exchanging whispered endearments and careful touches. We moved on to a small pub whose interior walls were panelled with dark wood – the kind of decor that you'd assume was fake if you saw it in England. We planned our half-hour set, which had a new song we'd only played in rehearsal. We didn't exactly sober up, though Karl was chain-smoking in order to limit his drinking and keep his stage fright under control. I'd seen him perform when far more drunk than this, but it tended to fuck his timing.

After a quick trip back to the hotel for our guitars and Ian's drumsticks – the special pair he'd bought at Glastonbury, and only used for gigs – we got to the Mean Fiddler just in time for our soundcheck. It didn't go very well: both guitars were murky and unclear, with strange dips in volume. It was like hearing church bells under water. Instead of crackling at the edges of the sound, the distortion came through it in waves. The sound engineer blamed our playing, then said it didn't matter live. Karl deliberately made his guitar sound harsh and ragged to mask the lack of clarity. We were beginning to regret coming without any road crew: it was easier without Martin, but we could have done with Alex or Jim. Backstage, I tried to encourage the other two: 'Just play up, keep it hard and tight. It sounds better with an audience anyway. They soak up the echoes.'

'That's what they're there for,' Karl said. 'The music's not real without them.' We took our cans of lager through into the bar, where a hundred or so people had gathered: kids in Nirvana and Hüsker Dü T-shirts, with spiky hair and dark, circled eyes. When The Black Stone came on, a lot more people suddenly appeared from nowhere. This was evidently a local band: a punky five-piece with two vocalists, a boy and a girl. Everything they played sent the faithful into a moshing, shuddering frenzy. The sound was raw and percussive, but the vocals came through pretty well. I liked the use of two voices, one picking out strands of melody and the other stalking her with ominous, repetitive muttering. The songs drew their images from folklore or horror stories: crows, drowned women, burial. At least, that's what I thought I could hear.

When their set finished, we hurried backstage and downed some more lager while tuning up. Hidden Bruises, four quiet- seeming lads from Cork, were passing through and said hello. Their manager, Paul, was a friend of Karl's; he'd set up the gig for us. Karl cracked a can for him and we sat around a low table, listening to the new Cure album thundering out over the PA. The first song, 'Open', was the most powerful song they'd ever written. It followed the downward spiral of a drunk at a party, crashing from manic excitement into numb despair.

Our set went surprisingly well, given that we must have been complete unknowns. 'Third Flight' had a couple of punks crowdsurfing, though the second pause/blast sequence near the end caused them both to drop from sight. The sound was still murky, guitar and bass hardly distinguishable, but Ian's drums crashed through with a cold finality. Next, we played 'Stranger Key' while standing in darkness, our backs to the audience; when Ian laughed into his microphone, Karl and I turned round and played a hard-edged, metallic finale. Then, without pausing, we went into a streamlined version of 'The Answer'. The audience were jerking madly in front, motionless and silent behind. I was shaking with adrenaline, wishing I'd had less to drink.

Next, we played the new song: 'Made of Clay'. We never recorded that one, though it would have made a good B-side. It was short and fast, with a hard bass riff and feathery guitar hooks. Karl chanted the words like an incantation. He was singing about the murder of a child on a building site. This was before the Bulger case, and I don't think he had any real child in mind. The ending was bitter and confusing: *Torn up and thrown away / Your puppet, made of clay / Your lover, made of clay / Broken and blown away / These people, made of clay / Our children, made of clay.* These last words were spoken over the hammering of drums. We followed with a stark version of 'His Mouth', then 'Still and Moving Water'; with the new ending that Karl had used in Hanley. By now, several people at the front were staggering and bleeding from the random violence of the moshpit; rows of pale faces surged back and forth whenever the volume rose. Karl seemed oddly calm, as if the fury of the audience had neutralised his own rage.

Addressing the audience for the first time, he said: 'We're Triangle, and it's good to be here. We'll see you again. One. Two. Three. Four.' We closed with a brittle version of 'Curfew Town', its stillness holding the audience like a flashbulb. Karl and I unplugged our guitars and took them offstage while Ian played a brief and jittery duet with the drum machine we'd borrowed from Furnace Records. Then he joined us in the dressing-room, where an open can of Special Brew was ready for him. Paul had a cheque for us; it didn't cover our expenses, but we weren't complaining about the deal. As the Cure album came back on with 'Trust', Rachel joined us. She kissed Ian aggressively, going for the corner of his mouth. Karl and I slumped together, each of us looking for a strength the other didn't have. As usual.

The Black Stone dropped in, all smoking weed and talking across each other. As the only wholly non-Irish member of Triangle – Ian has an Irish mother, though his accent is pure Brummie – I felt a bit out of place. Their bass player quizzed me about Birmingham's music scene. 'You know, you gave the world heavy metal. And the world took it and turned it into a bad joke. But that's not your fault.' He told me they were playing Birmingham soon; we'd have to meet up and get pissed. I took a puff of his joint; he took a swig of my industrial-strength lager. 'Tell me,' he said, 'you and Karl are knocking it, yeah?' I nodded. 'That's okay. At least you're making real music. You're not into fucking shite. Well, you might be literally, but not in musical terms.'

Karl, meanwhile, was locked in a deep discussion with the female vocalist. 'I read that thing in the *NME*,' she was saying. 'About how your songs use themes from folk music, but express them through something harder. A city sound. That's what we're doing too. It's what Sinéad did on that first album, but nobody got it.' Someone opened a door, and The Cure's 'End' blotted out Karl's response. I watched his face, lit from behind, tilting towards the girl's ear. She had cropped black hair and sharp teeth. *Karl's type*, I thought in a flash of paranoia.

We all slipped behind the bar to see Hidden Bruises. The audience were drunk and impatient, boys holding their girlfriends protectively from behind. The band made a low-key entrance, picking up their instruments and trying a few notes before stumbling into a rhythm. The singer's voice, high- pitched and angry, gave their sound a punk edge which the band occasionally followed up, blasts of chaotic rage falling back into the solemn basslines. *Take the money / Take the money / Help you fly before you run / Sell your body / Sell your body / You can buy another one.* They were good but repetitive; after a while, you lost the sense of where each song ended and the next began. Ian and Rachel were standing beside me, heads nodding in unison. I glanced around to see where Karl had got to. He and the singer from The Black Stone had both disappeared.

I made myself check the men's toilets first. No sign. Then I went back to our dressing-room. The door was open, but the light was off. They were sitting in a corner, faces moving slowly. It looked as if they were singing into each other's mouths. The kiss pulled their shadows back and forth. In the half-light, I could have been watching some terrible insect shedding its skin. Then Karl opened his eyes and saw me. He dropped his head onto her shoulder. I picked up my guitar case and walked out. An unlit corridor led me to an exit.

Outside, the rain glittered like sleet in the moonlight. Clusters of drowsy youngsters floated along the luminous pavement. Beggars huddled in shop doorways. Some of the streets were cobbled and admitted no traffic; in one of these, I saw two well-dressed girls with tall hair being pulled along in a home-made rickshaw by a lad whose white shirt clung to him like polythene. Either a damning indictment of Dublin's unemployment or a weird post-colonial joke. Just as my pocket map was becoming too wet to use, I got to a familiar bridge. As I crossed it, the wind shook me. Thumbprints of rain blurred the lamps. A grey-faced man in a dark coat was coming towards me, weaving from side to side. Just before we collided, his face dissolved into rain. The only trace of his passing was a coil of cigarette smoke that stung my eyes.

When I got back to our hotel room, Karl was already there. He must have caught a taxi. I dried my hair and put on a clean shirt while he sat on his narrow bed, tuning his guitar. Finally, I stopped and looked at him. 'I'm sorry,' he said. 'We got carried away. We weren't going to fuck, you know.'

'I don't...' *Care* or *understand?* One or the other. My anger was already turning to depression. 'This is fucked.'

'What do we do now?' Karl put down his guitar and looked at me. His eyes were red at the corners.

I shrugged. 'Long talk? Trial separation? Solo projects? Your long-overdue tragic premature death?'

'I meant now, as in tonight. We're not going to sleep like

this. Let's go out.' I glanced at my watch; it was past eleven. 'They have late-night bars here, you know. Free to get in. It's not a temperance chapel like Birmingham.'

'I've got a better idea. Why don't I break your guitar in half and shove the fretboard right up your arse?'

Karl smiled. 'You're not usually that inventive.' Then he stood up and gripped my arms. 'I really am sorry, you know. If I hadn't been so pissed…'

'You're always fucking pissed.' We stood apart in the lift, then walked silently out of the hotel. I tried to shut myself off: be cold, as if I'd just been put down by some smirking queen in the Nightingale and had to save face by ignoring him. It didn't work.

Back across the Liflfey, we walked through Temple Row: a long cobbled street with rotting sealed hulks casting shadows from above the cafés and bars. Music spilled from doorways; buskers played modern jazz on street corners in the rain. There were no pools of vomit, no couples squaring up for a fight or a spell of foreplay against the crumbling brick walls. Karl led me to a bar called the Foggy Dew, which looked impossibly crowded from the doorway, but once we got past the main bar, it was no worse than a nightclub. With patience, you could tunnel through in any direction. Karl got us both a large whiskey from the bar at the back, while I looked around in some amazement.

The Foggy Dew was a maze of wood-panelled rooms and alcoves with framed pictures. Across the steps, I could see de Valera scowling at his own reflection. All around, every square foot of this huge pub had someone in it. Drinks were being poured, paid for and knocked back at a hectic rate. But no one was out of control. The security men, dressed in black jackets, stood calmly beside the bar. The music was less loud than in any Birmingham bar after nightfall. The crowd were mostly young, but not exclusively. They were casually dressed: nothing expensive or tarty. Only one detail bothered me. There wasn't a single black or Asian face in here.

'This is incredible,' I said to Karl. 'You could never let a Birmingham pub get crowded like this. There'd be fights every fucking minute... It's nothing like a Brummie Irish pub either.'

Karl smiled, with some sadness. 'People here know how to take their drink. The pub culture goes deeper than the rivers. You get banned from a pub here, your social life is finished. So all the fuckups, the meatheads, the brawlers, go to England. They fit in there.' He took a gulp of Jameson's, wincing at the harsh flavour. His eyes were red all the way round now.

'The people look wonderful,' I said, unconsciously offering him a truce. 'So relaxed, and they're all so attractive. But are there no black people in Dublin?'

'Not many. Mostly because there's no work. But then, they used to say Ireland was the only country that never persecuted the Jews. It never let them in. Maybe it's still like that. I don't belong here either.'

'Where *do* you belong?' He didn't answer, and looked so depressed that I gripped his arm. 'Take it easy.'

It was past midnight now; the crowd was thinning out a little. I bought another pair of large whiskeys, and we dissected the gig. We both liked the stripped-down versions of 'His Mouth' and 'Curfew Town'; but Karl thought 'Made of Clay' needed to be fleshed out instrumentally. I said I didn't think the lyrics would stretch far enough. 'Anyway, what the fuck are they about?'

Karl looked uncomfortable. 'I don't like explaining the words,' he said. 'They mean what you hear in them.' I don't remember what either of us said from then on. It was Karl's round again; then, in all probability, it was mine. I'm not sure by what route we got back to the hotel, but I remember Karl deliberately getting into my narrow single bed and embracing me from behind. I don't usually like to sleep in contact with anyone, but that night, it seemed unavoidable.

When I woke up, a few hours later, it was still dark. Karl's arm was folded over my waist; his breath echoed my own. I slowly freed myself, went to the en-suite bathroom, filled a glass with water and drank it. Then I heard a hoarse voice behind me: 'David? Can you get me some water? Please.' He sounded as dry as paper. I half-filled the glass, went over to the bed and poured the water over his face. 'Bastard.' He pulled me down beside him and kissed me fiercely. I dug my nails into his skinny ribs, bit his neck in a way that I knew would bruise. 'Go on,' he said quietly. I rolled him onto his back, lifted his knees and fucked him – without lubricant, without protection. It must have hurt like Hell, but he came into my hand in less than a minute. I didn't feel my own climax, but I knew it had happened.

Then I withdrew and said, 'Are you okay?' He grunted. I got into the other bed and went back to sleep.

In a dream, I was looking for Karl's body. It was somewhere in New Street Station. I kept finding bodies hidden like bombs: curled up behind the chocolate machine, in a toilet cubicle, in the guard's van of an empty train, in the loudspeaker above the concourse where travellers went about their journeys with no concern for what had happened. Every body I found looked like Karl from the back; but the white, drained faces were never his. When I woke up for the second time, the curtain was edged with daylight like a cinema screen. My face was wet. I thought it must have been the water from the glass, soaking the pillow. Then I remembered I'd switched beds; I must have been crying. Confused, I glanced across at Karl's bed. It was empty.

I was drinking my third cup of coffee in the breakfast room when Karl walked in with Ian and Rachel. They'd been out for a brisk morning walk down O'Connell Street. 'A note would have helped,' I said. Once again, it occurred to me that it was easier for Karl to adjust to himself than for me to adjust to him. We had half a day to kill before the trip back; Ian and Rachel wanted to go to the coast. After some awkward negotiation between the four of us, it was established that nobody felt the need to be alone with his or her partner. So we caught the train as a group.

On a rainy morning, the promenade at Bray was a bleak but oddly calming place. Spray lashed the steps on the harbour wall. Waves churned and broke like a feedback solo. Gulls cried fragments of melody. We walked along, talking about non-music things: our families, favourite places, beliefs. I remember Karl staring at the mist of spray and saying: 'Nobody really belongs anywhere. I don't think we go where we belong when we die. It's more like… like the airwaves, messages drifting around. That's what's left of us, messages. Code.' A lot of the time, Karl didn't say much; he'd seem okay, and it wasn't until he spoke that you realised how down he was. I never knew how to react. Laughter and sympathy both seemed inappropriate.

Later, we had lunch in an old-fashioned pub. I noticed Karl's hand shaking as he lifted his first drink. His lips were dry. Rachel took a photo of the three of us, then got me to take a photo of her and Ian. I think she was trying to make the point that she was with him, not 'the band'. Across the road from the pub was the entrance to an indoor market: a huge and poorly lit barn with stalls selling old books, records and so on. One trader had a few second-hand guitars, acoustic and electric. Karl bought a Fender Stratocaster for two hundred pounds; he didn't have enough Irish money and had to use a credit card, but the trader didn't mind. 'You can't truly buy this guitar except with dollars,' he said.

This remark became the focus of much discussion on the train back to Dublin. Rachel argued that you couldn't truly play the Strat unless you'd just come off a shift at the Detroit car plant and had oil stains on your check shirt. Ian suggested the credits on our next album should say *Guitars played by Karl Austin and the soul of Jim Morrison*. I said we could call the album *The West Midlands Will Rise Again*. Ian said, 'What do you mean, again?' Karl said he wished he'd never touched the fucking thing. I said he would again when he had to carry it home along with all his other stuff. Rachel said that it wouldn't be truly carried unless the plane crashed with no survivors.

'No,' Karl insisted, 'it can only be truly carried on the train.'

That night, in his flat, Karl played me the basics of a new song: 'Broken Strings'. Without amplification, the Strat was a ghost: the rusting hulk of a car without wheels. The song was dislocated and strange; Karl sang it in little more than a whisper. *Where do they go, where does their time belong? / Swimming through the river underground / Past the stinking bodies and the photographs / Until there's nothing left except a sound.* By now, we'd more or less patched it up. I knew he was using alcohol as an excuse for selfish behaviour, going for every chance and hiding from the consequences; but what worried me more was that the alcohol seemed to be taking over. I could live with his games: I'd been through worse. Deep down, I hoped that by accepting this I could keep worse things away. If he slipped the catch from the razor of his needs, who would it cut?

The Black Stone played the Digbeth Irish Centre a few weeks later. The four of us went to see them. It was a good gig, though the audience was small and largely unresponsive. Spiky outbursts of thrash guitar and rapid, angry drumming created a sense of attack; but without an audience of punks, it didn't seem to define the band. Afterwards, we went backstage to say hello. They shared their Guinness with us, displaying hospitality even on foreign soil. Karl and the singer, Bernie, exchanged phone numbers or something. On the bus home, I remarked that punk was like blues: it had once been a state of mind, but was now just a set of techniques. Karl looked at me wearily. 'I'm getting tired of hearing you say things like that.'

The day that *Hard Shadows* was released, we played a one-off gig in Amsterdam. Alan Winter had set it up, and it was really an excuse for him and other Furnace people to spend a weekend in the Disneyland of adult recreation. Due to the last-minute booking, our party were spread over three hotels in the Rokin district (arf arf). None of the band had been here before. I'd been to Paris when I was with Adrian; and Amsterdam seemed oddly similar at first, even down to the white Ferris wheel visible from the hotel. Like Paris, it had evolved from the ground up. Karl and I were in a hotel so narrow it had no lift or central staircase, only flights of stairs that joined up the landings at unexpected points.

In Paris, Adrian and I had booked a twin room in a small central hotel. We'd arrived, unpacked and had a short rest before going out. The manager had stopped us in the lobby to say that she'd had a complaint about the noise from our room. Adrian had said it was a mistake: we hadn't made any noise. He'd been puzzled. I'd had to explain to him that it was a pre-emptive strike by the management against gay sex, and was probably standard policy. I didn't anticipate any such problems in Amsterdam. (Nor was I wrong.)

We were all due to meet up at the venue, a central nightclub, around eight. Webbing, our support band, featured Matt Pearce on keyboards; they were a fairly psychedelic outfit, and planned to be more so by this evening. Ian, Karl and I had less ambitious plans. We bought an ounce of Moroccan hash at a nearby café, shared a narrow spliff and saved the rest for later. Then we found a bar and sat drinking neat measures of jenever, feeling the mellow vibes drift through us. Jenever is a smooth, upbeat version of gin that Matt had recommended. We huddled together in a corner, planning our set, unconsciously mimicking the *Hard Shadows* sleeve picture. The looping basslines and splintered chords of New Order's *Low-life* album stalked around the bar.

The gig was a bit low-key – 'intimate' if you were feeling generous, 'wasted' if you weren't. Not that the audience of stoned dusk-dwellers in the narrow, smoky venue could have given a monkey's joss. Webbing came apart at the seams:

when they managed to play the same song, in the same time, it had the brevity of an accident. John, the guitarist, stared at the overhead lights until Alex was forced to reduce them to the brightness of candles. Matt was clearly accompanying the voices in his head, which included a church choir and Napalm Death.

We did a slightly drowsy run-through of all the album songs except 'Fugue', with 'Made of Clay' and 'Broken Strings' added. It was strange how old the *Hard Shadows* material sounded, now that we had the recorded artefact in boxes by the exit. Karl fumbled a few chords, and wrongfooted me and Ian by reverting to the studio version of 'Still and Moving Water'. We'd planned to encore with 'For the Distance', but instead tacked it onto the end of our set. After the last line there was a deep scream of feedback and the lights went out. Neither was intentional, but it wasn't a bad ending.

Afterwards, we smoked the remaining hash and drank countless bottles of excellent Dutch beer. Alan offered Karl a tab, but he turned it down – to my great relief. The thought of Karl on acid was intensely frightening. Various Dutch music business people and friends of Alan were nice to us. We started to envision a European tour in December, after the British tour which we were trying not to think about. The club was still open; industrial music threatened the motionless occupants, who were watching a film of darkness. Webbing had gone back to their hotel for an early night.

We missed breakfast the next morning, surfacing to drink some coffee and skip lunch. Some more jenever took the edge off our headaches. Karl stared at the clear liquid in a mood close to wonder. 'Why don't other countries drink jenever instead of gin?' he said. 'The suicide rate would collapse. The Samaritans should advertise it. Then again, how would that affect the population? We'd be overrun with manic-depressives. The economy would swing up and down every day. Leonard Cohen would be on *Top of the Pops*.'

We spent the afternoon drifting around, buying records and shirts with weird designs. Every bar we went into seemed to be playing a techno record with samples of something older: a soul vocal, a piano figure, a lonely trumpet. The ghost in the machine. We argued about whether sampling meant the end of real music or was just bringing theft out of its musical closet. Ian said: 'You're both just echoing the arguments you've read.' The three of us ate at an Ethiopian restaurant in the student quarter, mentioned in the *Time Out* guide; your meal was served on a huge pancake which you tore up and dipped in the sauces. After that, Ian – who'd been oddly quiet all day – went off somewhere on his own. Karl and I decided to visit the Warmoesstraat.

Two hours and several male-themed bars later, we went into a nightclub where most of the walls were mirrored. At one point, a reflection turned confusingly into a real bar. The music was the techno equivalent of speed metal. Men from all over Europe and America were here: denim jackets, leather vests, catsuits, G-strings, boxer shorts, glitter paint. Their dazed, serene expressions suggested that, whatever happened next, they were already where they wanted to be. Only a few – newcomers, the lonely – actively hunted for partners; the rest just happened to find them, like unexpected bargains in a record shop. The international language of foreplay replaced conversation. Some couples left together; others drifted towards the back of the club.

Inevitably, there was an unmarked door there. Like a fire door. A man emerged, red-faced, buttoning up his denim shirt. Karl tugged at my arm. 'Shall we have a look?' I shrugged uneasily. Two boys stepped out, arm in arm, the same smile on each face. Around us, tanned leathermen were drinking bottled beer. The walls were lined with huge Tom of Finland pictures – the figures nearly life-sized, the details not. The only seats were oildrums. The aircon was so powerful I could see my own breath. I shivered; a sampled diva wailed from the speakers in the ceiling. Karl drew me against himself. 'It'll be warmer in there,' he said.

It was, but only by virtue of body heat. A faint red ceiling light, like a permanent sunset, held the figures at the edge of visibility. The only furniture was a couple of tables with bowls, presumably containing tissues or condoms. The music was a slow, grinding house track, the same loop repeated over and over. I wasn't sure whether the moans and grunts I could hear were live or recorded. Couples were sprawled across the floor and against the wall, using each other or a third party as furniture. It wasn't like Tom of Finland. In fact, I thought of that other Finnish artist, Tove Jansson: her flabby Moomins and spiky-topped, staring ghosts. I reached out for Karl's hand. He was kissing someone.

I grabbed his sleeve and shook my head. His partner, a muscled boy with short blond hair, smiled at me. As if in a dream, I saw his hand settle on Karl's crotch and undo the zip. Karl reached out and gripped my hand, gently; then he began to caress the boy. I felt cold, as if I were reliving something that had already happened. When they began to masturbate each other, I backed away. A hand brushed my arse, stayed.

I thought *Fuck it.* He was stocky, dark-haired, possibly Welsh; the only word he said was 'Yes'. I backed him against the wall and kissed him, trying to blank out my mind. He stroked my crotch, but I wouldn't let him unzip me: it would have been too much like my 'exposure' dreams. Instead, I went down on him so fiercely that he came almost at once, his thrusts in time to the pounding music, his fingers tangled in my hair. Then I crouched by the wall, my hands covering my face. After a while, I felt a hand on my shoulder. It was Karl. 'Let's go,' he said.

We walked back to the Rokin district in silence. It wasn't raining, but the air was cold. Black-veined prints of leaves marked the yellow pavement. The canal was a ribbon of darkness, streetlamps glowing through it like cars in fog. Most of the bars were still open, but the cafés were dark. Finally, Karl stopped outside the entrance to a basement bar; a green neon outline of spiky leaves covered the black-tinted window. 'Do you want a smoke?' I stared at him. 'Come on.'

Inside, the light was webbed with motionless 3D shadows. A Bob Marley album played softly from behind the bar. Most of the tables were occupied, but no one was speaking. After a glance at the handwritten menu card on the bar, I bought two joints of House Red. It was good stuff. Very, very… good. My anger became something tiny and fragile, the ornament rather than the fire. Karl watched me through a cloud of bitter smoke. 'Why didn't you stop?' I said.

'To make you understand something.'

'What? Understand what?'

'To make you see. If you have to ask, then you didn't get it.'

'I saw what you wanted me to see. You and that boy getting down to it like a pair of cottage queens. But for fuck's sake, what did you... Jesus fucking wept.'

'I wanted you to understand something. About me. About what happened with Dean. About yourself. I can't find the words for it. I never can. But I think you got something. Because you didn't just look. I saw you.'

We sat there for a while, smoking. Light smeared across the pale ceiling. Behind us, Marley sang about being taken from the bottomless pit. I listened and felt something well up inside me, a kind of grief. I reached across the scratched table and gripped Karl's hand.

When we left the café, we were both a little disorientated. The street was empty. I looked at my pocket map, but couldn't make sense of it. Karl started walking faster, then going in what I knew was the wrong direction. When I tried to stop him, he muttered 'We're being followed.' I glanced behind us and saw a figure going the other way. We crossed another canal and found ourselves in the red light district. Pink neon vaginas flashed above doorways; naked women stood behind plate-glass windows, moving slowly like fish in half-lit tanks. Karl pulled at my sleeve. 'Keep going. We'll lose them here.'

We hurried on through streets filled with staring tourists, half-dressed prostitutes and doormen in leather jackets. Then we reached another canal. The far side was dark. Karl turned left, then left again, heading back towards Rokin. Suddenly, the porn shops and fuck bars ended and we were in a normal district, lit only by old-fashioned streetlamps. Crossing a bridge over the canal, I saw a body slumped in the black water. It had no head. When I stopped, I saw that its shoulders were the rounded front end of a submerged boat, its keel exposed like a muddy spine.

Soon we came to another canal, hardly different from the last one. We hadn't passed anyone in several minutes. Karl paused and glanced over his shoulder. 'There's no one following us,' I said.

'They don't have to.' His eyes were wide with fear. 'Can't you see where we are?'

'Not exactly. But the hotel can't be—'

'Fuck it, David. Can't you see? Where we *are*?' He looked around desperately. 'This isn't what you think. It's not Amsterdam. He's here. He's waiting for me.'

We'll laugh about this in the morning, I thought. The morning seemed a long way off. I put my arm around Karl's shoulders; they felt like wood. He closed his eyes and shuddered. 'Help me. Please help me.' I took out my map and forced it to make sense, drawing the route in my head. The hotel was only four streets away.

The next morning, all of us were sitting in the departure lounge at the airport; bad weather had delayed the flight by an hour. Karl sat next to me, inhaling the fumes from a plastic cup of coffee. I was still thinking of Marley's 'Redemption Song': how we have to free our minds. Then I thought of 'Fugue', a song we hadn't played at the gig. Scraps of it had been running through my head all morning, sampled by the traffic, the airport PA, the crying of babies. I glanced at Karl and realised that he, like me, was listening.

CHAPTER 8

talking blues

And I was wearing the mask of honesty
— Felt

The sleeve of *Hard Shadows* was put together in a hurry, on a tiny budget. It was designed primarily for the LP version: although CDs were already dominant in the mainstream, small independent labels were still doing better with vinyl. Within a year or two, of course, that would change completely. The front cover was an adaptation of the old Triangle poster: the same three silhouetted faces, but inside a red triangle. I liked it because it reminded me of the first Tom Robinson Band album, *Power In the Darkness*. On the back, the song titles were reversed out against a grainy black-and- white photo of the Hockley flyover. On the inner sleeve, there were three separate pictures of Karl, Ian and me, plus three more Birmingham scenes: the canal walkway that starts in Acocks Green, the viaduct at Digbeth and a smashed-up tower block in Lea Bank. The cassette and CD sleeves had the same photos, cropped differently. There was no lyric sheet.

John Peel and Mark Radcliffe both played a few tracks from the album on their evening shows. Radcliffe remarked after playing 'Stranger Key': 'Not bad, that. What d'you reckon, Lard?' Riley paused, then said: 'Aye, not bad. That singer, though – I've had him. He's crap. Good guitarist, but can he play the oboe? Forget it.' The morning after we came back from Amsterdam, I went into Swordfish to see whether they had the album; as soon as I opened the door, I could hear 'Nowhere To Go'. I browsed through the dimly lit record stacks, listening to 'His Mouth'; at this volume, the tenor sax at the start and end was clearly audible. I wasn't working at Tempest Records any more, but they ordered a hundred signed copies of the LP. The cover was too dark to write on, so we signed the inner sleeve. For months afterwards, Mark in the shop would say whenever I walked in: 'Still plenty left, our kid.' He pronounced it *orchid*.

The first reviews were in the weekly music papers. *Melody Maker*'s Judi Smith gave us the benefit of the doubt:

> Is Triangle's irony-free blend of rage and reverb truly relevant to the 1990s? Are they wearing combat jackets or anoraks? The answer lies not in their oddly dated music, but in those moments when Karl Austin puts his soul – and his arse – on the line. He's a non-celibate Morrissey, a wired witness of urban violence and repression. These are songs in the dialect of fear. Someone should tell Triangle to keep pressing the panic button. And leave the effects pedal alone. ***

Stuart Harvey in the *NME* said the same thing in a different way:

> Triangle's rhythm section provide a quietly powerful vehicle for Austin's voice, grounding it in a familiar place. But the voice – like Austin's manic, hit-or-miss guitar playing – comes from another world: beyond the blue, in the black. This album's reference points – New Order, Van Morrison, Peter Hammill – seem part of a desperate attempt to find a history, an explanation for a state of mind which belongs nowhere. (8)

Karl's only reaction to that was: 'But I fucking hate Peter Hammill.'

Both reviews praised 'Stranger Key', and Furnace were keen to release it as a single. Karl and Pete Stone spent a couple of days fucking about with the master tape of 'Rise and Walk', an outtake from the album. It was the track we'd abandoned after a futile day in the studio. They overdubbed screams and distorted vocals onto the master, then mixed in basslines and drum patterns from other tracks. The result was five minutes long and completely unlistenable. Its use as a B-side was vindicated when the *NME* called it 'mesmerising', while dismissing the A-side as 'more of the same'. *Melody Maker* had someone from a boy band helping out their singles reviewer that week; as far as I can remember, Boychick said 'Oh, this is really serious. Do we have to say we like it?' and the reviewer said 'No.'

The monthly music papers gave the album fairly lukewarm reviews. *Q* praised 'the Wire-tight rhythm tracks', while *Select* described us as 'a kind of fuzzy Felt'. The *Time Out* review seemed to have a regional agenda:

> Triangle's debut album is a cry for help from the blighted
> landscape of Birmingham. In tracks as dark and tangled
> as a road map of the West Midlands, this talented but
> doomed guitar band explore their bitter heritage. As one
> of their most frightening songs declares, there is *nowhere
> to go*. In Birmingham, no one can hear you scream. But
> thanks to the miracle of recording technology, these lost
> voices are saved for our bleak entertainment.

Brum Beat's Helen Fell, who'd reviewed our Barrel Organ
gig at the start of the year, gave the album its most direct and
positive review:

> Not since REM's *Murmur* has any band made such
> a powerful debut. Triangle are three men who play
> angular, hard-edged rock to express the non-macho
> emotions of pain, fear and loss. The scars left by a cruel
> lover; a closed community turning against an outsider; a
> man released from prison to find that he carries his own
> prison with him. But this is no Oprah-style confession:
> for every trauma revealed, others are left unspoken – or
> spoken only through the music. Behind the hard shadows
> of this record, there is a strange and terrible light. These
> are songs that Triangle needed to play, and that deserve
> to be heard.

Just after that review appeared, we got a message from
Martin that Helen would like to interview us. She came
down from Wolverhampton to meet the band at Zebedee's
Café in Alum Rock – an anarchist centre in one of the
toughest areas of North Birmingham. It was more punk
than hippy, more Class War than CND. The four of us sat
around a white table, eating vegan pizza and drinking bitter

non-corporate coffee. Helen was a pale, rather stern young woman with a Yorkshire accent. We spent the first half-hour talking about the new REM album, which had just been released. Too many singles were drawn from it later on. We all had different favourite tracks: Helen's was 'Star Me Kitten', Ian's 'Man On the Moon', Karl's 'Nightswimming' and mine 'Ignoreland'. I was still playing that album every day a month later.

The discussion moved on to Triangle and the album. I tried to explain how Pete had broken each track down into its components, then fitted them back together. 'When we play the songs live, it's simpler. There isn't the extra stuff going on in the background.'

'It's not a natural album,' Karl said. 'But it's real. I mean... you can't be real all the time. You can't be live all the time. On the album, the sound is what's real. That's why it's called *Hard Shadows*. Do you understand?'

'Not really,' Helen said. 'Can I ask you about "His Mouth"? What were the ideas behind that song?'

'Well, it was...' Karl gulped his coffee thoughtfully. 'It was a blues thing, like Van Morrison. Very male. It was David's track, really. I just wrote words to go on top of it.' I gave him a confused look: *you wrote the words first.* 'It came out of, like ... you know the way The Cure used jazz elements without lightening their sound, a kind of negative jazz? That kind of approach.'

Helen smiled. 'You're breaking the rules. I do the references, you do the revelations. All right?' Karl shrugged. 'I meant, what were you trying to get across in that song?'

'How you want to love someone and in the end, all you can do is suck his cock.'

'Er, we can't print that...' Helen tried another tack. 'The theme of victimisation comes up a lot in your songs. Is that something you've experienced?'

Karl stared at the table, then muttered something incoherent about the threat being in the music. Ian said: 'Everyone's been through that in some way. Haven't they? In school, at work. There are bullies everywhere.'

'Do you have a lot of pent-up aggression?' Helen asked. We all said 'Yes' at once, then looked at each other. 'That comes across on stage. But it's *still* pent up, isn't it? You don't just let go, the way a band like the Manics do. There's a kind of tension.' Karl's posture at the table was a perfect image of that, I realised: head forward, spine curved, his hands clutching the mug a few inches in front of his face. He lit a cigarette; the lad who was clearing the tables came across the room towards us, and Karl stubbed it out without a word.

Helen asked us some neutral questions about guitars and recording techniques. 'Our readers like to know these things. Sad fucks that they are.' Then she bit her lip and said to Karl: 'There's a lot of religious imagery in your songs. Images of, like... punishment and redemption, Hell and divine judgement. Children crying to God. But do you feel there's a conflict between religion and sexuality?'

Karl's face went blank. 'I don't... no. They're both very powerful things. But not in conflict, no.' He paused for a while, then shrugged and looked away. Helen gestured to me, inviting some comment. I made an inane remark about supporting the New Testament view of sodomy: it's better to give than to receive. Karl gripped my knee under the table. 'You never told *me* that,' he said, smiling innocently.

The mood lightened enough for us to move on to politics.

We exchanged vivid and unprintable views on the prospect of another five glorious years. Ian's image of Norma Major buggering her husband with a cricket stump while he cried out 'Please, the handbag! It's time!' was one of the milder comments. Then Helen asked Karl about his family background, his Irish roots. Did he think the Ulster peace process was going anywhere? Karl gave her a weary look. 'I'm not qualified to comment,' he said. 'And neither are most of the arseholes writing in the English press. It's like everyone's got to have an angle.'

Somewhat inevitably, the interview appeared in the next issue of *Brum Beat* under the headline 'Everyone's Got an Angle'. Helen had done a good job of making the interview seem coherent, paraphrasing most of our responses and filling out the page with information about the band. There was a photo of us standing outside Zebedee's in a wash of sunlight which came off the reinforced glass, reducing the inside to a shadow with glints of wire. After the interview, Ian caught the bus into town; Karl and I made for the nearest pub.

Where Triangle's reputation really took off, of course, was Mike West's interview for the *NME*. Alan Winter let us borrow his office for an hour, sharing a bottle of Napoleon brandy. Mike asked some interesting questions about the band: what we listened to, how we worked together. He told us our songs were set 'in a landscape of dead industry, a Black Country of the heart'. His thick Scots accent was strangely reassuring, though his stammer made him leave sentences unfinished or change them halfway through. 'I think the album's like a journey into... you know, leaving home, then turning back to see the... Where are you headed?

What kind of journey have you made?' Some of the links were lost in the unspoken bits.

Karl did most of the talking. He was in that energised phase of rapid drinking that came before the darkness of being properly drunk. At one point, Mike asked whether we minded being seen as like The Smiths, a band peddling an old-fashioned concept of musical 'authenticity'. Karl flinched at the word. 'It's not about having a particular kind of sound,' he said. 'All sounds are real. Not all people are. I mean, Dylan was attacked for playing rock music, because electric guitars weren't "authentic" – but his songs were more real than someone like Donovan could ever be. It's about the meaning, not the technology. You can't explain to a metal fan why Nirvana are real and Iron Maiden aren't. You either hear it or you don't.'

'Are you saying it's wrong to see the funny side? For a rock band to have a sense of humour?'

'A sense of humour about what?' Karl said uneasily. 'If you're taking the piss out of your own music, then you're admitting you have no self-respect. Real humour contains anger, it contains a sense of danger. It's not about fucking entertainment. It hurts.'

'Are you into pain?' Mike said. Karl didn't answer.

We finished up the brandy between the four of us, made some vague conversation about plans for the future, and drifted out into the surprisingly cold Hockley streets. Paul the photographer, who'd spent the last hour out here taking location shots in the dying light, accompanied us to the flyover. We posed for a joint headshot at the north end of the concrete walkway, cars hurtling past us into the night like red fragments of a meteorite shower.

Mike's article, 'Point of Departure', appeared three weeks later. It was hard to connect his rather formal, scholarly prose with the rushed, stumbling voice we'd heard; as if Billy Connolly had become Greil Marcus (which he hadn't, not by then). He was obsessed with the idea of an industrial folk music: 'not a music of fiddles and harmony, but one of machines and discord... a music through which the urban landscape is transformed into myth'. He placed Triangle at the end of a chain which ran from American blues through The Doors, Iggy and the Stooges and Lou Reed to The Fall, Joy Division and The Triffids.

> *Hard Shadows* is a journey through dead space and wasted time: a journey through the deaths we all know. Children die and become adults. Communities die and become individuals. Lovers die and become you and me. As Karl Austin says: 'A child is innocent. That innocence is dangerous. It's nothing to do with original sin. The innocent have no sense of right or wrong.'

The photograph they used had come out badly: our three faces were almost blank against the shadow of the flyover, like negatives.

We played two gigs in September: one at the Felch and Firkin in Birmingham, the other at the Islington Hope and Anchor. Martin was keen to get us known in London before we played there at the end of our October tour. The Brum gig was okay, if a bit too guitar-heavy; we were trying for a hard, brittle sound, but the low ceiling meant that the vibrations all but deafened us. We played with a local punk band called Blinder. Stefan and James, Karl's friends from Stourbridge, were at the gig. They came backstage, but didn't say much besides 'Hello?', 'Got any dope?' and 'Cheers.'

Diane was there too; she told me she'd split up with Andy. 'We were getting into heavy shit,' she said. 'Downers, then smack. I wanted to stop and he didn't. So we called it a day. You can't go out with a user and not be one. The band's still going, though. You never know, we might do better now. Nothing to lose.'

The London gig was a bit of a mess. Karl got pissed to overcome his stage fright, and his timing threw me and Ian off balance. It's funny: when Karl was on form, Triangle worked well as a unit; but when he was fucked up, Ian and I just felt like his backing musicians. Still, the rage was there even if the control wasn't. The support band were a local sound system outfit called Dire Tribe; they played jagged, murky rhythms on tapes and drum machines, like the ghost of a band. It made us feel vaguely out of place. After the gig, an A&R man from London Records told Karl that Triangle could be the new Smiths. 'Who are The Smiths?' Karl said, deadpan. The A&R man backed away.

While we were in London, we did an interview with a gay lifestyle magazine called *Flounce*. Their music reviewer, Matt Gray, had contacted Furnace Records after seeing a review of *Hard Shadows*. It took us a while to get to the magazine's offices in Baron's Court from our hotel in Tottenham; though he'd lived in London for a year in the eighties, Karl was confused by the stone labyrinth of the Underground. We were both hung over, subdued. Ian had decided not to come with us. When we arrived, half an hour late, we had to wait in reception as if we'd come for a job interview.

Finally, Matt appeared: a tall youth of twenty or so, with bleached hair and a Kylie Minogue T-shirt. He led us into an office whose floor was nearly covered with magazines and CDs. We sat down on a fake-leather couch; Matt faced us from a swivel chair. Behind him, the blank screen of a huge TV set reflected the grey autumn sky. 'I'm afraid we haven't got long,' he said. 'So, Triangle. You two are lovers, right?' Karl muttered an assent. 'Feel free to snuggle up on the couch, I don't mind. How about your drummer? Is he one of us?'

'No,' Karl said. 'He's one of *us*. We're a band, first and foremost. The fact that—'

'That's what bothers me about you,' Matt interrupted. 'That's why I wanted to establish that you're both card-carrying homos.'

'You're taking a lot for granted,' Karl said. 'Look, can we talk about the music?'

'Of course. Your album has a very homo-erotic song on it, "His Mouth". About the master-servant thing. Is that important to you?'

'It's more about sharing,' I said. 'The lover only becomes, like, an icon through remembering. The way you hold onto particular details and they become, like, magical.' Matt raised his eyebrows, as if amazed to get a meaningful answer from a bass player. Karl didn't add anything.

'Mmm. Know what you mean. But that's the only real gay song on the album, isn't it? Unless you count "Stranger Key". And in "Third Flight", the guy who gets beaten up, that's obviously queerbashing.'

'Not really,' Karl said. 'I was thinking of a black guy who was almost killed by a gang of neo-Nazis in

Birmingham last year. They chased him into the tower block where he lived and pushed him out the window of his flat. Then they came down the stairs after him, and he couldn't run away.'

'You should have put more of that into the song. I mean, you use stuff but you don't explain it. You've got gay themes, but there are hetero themes in a couple of the songs – "Road Into Fire", the guy's got a woman and child waiting for him. That's not you, is it?'

'Well, I was married once. I've had more girlfriends than boyfriends. Besides, it's a character.'

Matt raised his eyes to Heaven. 'Please, save that for the music press. I'm not convinced. In my experience, all so-called bisexuals are either lying straights or lying queens.'

'You should get out more,' I said. Karl laughed.

Matt glared at me, then returned his gaze to Karl. 'How can you say you're bisexual with such a cute boyfriend?' I felt myself blushing. Christ, this boy knew how to manipulate people.

Karl tried again. 'Sexuality is just one part of your life. The songs are trying to look at a bigger picture. It's not denying your sexuality to recognise that other things are important.'

'You just contradicted yourself,' Matt said bizarrely. 'If you're not really queer, it's just an *experience*, why don't you write songs about hetero subjects like lager and football? Why are you borrowing ideas from gay culture—'

'*What?* Karl was looking dangerous now. Half of me found this situation horribly depressing; the other half was struggling not to laugh. 'So I need your permission to suck someone's cock?'

'Unless it was mine, no. All I'm saying is that you're

denying your gayness in this music. It's just standard indie-rock with some homo sex thrown in. There's no real sign of a gay sensibility. No element of drag or camp.'

Karl took a deep breath, then slumped wearily on the couch. 'If you want to know how gay I am, just turn around and bend over. Can I ask *you* a question? Why do you review music when you're not interested in it?'

Matt glanced at his watch. 'I'm wasting my time here.' He stood up and straightened his T-shirt, every inch the professional. 'Come on, boys, I'll see you out.' He led us back to the reception area, then stepped aside to let us pass through. As I walked past him, he patted my bottom; I resisted the urge to smack his face. 'I probably won't use any of that,' he said. 'It was your fault. You walked in here with a negative attitude.' Once again, it felt like a job interview; the kind where you know you've failed the moment you leave.

On the way back to the hotel, Karl was tight-lipped and silent. Apart from giving Ian a brief account of what had happened, we didn't discuss the interview until late that night. The two of us were back in Birmingham, drinking in Karl's flat, listening to the Kitchens of Distinction album *Love Is Hell* Karl looked up at me from an empty glass, shaking his head. 'I wasn't hostile. He was controlling it, all the way through. How many bridges are there between the rock world and the gay world? The Kitchens, Hüsker Dü, Tom Robinson? Most queens only listen to shite like Eartha Kitt and Dannii fucking Minogue. It's like saying, because you love someone you've got to change your appearance, your music taste, your whole personality, just because of that. But you don't.' He stared at me, then reached out and took my hand. 'I do love you, David.'

'I love you too,' I said, my mind cloudy with wine and foreboding. It was the first time we'd said that to each other. Perhaps we hadn't needed to. I bought the next two issues of *Flounce*, but the interview didn't appear.

———————

We'd intended to spend the rest of September rehearsing and working on new material for the tour. But Karl and I weren't writing much. I needed his lyrics to build music around; and whatever Karl needed, it wasn't there. When we booked rehearsal time at Rich Bitch Studios in Edgbaston, it got frittered away on experiments with backing tracks or alternative arrangements. One song we demoed at that time, 'The Lost View', was inspired by one of our favourite walks in Erdington: past Witton Lakes to the top end of the Brookvale estate, where you could see down past Spaghetti Junction and through Aston to the city centre. *The day your home came apart / You ran down the burned slope / Looking for the pieces / But all you found was this*. We didn't think it was strong enough to include in the live set.

After the *Flounce* disaster, Karl didn't want to do any more interviews for a while. 'We're getting trapped in talk,' he said. 'It's all second-hand. We've got to just play. Let the music talk for us.' He was drinking more than ever, but showing it less and less. Occasionally he'd get shaky around lunchtime and start to sweat; he blamed it on a persistent stomach bug he'd picked up in Amsterdam. I got worried and talked him into going for an HIV test at Birmingham General Hospital. He insisted that we take the test at the same time, though I'd been tested in 1991 and he'd never been. 'We need to start on level ground,' he said. 'Know exactly where we both stand.'

Both of us came through negative. But the experience depressed Karl so much that he went completely off sex for a few weeks – which I found more difficult than his being unfaithful. To compensate, and to even up the relationship, I tried to keep up with his drinking. I failed. Karl never had my sex drive, but I never had his drive in anything else. Towards the end of September, he went off on a succession of visits, all arranged at short notice: his parents in Coventry, his wife and daughter in Oldbury, friends in London and Manchester. As if he was unable to keep still, but had nowhere in particular to run to; he needed a sense of being on the move, and the booze wasn't doing that any more. He told me that he'd told his parents about us. His father had asked him: 'So which of you is the man and which is the woman?' He wasn't keen for me to meet them. It's odd how we do that. Break up our lives, as if they were tracks we could remix later.

CHAPTER 9
episode

Daylight touches the cold stone
Sets your blood on fire
— Triangle

The first weekend in October, I went to stay at my mother's flat in Exeter. She was living alone now, but had a lot of friends – and a grey cat whose face had the weird stillness of early films. I got back to Birmingham on Sunday evening, and phoned Karl from New Street Station to suggest meeting for a drink. I'd last seen him on Friday morning, after stopping the night. Stefan and James had dropped in, and I'd left him talking with them and gone to bed. When Karl joined me, he didn't wake me up. He'd been as uncommunicative the next morning as he'd been all week; I'd left him in bed and gone home.

His phone rang a dozen times with no answer. Karl hated answerphones. I wanted to see him, check he was in a reasonable state. The tour was starting on Tuesday; we could do with another rehearsal. For a control freak, Karl was showing an odd lack of interest in the band. Maybe when he got back into playing with Triangle, he'd want to sleep with me again. After all, the music had brought us together. It was another seven-date tour: Glasgow, Newcastle, Leeds, Manchester, Liverpool, Leicester, London. Not a triangle, more like a distorted Z.

I decided to go over anyway. My Rockwood bass and a lot of my clothes were at Karl's. I'd been on the verge of moving in for weeks, but Karl's moods had delayed the transition. Moseley was getting more run-down all the time, the culture shifting from friendly lawlessness to hard-faced villainy. A hippie who'd sold grass in the local pubs had recently been beaten to death by a professional dealer. Nowhere felt like home. I was lonely and in an impatient mood. The dark, stony landscape of Erdington – part futuristic, part Victorian – calmed me down a little.

Karl was still out. I made myself some coffee and waited, imagining the depressing scenario of him bringing someone else back here later. Maybe I should go, to make sure there wasn't a scene. But it was more likely that he'd come back alone, drunk, perhaps needing to talk. I'd lost the thread. There was a broken tumbler in the kitchen sink, grains of red wine stuck to the fragments. I switched on the radio to hear the Evening Session; no sound came out, though the red light was on. The speakers were disconnected from the stereo. I wondered if there'd been a break-in. But nothing seemed to be missing. I went to check the bedroom. As I switched the light on, the room blurred somehow. A kind of distortion or twist in the light, something I couldn't make sense of.

The bed and the floor were littered with magazines and sheets of paper. He'd evidently been looking through his boxes of old stuff. There were letters, photos, press cuttings about Karl's favourite bands, old music papers. Among the things on the bed were some pages cut out of porn magazines, both gay and straight. They were curled up at the edges, a decade or more old. There were yellowed pages of song lyrics or poems in a more childlike version of Karl's handwriting; some were marked with chords. None of it seemed recent.

Back in the living-room, I poured myself a large vodka and sat at the table. His glass, his chair. I felt like a stalker. Then I saw a small red notebook on the windowsill. It was full of recent lyrics, including several versions of 'Broken Strings'. Sometimes the writing got disjointed and almost unreadable when he was drunk. The last page was like that: several lines running at an angle, ending with the words *all going to loss / empty and element*. The phone didn't ring. Around one a.m. I gathered together all the papers in the bedroom and stacked them against the wall, then went to bed.

I slept badly, aware that Karl hadn't come back. Surely he'd have told me if he was going away? I'd said I'd call him on Sunday night; obviously he'd forgotten. I kept imagining his arms around me from behind. His lips brushing the back of my neck. The morning light was chilly, tinged with a pink that seemed artificial. I phoned Ian, who said he hadn't seen Karl since the London gig. 'Is he okay? I know he's been quite down recently.' I said I hoped so. 'Let me know when you see him. We've got to be on the Scarab by this time tomorrow. How do scarabs get to know each other?' I said I didn't know. 'They do lunch.'

By now, I was feeling quite worried. You can't go out with someone and not have some sense – conscious or unconscious of how things are with them. I didn't know the melody, but I could hear the backbeat. The front door rattled, but it was only the post: an electricity bill and a Council Tax paying-in booklet. I rang Martin, but didn't say anything to his rather self-satisfied answerphone. Then I tried Diane; there was no response. I put the phone down, and it rang. It was Alan. 'Hello? Karl? Oh, hi David. I've got some exciting news. Bob Mould wants you to tour with his current band, Sugar, in the New Year.'

'Fucking Hell. Karl'll be in Heaven. He loves Bob Mould. By the way, you don't have any idea where Karl might be? He's not here, hasn't been since yesterday.'

'No, I haven't seen him since Saturday. He dropped by to borrow the keys to the studio in Fazeley Street. Said he wanted to demo some new songs before the tour started.' Something rang like an echo in the back of my mind. 'Have you got a second set of keys?'

'Sure. But if he's there, you won't need them.' There was a pause, then he said: 'Shit. Look, stay where you are. I'll pick you up and bring the keys.'

Half an hour later, we parked outside the studio in Digbeth. The door was locked, but the staircase light was on. I could hear the rhythmic thudding of machines in the factory next door. Alan muttered a phrase in Hebrew. We rushed up the cold uncarpeted steps and along the corridor. The studio door was unlocked; when I pushed it open, the first thing we saw was electric light. The first thing we heard was silence.

The floor looked as though someone had torn apart a

huge bouquet of red chrysanthemums, then left the petals to dry in the sun. Clusters of broken glass were scattered between the walls. There was blood everywhere, dried to a thin crust. The smell of dead meat was mixed with the thin smell of whiskey. I could see labels on some of the fragments of glass. The jittering mercury light reflected from broken edges, like a dying fire. It was strangely beautiful.

At the back of the studio, the mixing desk was crowned with bottle-ends like stubbed-out cigarettes. Cables had been slashed through. A row of speakers had been cut open to expose black mouths full of wires. Karl was standing behind the mixing desk, his back to the wall. He was wearing a black denim shirt and jeans. His hands were covered with blood, and he was staring at them.

As I walked towards him, I could feel glass crunching under my feet – and worse, blood sticking to my shoes from the floor. He didn't seem to notice me. His breathing was slow and even, as if he were asleep. 'Karl. *Karl.*' I touched his arm; it felt stiff and cold. Could you die and still breathe? There was a blue tinge to his lips. His breath smelt of whiskey, as usual. Tiny crystals of glass were embedded in his hands, but the blood had stopped flowing. 'Come on, man.' He glanced at me dully. I put my arm around his back, gently pushed him forward. 'Please, come on. Let's get out of here.'

Alan was still standing in the doorway. He looked like he was going to be sick. 'Should I phone an ambulance?' he said. 'I don't mind driving, but…' He looked away from Karl.

'It's probably quicker if you drive,' I said. 'He's not bleeding much. But he's in shock.' I walked with Karl down the staircase, forced to mimic his zombie movements. His hands were bleeding again; I fished a thin wad of tissues from my pocket, and he crumpled it absently. I thought of a Bunnymen gig I'd been to where the backdrop was a projection of snow- covered mountain peaks: when the light changed to red, the mountains became volcanoes. Thinking of that helped me to focus on the task of getting Karl out of the building and into the car. He didn't speak.

Alan was usually a reckless driver; but this time he drove cautiously, afraid of giving way to his nerves. The A&E department of the General Hospital was only ten minutes' drive from the studio. Its glassy frontage was screened by a line of reddish bushes, their leaves on the way out. Alan spoke to the receptionist. Karl's breathing was more normal now; when I touched his shoulder, I felt him relax slightly.

The waiting area was half-empty. There was a child with a clumsily bandaged finger; another with a cut face. Several unshaven, silent men whose wounds from the night before were bruised and swollen. Alan paced back and forth, looking up expectantly whenever a nurse passed by. Karl plucked a few splinters of glass from his palms and wrapped them in the stained tissue. I'd realised in the studio that he wasn't badly hurt; but an appalling question waited at the back of my mind and wouldn't let me speak to him. *Where did all the blood come from?* I took my jacket off and put it over Karl's shoulders at the front.

After only a few minutes, a nurse called out 'Karl Austin?' He didn't respond, but I waved and then stood up. The nurse, a young man with hair dyed red, came towards us. 'Are you okay to come through, or do you need some help?' Karl stood up, wavering slightly. Then he turned to me and Alan. 'It's all right,' he said. 'I can do the tour now.' The nurse took his arm, led him down a corridor and through an open doorway.

Half an hour passed. Alan went to the drinks machine, returned with two plastic cups of coffee and two small packets of biscuits. The biscuits were engraved with china teapots; they tasted stale. 'Have you any idea what happened?' he asked me.

I shook my head. 'I'm sorry. I should have realised something like this might happen. Karl's been very strange lately. Hard to be with. I should have got him to talk. Somehow.'

'You can't catch a bullet with your teeth, David.' Alan sipped his coffee thoughtfully. 'I lost a boyfriend three years ago. Gary. He threw himself off a tower-block balcony.'

'God. I'm sorry.'

'He was HIV positive, still in good health. They have much better treatments now. He'd probably still be alive. Before he did it, he pissed me off so I wouldn't feel bad. But I did.'

I thought back to Karl's HIV test, how scared and yet fatalistic he'd been. Which was when it hit me. Blood samples. I choked on my coffee, and Alan had to punch me on the shoulder blades. At that point, a bearded doctor appeared and asked if he could have a word with us. We followed him down the corridor to a consulting room. Karl was nowhere in sight.

'Karl's okay,' he said. 'I've given him a sedative, and he'll need a few stitches in his hands. We're also sorting out a blood transfusion for him. We think he's been drawing blood from himself. There are needle marks in his arm, going back to yesterday and the day before. I gather you two found him. Can you tell me what happened?'

I explained briefly about Triangle and the tour. 'Karl suffers badly from stage fright. And some kind of depression.'

I told him what Alan and I had found in the studio. 'There was so much blood. It's obvious now.' The doctor looked confused. 'The bottles he smashed. They could have been quarter-bottles, miniatures even. He bottled his own blood, sampled it, like he was making a record.'

Alan laughed in a shocked, desperate way. 'That boy needs help.'

'Probably,' the doctor said. 'We'll take out the stitches in a week. He'll be able to play then. Whether he can go on stage is up to him – and you. We have to refer him to a psychiatrist, but he's a free agent. Unless the police get involved in what's happened.'

'They won't,' Alan said. 'It was just a rehearsal that went wrong.' Our eyes met, and I could tell we were thinking the same thing. *A rehearsal for what?* The last words in Karl's notebook came back to me, as if I could hear him singing them: *All going to loss / Empty and element.* They made as much sense as anything else that morning.

CHAPTER 10

break

Everywhere around
Is telling me something
Breaking me down
— Strangelove

The tour was cancelled. We could, in theory, have made the last four dates, but Alan said the risks were too great. 'If anything went wrong, we'd be in a legal and financial nightmare. We're only insured if we give up now.' To be fair to Alan, he did his best. He got Karl admitted to a private clinic and put all Triangle plans on hold. He never said anything to us about the money Furnace were losing. Martin didn't want to get involved. After leaving the A&E ward I went round to Ian and Rachel's house in Acocks Green. Ian was there; I told him what had happened. He wept. I don't think his crying had anything to do with losing the tour.

I went round to Karl's flat and did some basic tidying and cleaning. Until that point I hadn't realised how manky the place had become: layers of dust in the bathroom and kitchen, rotting fruit at the bottom of the fridge, magazines piled up everywhere. Karl was very bad at throwing stuff away. For the first time, I noticed that his collection of various-sized empty bottles had disappeared from the kitchen. Which made me wonder: *Where did he get the syringe from? What was he doing with a syringe anyway?* I took my clothes home in a suitcase. If he wanted me to move in later, fine; but I couldn't take anything for granted. He was mad. I didn't know what that meant.

The weekend after he was admitted to the clinic, I went to visit him. It was an old building in West Heath, probably a Victorian doctor's surgery; the rest of the street had been converted to industrial units. Karl was sitting in a day room with brown fabric-covered chairs, a low table and a TV set. The walls had faded semi-abstract prints: clouds, waves, stars. Karl hardly moved as I came in and sat opposite him. Either he was under heavy sedation or he'd had enough of the decor. His hands were unbandaged; stitches gleamed along one finger. 'How are you feeling?' I said.

'Okay. It's quiet here. They've given me a soundproofed room. Whatever goes on, I don't hear it.' He tried to light a cigarette, but couldn't get the match to strike; he wasn't gripping it properly. I lit it for him. 'Cheers.' The nurse watched impassively from the doorway. 'How are you, David?'

'I'm fine. I went round to your flat. Everything's okay there. And I paid the landlord your rent for this month. Can you pay me back?' He nodded. There was a pause. 'Karl... Do you remember what happened? In the studio?'

He nodded again. 'Why? I mean, why did you do that?'

Karl smiled with the left side of his mouth, the way he did when he was completely worn out. 'That's like asking *Why did you record that song?* or *Why did you play that chord?* I had to make something, and I made it. Even if I cheated.'

'How do you feel now?'

'Like I said, it's quiet here. It's safe.' He finished his cigarette and tried to stub out the end; it slipped from his fingers and lay glowing in the ashtray. 'I want to go home, but not yet.'

'Home to Erdington?' He nodded. 'You know we're not touring. Maybe in the New Year, if you're ready. We got an offer from Sugar to tour with them.'

Karl's face jerked up. 'No. I'm not going to. They always said it would harm me. The music. My mum and dad. They knew.'

'It's only stage fright, Karl. The audience, not the music.' I'd never seen him afraid before, except that time in Amsterdam. Drugged; that was it. 'We don't have to tour, you know.' It was hard to keep the confusion out of my voice. Triangle was Karl's obsession. Had been. 'It's up to you.'

He looked at me blankly, then lit another cigarette. The flame sparked in his eyes. 'Thanks for coming to see me. I'm sorry about what happened.'

'Just don't do it again.' We sat for a while, talking about nothing much. Eventually, I stood up. 'Better go. Take care of yourself.' I kissed him briefly, tasting smoke on his lips. He usually smoked Marlboro, but these were menthol. Schoolboy cigarettes; they smelt like cough sweets. 'Sorry, I forgot – the rent cheque.'

'Wait here.' He got up and walked to the door, his

arms hanging at his sides. The nurse went with him. They returned a minute later with his chequebook; it took him ages to write out the cheque, his hand moving deliberately as if he were trying to fake his own handwriting. He passed the cheque to me and gripped my hand for a moment, then stood to watch me leave.

Outside, it was getting dark. The buildings were tall silhouettes with no age or function. A few premature fireworks exploded behind one of them; echoes jarred the still air. Nothing seemed real. I hadn't really seen Karl or talked with him. I'd almost rather have faced a mad, dangerous Karl than this passive ghost. As for the tour and the band's future, I didn't know what to think. I felt a deep sense of confusion; a need for sleep.

That evening, I got a call from Mike West. He said Martin had given him my number. 'There's a lot of rumours flying around. About Triangle, the cancellations. Furnace Records are no saying much. I wondered if… if I'm intruding, just tell me to fuck off.' I gave him a brief version of what had happened, leaving out the studio incident: Karl had been behaving strangely, was having some problems and needed to rest. 'He really is ill, then?' Yes, I said, he was. 'Look, I don't want to pry. But there's a rumour that he, like, trashed a studio.'

I took a deep breath. 'Mike, look. What happened… it wasn't that exactly. But it's private. Who cares about the details?'

'At the moment, quite a few people. Would you rather be unknown, have no one… reputations matter in this business. Give me something to print that doesn't sound too fucked up.' I said I'd get back to him.

Then I phoned Ian. He asked how Karl was; I described

our meeting that afternoon. 'He wasn't the Karl we know. I think he might be in there for a long time.' Then I told him about Mike's call. We agreed that we'd better find something to say. I said I'd phone Radio Scratching as well. After hanging up, I switched on the radio and searched for their elusive waveband. I might have missed it if the song hadn't been familiar. It was 'Nowhere To Go'. After that, they played Andy Fairweather Low's 'Wide-Eyed and Legless'. Halfway through it broke up into static, as if the record was too scratched to listen to. I moved the dial back and forth, but the station had gone. Their transmitter was probably fucked.

Over the next couple of days, Ian and I had several phone conversations with Mike. Prompted by his questions, we gave him an account of Triangle's past and present which he organised into a kind of virtual interview. When it appeared in the *NME*, some witty sub-editor had titled it 'Bizarre Love Triangle'. Mike wrote it as if he'd talked with both of us at once:

> *NME*: What's *Hard Shadows* really about?
> *David*: It's about the need to belong, really.
> *Ian*: And different kinds of love – love for men, women,
> music, living. In spite of the damage love can do to you.

The accompanying photo used the three pictures of Triangle members from the inner sleeve of the album, cut out and superimposed on one of Paul's background shots from Hockley. The article ended: *They'll be back. This isn't the last word.* What Mike had actually said to me was: 'Let's hope this isn't the last word. If Karl doesn't get it together, not only will your future be fucked, so will your past. Suicidal depression is a rock cliche. You know that's not what Triangle are about. So do I. But reputations work backwards, you know? Take care, man.'

The letters page in the following issue contained several responses, ranging from admiration ('Karl Austin expresses truths few of us could face. His suffering is the price of that truth') to contempt ('Triangle are just another boring indie-rock band with a vocalist who's in need of a good slapping'). The letters editor chipped in: 'Are Triangle the miserablist band of all time, or just Brum's answer to The Sisters of Mercy? Does Karl need medical help or just guitar lessons? Does it really matter? Does anything really matter?' I didn't feel angry, reading that. I just felt a sense of unreality.

By then, Karl was out of the clinic. He phoned me to say he wanted to be alone for a while, and was going away. 'I'm much better now,' he said. 'They put me on sedatives, then on anti-depressants. The difference is... well, quite a bit. I used to think you could pass through death with your personality unchanged. But in fact, you can't even go through medication. Is that why you didn't come back?' I said I was sorry; it had been ten days, and I'd been planning to see him that weekend. 'It's okay,' he said. 'I needed the break anyway. I still do. Look, I'll ring you. Bye now.'

He was gone until the end of October. Nobody seemed to know where he was. Ian and I avoided seeing each other. He and Rachel were just about getting by on her income and his share of the royalties. To pay my rent and alcohol costs, I needed more work. I did a few recording sessions at Rich Bitch Studios with an R&B band called Frozen Gin. They came from Coventry; their work had a fast-paced urban tension about it that I enjoyed. Radio Scratching played their 'Slipping Down' EP to death and limbo. When it came to touring, though, I backed out; didn't want to be seen as 'ex- Triangle'. I was paid per session, and always visited the off-licence on the way home from the studio. The streets of Moseley were getting quieter after dark. The dead leaves broke up, and the rain washed them away.

————————

Karl phoned me on a Saturday morning, just before Hallowe'en. 'Hi David. It's me. I'm back in Erdington.'

It was a relief to hear his voice. 'Karl! My God. How are you, man?'

'Okay. I've been with my parents. And Elaine. Retracing my steps.' He sounded brisk, confident. 'Look, we need to talk. Do you want to come round this afternoon?'

'Sure,' I said. This calm-voiced Karl was as much a stranger as the frightened Karl had been. 'Is the flat okay?'

'I'm not staying here long. Might give it up. I've missed you.'

'I've missed you too,' I said, bewildered. 'I'll be round in a couple of hours.'

Outside, it was raining in fits and starts. I considered buying some flowers, settled for a bottle of Chianti. Too late, I realised that it would remind him of blood. The traffic into the newly pedestrianised city centre, and out again through Snow Hill, crept from light to light as though pretending not to move. At last the tall buildings of Slade Road closed in the view.

Karl had put on some weight, though he was still thin.

We embraced in his hallway. His kiss was unusually gentle; at least he was back on Marlboro. We sat in his living-room and drank coffee. He didn't have the stereo on, which was odd: Karl hated silence in his flat. As we talked, I noticed that his voice and gestures remained calm, but his eyes moved nervously whenever I spoke. As if someone had told him that he wasn't allowed to show excitement. I gave him a copy of the 'Bizarre Love Triangle' feature, which he hadn't seen, and told him about the Frozen Gin project. 'Have you been writing songs?' I asked.

'Kind of. They're not ready yet. I don't know how they should sound. I'll show you them another time.' His uneasy gaze flickered across my face. 'I'm looking forward to working with you and Ian again. But I need to make some changes in my life.' There was an awkward silence. 'I'm sorry about what happened,' he said. 'It was the only way I could take back control. But it's over now.'

'Are you really all right?' He shrugged, smiling. 'What are you going to change?'

Karl went over to his stereo and fiddled with the settings, but didn't switch it on. 'We can't go on pushing Triangle like it's a brand of cigarettes,' he said. 'That interview you showed me, can't you see what a trap we're in? None of it means anything. And the band has to. It's about creating music that makes people feel. Makes people *know*. It's not about recreating some trademark sound. It's not about chart placings or career moves or trends. It's not about fucking entertainment. Are you with me?'

'I'm always with you. You know that.'

'Not always. It's not your fault, David.'

'What isn't?' He didn't answer. Rain was smearing the

windows, reducing the view to a grainy 1960s film. Karl went to the cabinet, took out a near-empty bottle of Scotch and poured two small glasses. We drank. 'Take it easy,' I said.

The rain on the window was a nervous, scratchy drum pattern. Like Ian's playing on 'Still and Moving Water'. The drink had brought a touch of colour to Karl's angular face. He stepped behind me and ran his fingers through my hair. I looked up at him. 'Let's go to bed,' he said with a fragmentary smile.

The bedroom was cold; we got under the duvet and lay together in the dark of the drawn curtains, exploring each other with careful hands. Karl's kiss was still gentle, passive. Our throats made sounds in counterpoint, gradually converging to a shared wordless coda. We came rubbing together, Karl above me. It had been a long time. I kissed the sweat from his cheekbones; his eyes were closed. Then he got up, wiped himself with a towel and started dressing.

'Karl? What's up?' He didn't look at me. I stepped past him to the bathroom. When I emerged, he was sitting in the living-room just as he had been half an hour earlier. Still no music. He lit a cigarette and gazed at the window. The sun was breaking through outside, which made the room seem darker.

'Theresa's just started going to school,' he said. 'She's bright. A bit shy, the way I was as a kid. I can't remember what it was like to be five. Nothing at all. Theresa hardly knows me, you know. I didn't want to be a father, so I wasn't.'

He paused. 'I made up my own family. You and Ian, Diane. I used music as a kind of sacrament. There's no going back. But sometimes... To move on, you have to break away.' He stubbed out his cigarette and drew another, but didn't light it. The window behind his head was tinged with cold fire. I remembered the clocks were going back tonight. 'Shall we go for a walk?' he said.

We turned up Slade Road towards the centre of Erdington, where most of the traffic was headed. 'Elaine wants me to stay with her for a while,' he said. 'She and her boyfriend split up a few months ago. It won't be permanent. Her and me, I mean. But she's the only person who really understands me. She looked after me when I got like this before, seven years ago.'

'I didn't know that.' Our voices were drowned by the traffic, like ghosts in my head. I could see Karl's mouth opening and closing. 'Sorry, I can't hear you.'

'Too many gigs, David. I said I'm sorry. Do you understand?'

'What about Triangle?' Karl turned left onto Rosary Road, going uphill towards the lakes. A few primary-aged children were kicking a burst football up and down the roadway; one shot narrowly missed my face, striking the wall with a dull slap. The pink sun glowed above the rooftops like the moon reflected in water.

'Like I said. We don't need to tour, that's all shite. We can go on making records. I've got plans.'

'You've always got fucking plans,' I said. We walked on, driven by cold and tension. The black trees around Witton Lakes reminded me of false eyelashes. Beyond the lakes, the grid of narrow streets lined with identical houses seemed perfect and unreal: a facsimile of a village. At the top end of the estate, the view stretched down over factories and tower blocks to the pale buildings of the city centre. A kestrel hovered above us, its body perfectly still as its wings flapped.

'I don't know what to say, David.' His face was stiff and expressionless. 'You're a good friend, but... Well, it's like drinking. The friends you drink with seem more special because of the drink.'

'I thought there was a bit more to it than that,' I said.

'That's because you think sex is a spiritual experience. Like with music, you think having the right techniques will get you there. You can't see that there's something beyond all that. Something more than the body. More than just the thrill of doing it.'

I could feel my face burning. 'That's not fair. It's not fucking *fair*. You can't see beyond your own obsessions. You're an arsehole, Karl. I know you've had a bad life, but why take it out on me?' Karl turned away and looked down the slope, hugging his arms to his chest. Nightfall was starting to blur the outlines in the distance. He shivered. The kestrel had gone.

On the way back down to Slade Road, I made one final attempt to get through to him. 'Karl, look. We need to talk about what happened. The studio. I was there, remember. I saw what you'd done. And the things you've told me...'

Karl shook his head. 'There's no magic in words either. Talking can't change what's happened. That's the new religion, talk. People think Oprah Winfrey is the new Blessed Virgin. It's such a fucking waste of time. None of it means anything.' We walked past the grey prison-like hulk of the mental hospital, then paused on the bridge just before Six Ways. Below us, the streetlamps had come on; the roads were bristling with rush hour traffic. 'Will you be okay to get home from here?'

'No problem.' A question came to me, prompted by the orange light and the black fumes of a waiting lorry. 'Do you remember that house in Stoke? The one that was burning?' Karl looked evenly at me. 'What did you see exactly?'

'The same thing as you. Or a different version of it. Don't you understand? I couldn't live with someone who could see things like that. It would drag me under. We're too much alike.' He stepped towards me, pressing his mouth briefly against mine. 'Take care, David.' I watched his head disappear going down the steps, then turned and felt the vibration of the traffic. A year of our lives, I thought. The first kiss under a bridge, the last kiss above one. It didn't feel any higher up. For a few minutes I couldn't move. As long as I couldn't see people's faces, it would be all right. The car engines, the wheels scraping tarmac, the angry horns were all in another world; I stood there, listening to a deep silence in my head that nothing could break.

CHAPTER 11

solo

Always corpses at breakfast-time
— Kitchens Of Distinction

The main bar at the Nightingale smelt of poppers and spilt beer. Red light glistened on the sticky floor and turned the antique mirrorball to a bloodshot moon. Beyond the swing doors, music pounded from the crowded darkness of the dance floor: happy handbag amplified and remixed into something hard and relentless. This bar and the upstairs bar, connected to it by a spiral staircase, were mostly male; the women tended to gather in the smaller bar and pool room, beyond the dance floor. It was after midnight. Some couples were making an early getaway before all the taxis disappeared; others, sweaty from dancing, queued for burgers in the restaurant area. A notice on the wall warned us to watch out for trouble in the streets around the club: several men had recently been followed and attacked. I knew one of them: Steve, a friend and ex-lover of mine who was here tonight with a new boyfriend. He was wearing a black silk shirt and a scar across his forehead; the skin there is hard to stitch.

There weren't many familiar faces tonight. New clubs had opened in Birmingham and Wolverhampton; the scene was getting more dancey, less social. I'd never quite felt I belonged, but now it didn't matter: I was here. Karl had taught me that. After a couple of pints (my budget didn't stretch to spirits in a nightclub), I got talking to a rather neatly dressed lad with a London accent. It turned out he was from Solihull, but had spent the last five years in London. 'I fucking hate this city,' he said. 'Nobody's got a clue what to wear. They think Armani's what backing singers do. I'm bisexual in London, but I wouldn't shag a girl in Birmingham. I'd be too scared of her white stilettos putting my eyes out. They haven't got a clue. Do you see white stilettos on a John-Paul Gaultier catwalk? I don't fucking think so.'

Later, he drifted off. I was thinking about going home when a drunken boy stumbled into me. 'Sorry mate. You right? Oh, it's you. Remember me? I used to work in Starlings.' I did remember him: an attractive, rather camp lad with an angelic smile. His hair was dark, with a blond streak in the middle. He was wearing a green rugby shirt and prefaded blue jeans, and was drinking Breaker. His name was Marc – 'with a "c", as in Almond.' He was a fan, especially Soft Cell. We chatted for a while and bought each other a pint. At one point, when he was going off to the toilet, he said, 'Don't run away' and slipped his hand under my shirt, just above the belt. His blue eyes held a friendly sense of conspiracy.

When he came back, instead of sitting down, he pulled me to my feet and then leaned against the wall of the staircase. We stood there together, Italian shoes passing within a few inches of our joined mouths. My fingers traced the outline of his cock. The alcohol slowed everything down, like watching a video frame by frame. By the time we had finished our drinks, we were both too excited to walk in comfort. 'Would you like to come back with me?' I said.

Marc shook his head. 'I'm sorry. I don't like going back to people's flats. Something happened to me once. But I know somewhere we can go.' He gripped my arm. The barman was still serving, but had pulled the wire screen halfway down to indicate *no more customers*. A few desolate queens were trying to cruise the cloakroom queue. It was time to go somewhere else.

Outside Pulse, teenagers were busy paving Hurst Street with vomit that was exactly the colour of the streetlamps. Marc, wearing a blue ski jacket, led me up the hill towards Colmore Row. We crossed New Street, where beggars lay huddled in shop doorways, and separated by a few yards in order not to look like a couple. Marc disappeared into the shadows of Needless Alley; I followed him. Opposite Swordfish, I could see the dusty blue sign of Starlings above the boarded windows. Originally part of the New Imperial Hotel, Starlings had become an independent gay bar with a female manager and a mixed, student-based crowd. Three years of my life had revolved around that place. When the hotel closed down, the demolition plans forced Starlings to close too. It had been closed for two years, but the building was still there.

Marc pointed into a narrow alleyway, made for access only. It led round the back of the dead hotel. Some repair work had been started and left unfinished: rusty scaffolding framed a bricked-up doorway with ragged sheets of tarpaulin hanging on either side like curtains. A streetlamp glowed at the corner of the alley. I glanced up to check for loose masonry, and saw a square of velvet sky. It was strangely like being inside a house.

Another sheet of tarpaulin was spread in front of the doorway, held in place by loose bricks. No doubt another couple had made themselves at home here. Marc stepped back against the rough brickwork, unzipping his jacket. 'You can go down on me if you want,' he said. I kissed him, then knelt and unfastened his jeans, reaching up to touch his nipples under the rugby shirt. His chest felt completely smooth. 'Don't take too long,' he said. 'It's cold.' I kissed his cock through his boxer shorts, feeling it stiffen against the thin fabric, then pulled them down. He stood very still, cradling my head in his hands; his breathing quickened as I sucked him, but then slowed again. 'Stand up,' he said.

When I stood up, darkness creased my vision for a moment; then I was okay. Marc knelt on the tarpaulin and unzipped me, then gripped my cock with his mouth. I stroked his hair, tracing the blond streak to where it vanished at the crown. He began to wank himself furiously; the rhythm vibrated through both of us. I was too drunk to come, and inhibited by the fear of being caught; but soon I heard Marc crying in the back of his throat, and felt his body stiffen. He let go of me and rocked back, closing his eyes, his hand still moving gently. Sweat glistened on his eyelids. Then he stood up, breathless, and pointed to my crotch. I shook my head. 'It's okay, I'm fine.' As we zipped and buttoned our clothes, I saw that my shoes and trouser bottoms were splashed with Marc's semen. I crouched and rubbed one shoe with the fingers of my left hand.

We said goodbye in Colmore Row, where Marc wanted to catch the night bus to Perry Barr. 'Will I see you again?' I asked. He said he'd be in the Jester on Friday night. I knew what that meant, knew I'd go along regardless. It was nearly three o'clock; I didn't want to sit on the crowded night bus to Moseley with Marc's come drying on my shoes and trousers, so I walked home. Along Bristol Street, with its kerb-crawling cars and boys pretending to wait for buses; Pershore Road, where girls stalked back and forth like the ghosts of prisoners and trees cast giant shadows across the roadway; Edgbaston Road, where the security lights jumped from house to house as I passed. Every now and then I paused to rub my left hand against my nose. It felt as though his orgasm had released me. As though he could feel my pleasure for me, taking away all feelings of shame or inadequacy. I didn't believe that, but I felt it.

The next evening, I went with Ian and Rachel to see a firework display in Senneley's Park. There was a bonfire, guarded by security men in orange jackets; in the distance, a Ferris wheel lifted tiny figures into the night. We shared a six-pack of K cider, clutching the dark bottles like microphones. There were no short-range fireworks: the whole display unfolded in the sky above us, dropping fragments of ash that were only visible in the firelight. A crowd of angels, all staring eyes and melting bones and crackling hair. A random percussion: perfect riffs but no underlying beat. Afterwards, the night seemed to press in around us, bitter with smoke.

We walked past the glowering husk of the bonfire to the crowded funfair, where Meatloaf competed with Take That. Teenagers wailed in chorus, strapped to the interior of a wheel that spun and then tilted. Ian was talking about shamanic rituals: 'They use drumming and lack of sleep to induce a visionary state. Throw a handful of dust into the fire and see the faces of the dead. Then the dead speak through them. The Chinese have used fireworks to induce visions for thousands of years.' I was in a deeply maudlin state, after two bottles of K cider on an empty stomach. Rachel winked at me and linked her arm with mine. Nothing seemed to help.

From the start of November, the shops were full of premature Christmas decorations and muzak carols. I was desperately trying to get a job before I ran out of money; without appropriate references there seemed little chance, though Tempest Records agreed to take me back on as a temporary assistant to handle the pre-Christmas orders.

Martin offered to help me find another band, but I thought that would be burning a bridge we could still cross. Alan was busy with his other bands – including Webbed, who were recording their album *Boys From the Key* – but was still very keen to get Triangle back on the rails. He seemed less wary of me now that I wasn't with Karl; I realised it was Karl he'd been afraid of.

Throughout November, I alternated between phases of going out a lot and phases of sitting at home with my record collection, drunk and tearful. I was determined not to sink into obsession the way I had after the breakup with Adrian. That had been a much nastier business, lightened only by the opportunity to make a few evil remarks: 'Maybe I'll find a partner who's heard of fucking. That'd be nice.'

This time, it was hard to work up any real anger. I felt lost and disorientated. Nowhere was warm. When I went out on the Birmingham gay scene, I found it easier to pick up than I ever had before, because I no longer cared. There was a passivity about me that got men interested, though it shut down any possibility of getting involved.

There were any number of false dawns, points when I felt it was all going to be okay. Like one night when I walked into Edwards No. 8 just as the DJ put on the EP version of 'Movin' On Up' by Primal Scream: scratchy guitar, deep bass riffs and Gillespie's blissed-out vocal. Or the Sunday morning when my flat's window let in the sunlight but kept out the cold, and I played all my Bowie albums from the seventies before remembering that I'd once masturbated over the cover of *Low*. I was twelve years old at the time. Thinking of that, I laughed so hard that I choked and spat black coffee over the sofa. I even checked the faded sleeve for any trace that a DNA test might identify as mine.

Karl sent me a postcard from North Wales: a green hillside dipping into shadow, with the silhouette of another hill behind it to one side. He'd written in his usual jagged, back-slanting script: 'David – hope you're well. It's quiet here, except when it rains or the sheep are frightened by something. I know how Agent Starling felt. I'm writing more songs. Thought the Frozen Gin stuff was good. See you soon. K.' It didn't explain why he was there or who he was with. The ending reminded me of a blues song I'd once heard, called 'Looking For Kaye'. Its chorus contained the line *If you see Kaye*. I wished Karl's puzzles were as simple as that. Maybe if I could understand him, it would be over. Then I could move on.

The *NME* was still getting letters about Triangle, mostly from fans who claimed they could 'identify with Karl's despair'. It made me angry. Depressed people are always blind to any emotion but their own. If they can't 'identify' with a point of view, it doesn't exist. Karl never trusted an emotion unless he could perform it in some way. At times, I wondered if he'd left me just to show me how it felt. To keep me playing the bassline to his guitar.

––––––––

At a PJ Harvey gig in late November, I ran into Diane and Matt. We had a drink together and exchanged tales of woe. The Vacant Lot still couldn't get a record deal, and tension between Diane and Andy was making it hard for the band to do anything. 'I wish he'd fucking leave,' she said. 'Everything I want to do, he finds a way to fuck up. I'd rather have a less good drummer who wasn't Andy. I keep praying for a Spinal Tap kind of thing to happen to him.' I wondered if Karl and I could still work together in Triangle. It had been a bumpy ride even when we were sleeping together. Diane had lost some weight and was looking tired, though her Goth make-up disguised it well.

The next evening, she phoned me. We talked about the gig, which both of us had loved. 'She sounds like a woman who's walked across burning coals,' Diane said. 'Like she could go on singing after her death, and wouldn't take orders from any fucking drummer.' We both thought she was far too good to be successful. 'Anyway,' Diane said, 'I just thought – would you like to come round for dinner on Friday?' Diane lived in Northfield: a grim district on the southern edge of Birmingham, full of slate-grey housing projects and high walls sprayed with swastikas. Her flat was on the second floor of a converted house, near the railway line. Inside, the walls were covered with posters and album sleeves. A cat's skull perched on a cabinet full of records; a complete rattlesnake's skeleton was stretched out along the top of the gas fire. 'I used to have red light bulbs,' Diane said. 'But the landlord made me change them. He thought I was a prostitute. I had to show him my P60 from Rackham's before he'd believe I wasn't on the game.'

We drank some red wine and ate some corrosive chilli, then sat on the couch listening to The Cure's live album *Entreat*. Every half-hour or so, the roar of a passing train echoed through the flat. The wine made Diane a bit giggly, and she did perfect impressions of Robert Smith and Siouxsie Sioux before picking up an acoustic guitar and playing a new song of her own, 'Still Friends'. It mocked the idea of ex-lovers remaining close: *You say we're still friends, but what you never said / Is that now you can't fuck me, you'll fuck up my head.* 'You know the really sad thing? I need Andy to play that song properly. That slow drum pattern of his, no one else does it the same way. But he won't play that song.'

That got us onto the subject of Karl, which called for a second bottle. 'You two never really seemed happy together,' Diane said. 'You're not good for each other. You admire each other as musicians, not as people. You could do better than Karl, anyway.'

'Better in some ways, maybe,' I said, watching the light shimmer on the death metal album covers that crossed the far wall. A cemetery, a pile of corpses, a ruined church. 'With Karl, there was something different. In the songs, the way he was sometimes. Like there were things inside him that he couldn't control but needed to share. I can't explain it. After him, someone… better might just seem bland. I suppose he's mad. But there's more to it than that.'

Diane laughed. 'Other people have madness. Karl has visions.' Suddenly she looked vulnerable, curled up on the sofa with the light melting in her eyes. 'But he can't follow anything through. He'll always run away. Did he tell you I had an abortion when we were together?'

'No. I'm sorry. I had no idea.' Somehow, I thought I should have guessed.

'It was an accident. The baby, I mean. A condom that broke.' She paused, breathing slowly. 'We both felt very bad about it. Karl didn't want me to have an abortion. But he didn't want to live with me. Said he'd already failed at being a father. He didn't leave me, but I could feel him backing off. Someone had to take charge of the situation. So I did.' She closed her eyes. Behind us, Fields of the Nephilim repeated the same blurred riff over and over. 'We went off each other after that. Guilt, resentment, I don't know. We couldn't touch any more. Once we'd split up we got on fine, because we weren't trying to be *friends*. There was no emotional blackmail. Karl's good like that. He knows about letting go.'

We refilled our glasses and sat for a while, letting the music's placid solemnity fill the room like temporary dust. Then Diane said: 'I told Karl he should work for the Samaritans. Because he's good at listening, but never gives advice.' We both found that intensely funny, for some reason. When we stopped laughing, we were in each other's arms. 'I miss him too,' Diane said. She kissed me. We kissed again. Close up, her face was almost still. Her eyes moved under the pale eyelids, and her mouth opened as if she were about to sing.

The next morning, I woke up in Diane's bed. She was lying with her back arched towards me, her spiky hair floating above the pillow. It was nearly midday. We'd made love during the night, and again just after dawn. It felt strange, but not wrong. We'd comforted each other. And taken precautions, obviously. Once you get used to condoms, they become a symbol of trust. I didn't feel the need to walk away asking myself whether I was a lying straight or a lying queen. The only thing that worried me was the irrational thought that I was still trying to be Karl's shadow.

———————

One morning in early December, I caught a train to Leicester. That had been one of the dates on our cancelled tour – De Montfort Hall, I think – but we'd never played there. I hadn't been back to Leicester in twenty-two years; my images of it were murky, as if I'd only seen the place by night. The railway station backed onto a canal whose black surface was lumpy with almost-submerged rubbish.

It was near the museum, I knew that. I followed signs through the city centre, whose narrow streets were choked with traffic. A tower block was covered in some rough white material, like fossilised bandages. The sign above a record shop declared that it sold PROGRESSIVE MUSIC. It sold retrogressive music. Further on, as the buildings became older and darker, I began to feel a confusing sense of half-familiarity. A tiled subway led me to the museum. Here and the library had been two of my favourite places.

The silent places. I could remember an upstairs gallery where birds of prey had crouched or hovered above rocks and trees: owls, falcons, eagles, hawks. But they were gone now. An assistant told me the bird collection had been sold to another museum.

Imagining cries I'd never heard, I walked slowly round the block that included the museum. The air was bright and cold; my breath left traces of pale vapour. I turned a corner and looked up a long avenue of trees, flanked by taller buildings. A line of bollards protected the gravel-laid walkway. I was there. The tenement house – or was it a short block of flats? – was less than halfway to the upper end. The walkway was patterned with dead leaves: sycamore and horse-chestnut. The echo in my head made the street seem more than real. There was a low wall I'd walked along, balancing with my arms. Or was I making that up? It was next door to the house where we'd lived.

Which wasn't there. Roughly where I thought it had been was a new office building with pebble-dashed stone fins. Why did all this new architecture look so archaic? Confused, I walked on. There was the narrow path that led back through the park to the museum. And there, in the wrong place, was the house. Dark walls, darker than slate. A basement with spiked railings coming up to street level. Two balconies overhead, each with a black-painted iron moulding shaped like a rose. An old woman was standing on the first-floor balcony, watering some pot plants. I stepped forward and waved from the street.

'Excuse me.' She looked down. 'Sorry to bother you,' I called. 'Did there use to be another building like this, but further down the street?'

I could see her nodding. 'Yes. It was knocked down about twelve years ago. There's an insurance building there now.'

'Were you here in the early seventies?'

'Yes. I moved here just after the war.' I couldn't see her face clearly; her hair was a dull grey, the colour of smoke.

'Do you remember a Mr and Mrs Pelsall? A dark-haired man and a fair-haired woman? With a small child?'

'No,' she said. 'I didn't know anyone from that building.' 'Thanks very much for your help,' I said, and waved goodbye. She didn't wave back. I walked on up to the bollards that marked the end of the walkway, and on through jagged streets full of semi-detached houses, tiny hardware and grocery stores, grey prefabs displaying washing lines and satellite dishes. I didn't know where I was going, but I didn't want to stop and think.

We lived in Leicester for about two years, in a flat on the first floor of that house. I remember it was dark, and not very warm. The stairs seemed to go on for ever. My parents let me run around in the street outside, because there were no cars. My sister was born there, but died after a few weeks. In the time that followed her death, it somehow emerged that my father was seeing another woman – had been for more than a year. After weeks of screaming, he moved out. I've seen very little of him since. My mother got a job in Birmingham and moved there with me. I was five years old.

I walked until I could hardly feel my feet. The sky was darkening, but it was too early for the streetlamps. All around me were damaged buildings: a boarded-up pub, a neighbourhood office with a shattered window, three houses in the process of being demolished. The wind blew through the teeth of a blackened staircase. A square of canvas flapped from rusty scaffolding, a coat over a lack of body. I stopped, unable to move or look away.

Empty. Like nothing. like not being there. This was worse than crying. The ruined houses were more real than I could ever be. Something moved under the staircase. I saw it, but I was nothing. The light fell through me. If I had to go on feeling like this... Feeling what? An echo of pain. I was shaking. And then, suddenly, the world came back, or I came back to it. In a single moment, a memory: the building site. Marc's body. His drying semen on my hand.

I walked on, looking for a signpost. Around the corner, a man was wringing his hands in an agony of guilt. Then I saw the cloth in his hands, the bucket, the van he was trying to clean. Up ahead, I could see the canal and the back of the railway station. The rhythm of the traffic drove me forward.

three below zero

My hands came back today
Trying to set themselves free
— Tindersticks

Martin phoned me a couple of weeks before Christmas to say that Karl had been in touch. He wanted to start work on a new Triangle album. I said it was a bit odd of Karl not to contact me directly. 'You know what he's like,' Martin said. But I didn't seem to, not any more. Fuck it. I had a chat with Ian and we both agreed to start right away. Martin fixed up some time at Canal Studios for us to work on the arrangements and demo tapes. The Digbeth studio didn't seem like a good idea. We didn't need a producer at this stage: all we needed was a room and some half-decent alcohol.

It felt strange, waiting for Karl in my cold Moseley flat. I did some basic tidying, so he wouldn't imagine I'd let things fall apart. The upper panels of the bay window were leaded, with tiny panes in deep blue, red and green. In a vase on the mantelpiece were some dried-out flowers whose water had long since evaporated; I threw them away. Karl was half an hour late, as usual, and wearing the same black coat he'd worn last winter. He looked tired: there were shadows under his eyes like bruises.

We embraced without kissing. 'It's good to see you,' he said. 'Mind if I turn the fire up? It's fucking froze out there.' An angry wind was shaking the tree in the neglected front garden. Karl stood in front of the gas fire rubbing his arms, unable to get warm. I made some coffee with brandy. He got me to play my copy of 'Slipping Down', which he hadn't heard all the way through. 'Not bad,' he said. 'Blue Away had a better guitarist, didn't they? I like that fast track, "No Witnesses". Bit like The Specials before they got bored. Or Nine Below Zero. Like this flat.' It was good to hear him sound so normal. I drew the curtains and we talked for a while. We'd arranged to meet Ian at the K2 later on.

Karl said he was living with Elaine, but he was away a lot. 'I went to Clwyd for a while, to sort myself out. We bought a fixed caravan there a few years ago. A good place to be alone.' I remembered the postcard. 'I'm off that medication now. And back on the booze – but not like before. I don't need to drink myself unconscious. But it's hard to sleep without something.' I gestured to the brandy on the sideboard; we both had a small glass, no ice.

Feeling a little more at ease, I gave him the radio edit of my recent life. I described Marc and two other conquests (without the fine details), but didn't mention Diane. If he was jealous, he didn't show it. 'Jobwise, nothing much has worked out. When you've been sacked, it takes a while to get back into work. Easier to find a new lover. They don't want references. Be good to work with you and Ian again. How much stuff have you got?'

'Sorry I phoned Martin instead of you,' Karl said. 'I thought you might not want to talk to me. It's been a strange time, you know? I've got a lot of stuff – lyrics, chord sequences, melodies. You know I can't write sheet music, not properly. I'll show you when I can plug in a guitar and play some of it. There's maybe a dozen songs worth doing something with. Plus "Broken Strings" and maybe that outtake from the album, "A Yard of Skin". There's enough for an album, I hope.' He sounded much less sure of himself than he'd been over the *Hard Shadows* set. But that wasn't surprising.

That evening, Triangle met for the first time since our last dodgy rehearsal in September. We had a pungent curry and some beers at the K2 restaurant in Moseley, a favourite haunt of ours from the early days. Karl explained his ideas for the second album. 'It's going to be quieter than *Hard Shadows*, I think. Not as clear about who or where or why. I'd like to call it *Dead Space*… you know, like a dead nerve or a disconnected line.'

'It's a bit risky to call it *Dead* anything,' I said. 'We're already getting a reputation as Sorrows R Us.'

'I like the idea of dead space, though,' Ian said. 'It makes you think of, like, ancient geometry. The Druidic religion … Why not call it *Off the Map*?'

Karl smiled. 'Brilliant. You're a genius, Priest. I'd kiss you, if you weren't so fucking ugly.' Ian was not ugly. In the past, Karl and I had discussed possible ways to entice him into a threesome. Fear of an angry Rachel had deterred us.

'I'd let you if you cleaned your teeth occasionally,' Ian said. 'It's good to have you back. How do you feel about playing live?'

'I don't know.' Karl gazed uneasily at the green beer bottle in his hand. 'Not yet. I'll let you know.'

We broke up mid-evening; Karl had to get back to Oldbury. Ian and I went for a swift half at the Fighting Cocks. 'He's not really better, is he?' Ian said. I didn't know what to say. There was something inevitable about the change, like getting older. Karl didn't have a 'normal' to get back to. He'd been running from something, but now it had caught up with him.

———

We had five sessions at Canal Studios: three evenings and two Sunday afternoons. The Yardley cemetery was sprayed with frost; the canal was frozen over. A new hairdressing salon across the road had the sign JULIE FORLETTA – Karl said to me, 'I wonder what her staff call her?' He was sleeping badly, always tired, relying on coffee to get him wound up and alcohol to help him chill out afterwards. I was glad we weren't touring.

At first sight – or first sound – Karl's new songs were musically undeveloped. The lyrics seemed too cold and distant: they didn't suggest rhythms or dynamics, anything to grab hold of. And Karl didn't want to play as much guitar as before. But after a while, a few arrangements came together that set off the icy lyrics instead of just echoing them. Ian's drumming was light and rapid; Karl and I played in counterpoint, one carrying a soft melody line while the other broke in with hard riffs. The result was a brittle, repetitive sound, more offbeat than downbeat. I thought we needed a keyboard player to give the songs more structure. Ian's suggestion was more immediate: 'We need to play this stuff live, Karl. Before we record it.'

Karl's voice was gentler than before, a bit too high, with a breathy quality that came from a persistent cold. The note of fear he'd had on songs like 'Curfew Town' was there in the new songs, but mixed with a kind of helpless acceptance. As if he'd fallen in love with pain. We demoed four tracks. 'Blue Glass' was a slow, dazed piece with Karl using a tremolo arm. His voice sounded like there was something nasty in his mouth that he couldn't wash out. *Drink the blood from this glass / The blood is a bruise / From all the years past.*

Then there was 'Oubliette', the strangest track we ever recorded. Karl said an oubliette was a kind of stone pit they used in medieval times where a prisoner would be stuck, unable to lie down, standing in his own shit for as long as it took him to die. The lyrics had an edge of madness: *Standing alone in the dark / I don't know whose body this is.* What upset most people about 'Oubliette', when it was released, was the overdub. Karl taped himself screaming, then put it behind the whole track at a low volume. It was a terrible, sickening sound, but you could only just hear it.

The other two songs on the demo tape had stronger arrangements: gentle tunes broken up by violent bursts of noise, as in 'His Mouth'. Even so, they were rather static – the sound of something breaking apart, rather than something coming together. 'The Ruins' was about this place Karl had seen on a moor in Clwyd: *The house of the master / A crown with no head / The timbers are rotting / The bulldogs are dead.*

Karl had a phobia of dogs, especially the hunting kind that
morons keep in heavily built-up districts. He once showed
me a report in the Birmingham *Voice* about missing cats
being found skinned on patches of wasteground: bait for
nocturnal fox-hunting with dogs.

'Punishment' was a violently sado-masochistic song,
though there was no violence in Karl's voice. *I feel the bark
against my skin / His hands break me open / He bites deep inside
me / And never lets go.* When we'd finished recording that,
Karl was very down. I wanted to kiss him, but couldn't.

Alan wasn't too keen on the demo. He said the music
was flat and the lyrics were maudlin. 'It's not healthy.' He
said we should tour and then write some new material
'while the fight's still in you'. But Karl was even less
willing to play live than before we'd recorded the demo.
He seemed unable to take charge of things, unable to front
the group in any sense.

Martin persuaded Alan to set up a month of recording
time in the spring, with Pete Stone as producer. We discussed
trying to get other musicians involved: Matt Pearce, Felt's
Martin Duffy, maybe Diane from The Vacant Lot on backing
vocals. Diane was quite happy to do it. I wish that had
happened. Later, Martin told me he'd hated the demo tracks.
'I just had this feeling that we shouldn't waste time.'

———————

After one of the Sunday afternoon sessions, we went
for a curry and a few beers in Acocks Green. It had been
dark since four; the streets were metallic with frost. The
pubs all had security staff, grim-faced boys playing pool,

Haddaway's 'What Is Love' blaring and MTV on a screen with the sound off. Outside, men walked their dogs and inadequately-dressed girls stood around telephone boxes, shouting. No car seemed to move at less than 50mph. Acocks Green is a handy crossroads of bus routes going to different parts of the city. There isn't much else you can say for it. By ten o'clock we were bored, sick of talking about music, and not quite drunk enough to call it a day. I was at the bar, getting our fifth or sixth round in, when a glass shattered not far behind me.

It was hard to see what was happening. People were backing away, raising their hands to protect their faces. One man had backed another against the wall and was threatening him with a broken glass. He made quick stabbing movements in the air, foreplay before penetration. Then a flying glass struck the back of the attacker's head. He turned and saw Karl struggling to his feet, a bottle poised in his hand. The other man backed off, bleeding across his face. A bouncer ran in from the doorway, shouting. Karl overturned the table, scattering beer and broken glass across the floor. The bouncer grabbed him from behind. The man with the glass lunged at Karl, but tripped over the edge of the table and fell hard. Before he could get up, the barman's foot was on his shoulder. He screamed 'Fucking wankers!' in an oddly high- pitched voice.

Karl had gone very pale. Flying glass had cut the left sleeve of his jacket; there was blood on his hand. No one spoke. The man on the floor curled up on his side and lay still. The back of his shirt was covered with blood. This all took a few seconds, while Madonna was singing the chorus of 'Fever'. The Christmas decorations – fairy lights and tinsel-coated balls – glittered like the lights of a distant city. Karl turned and looked at the man who was holding him. The bouncer stepped back warily. Then Karl made for the exit. Ian, returning from the toilet, stopped and stared. I pointed towards the door, and we followed Karl out into the icy street. He walked quickly down a side road, then glanced behind him and saw us. He started to run. I called out: 'Karl, it's us.' He stopped, his back to the chain-link fence around the Post Office depot.

His left hand was dark with blood. I wanted to apologise for not getting involved, but didn't know what to say. Some inner reflex had frozen me. It had happened too fast. But Karl didn't seem to care. He stared at his hand and said: 'That cunt was holding me. Just holding me from behind, like a sacrifice. So that fucker could glass me.'

'Why did he let you go?' I asked.

Karl smiled. 'I looked at him.'

'Let's get the fuck out of here,' Ian said. A police siren started wailing somewhere close by; then another, going in a different direction. Karl wrapped a handkerchief around his wound and put both hands in his jacket pockets. We walked up to the traffic island on the Warwick Road, where a fir tree was wrapped in coils of wire carrying beads of red light. Two girls in PVC jackets and brightly coloured leggings were getting out of a taxi. I waved to the driver and the three of us climbed into the back.

'City centre, please.' Neither Ian nor I had planned to go there, but it didn't matter. Karl sat between us, staring at the back of the driver's head. He was trembling slightly and his face was wet, as if he had a fever. I hugged him. 'Y'all right, bab?' He didn't answer. When we reached Digbeth, he insisted on going to New Street Station rather than the General Hospital. It wasn't his playing hand, he said. Neither Ian nor I felt like making any of the comments that came to mind.

———————

Just before Christmas, we took advantage of a gap in the studio bookings to fit in a gig rehearsal. Ian thought it would help Karl to overcome his stage fright: once he got into it, he'd remember how it felt. But the evening wasn't a great success. Karl turned up nearly an hour late, looking hollow; he said he'd been sleeping badly. I asked whether Elaine was keeping him up. 'David, will you do me a favour, sweetheart?' he said. 'Will you die?' Ian hid behind his drumkit, tapping out rhythms while Karl and I tried to agree on a set list.

We slogged through about half of *Hard Shadows*, plus 'Made of Clay', 'Blue Glass' and 'The Ruins'. With any number of false starts and bum notes. Karl sang well, especially on the new songs, but he played like a zombie. On 'Still and Moving Water', he let the instrumental coda break up into random bursts of guitar. In a cold and bitter version of 'His Mouth', he played false chords on purpose, corrupting the rhythm. As 'For the Distance' ended a few seconds early, Ian drumming over thin air, I unplugged my Rockwood and said: 'Well, thank fuck there was no one to hear us.' Karl crouched with his eyes shut, touching the strings of his Fender too gently to make a sound.

This being our last gathering of the year, we went for a quick drink at the Redhill Tavern in Yardley. The lounge was quiet, smoke-filled and comfortable. Karl lit a cigarette, then fell asleep in his seat. Ian and I chatted about our plans for the festive season, the brilliance of the new House of Love album, and a new TV series called *The X-Files*. 'All the episodes are based on true stories,' Ian said. Karl's cigarette had burned down to a stick of white ash; I stubbed it out. He hadn't touched his Guinness. Ian shook him gently; his eyes twitched under the lids, but he didn't move. His breathing was slow, but not deep. I'd watched him sleep many times, even in pubs; but there was something not right about this.

Ian looked at me, confused. 'Is he on medication?'

'Not officially,' I said. Then it sank in. 'Oh, fuck.' I slapped Karl's face, then struck the top of his ear with my knuckles. His eyes opened, blank. Nobody at home. He blinked at me and Ian, yawned, reached for his pint and drained half of it in one go. I checked my watch. There wasn't time for another round.

Ian caught the bus to Kings Heath; I went with Karl to New Street Station, just to make sure he didn't flake out. When he lit another cigarette, I noticed the wounds in his left hand hadn't healed properly. 'You should have got stitches,' I said.

'You know I'm not into nostalgia,' he replied coldly.

'Karl, what are you taking?'

'A break.' We were in the station concourse, which was crowded with motionless figures and their luggage. Karl looked up at the electronic display of arrival and departure times. 'My leave. Your heart with me, wherever I go.'

'I'm sorry I was a cunt earlier,' I said. 'Christmas always fucks me up. You know that.'

'Forget it,' he said. Karl never believed my apologies. Perhaps he was right. Our eyes met for a second. He gripped my hand, pressing the fingers together. Then he turned away, guitar case in hand. At the ticket gate, he turned and waved; but someone walked past, blocking my line of sight. If he called anything, it was drowned by the incomprehensible buzz of the announcer's PA system.

sleeve notes

The demons in your darkness
And the friends you never called
— Tom Robinson

We were due to start recording *Off the Map* in March 1993. By mid-February, when we still hadn't heard from Karl, Ian and I began to get worried. Not that we were expecting Valentine cards; but it was going to be difficult to go into the studio with only half the tracks even vaguely sorted out. I knew Karl wasn't happy with some of his lyrics, and was trying to write some more. Money was tight all round: we couldn't afford delays, and neither could Furnace. Alan was keen to put a single out, but didn't think any of the new songs would stand alone.

When I phoned Martin, he said he was sick of me and Karl using him as a go-between. I said I'd happily talk to Karl directly, if I knew how to contact him. Martin said that Furnace must have an address for him. 'I'm keeping out of it. To be honest, I think Karl dramatises his own problems. That's become what the band's about.'

'It never used to be,' I said. 'We've always been a team.'

'Meaning you gave, and Karl took. Look, David, I'm not knocking gay relationships. But your relationship with Karl was just like master and servant. To be honest, I think he's a very self-obsessed person. And I don't go for that "tortured genius" crap. I don't know anyone who does.'

I took a deep breath. 'That's really not the point. He's ill. He's not himself. And I think he's started using drugs. Needles.'

'Really? A rock musician shooting up? Unheard of.'

'Look, you know Karl. He likes a drink, but that's it. If he's on smack, then something's gone seriously wrong with him.'

'Why? It's a part of the lifestyle, David. Rock musicians have always helped themselves to vast amounts of drugs. And drink. And women, or boys. It goes with the territory. Look, David, I'm saying this as a friend. If Karl doesn't want to do the album, forget it. Find another band. Get a life. Know what I mean?'

A few days later, I phoned Furnace Records. Alan was away, but his assistant Stephen gave me the address in Oldbury that Karl had asked them to send royalty cheques to. I tried Directory Enquiries, but they had no phone number for Karl or Elaine Austin at that address; a recorded voice told me Elaine's number was 'unlisted'. I wrote to Karl, asking him to get in touch and reminding him of the schedule.

The first day of recording was a Friday. There was Ian, me, Pete, Jim and Stephen from Furnace. We worked on the bass and drum parts of the four tracks from the demo tape. It felt strange hearing Karl's voice in the studio and not knowing where he was. Being back at Canal Studios didn't help: the ghost of those miserable December sessions stood behind us, blankly imitating. At lunchtime, I wrote a short letter to Elaine, explaining the problem and asking her to phone me. Oldbury wasn't far away, but somehow I didn't want to turn up unexpectedly on her doorstep. We knew so little about the situation there.

No sessions were planned for the weekend. On Saturday morning, I got a phone call from Elaine. Her voice was quiet, with a soft accent that sounded more Worcestershire than Black Country. There's only a few miles in it. 'I've not been opening Karl's letters,' she said. 'We had a row, and he left. He didn't pack up, just took off. That was in November. I haven't seen him since.'

It had never occurred to me to ask why he was going to New Street Station when he could have got to Oldbury on the number 87 bus. 'Have you any idea where he might be?'

'He phoned me just before Christmas. Said he'd been staying with James in Stourbridge. An old school friend, you know. I asked him what his plans were. He said he might go back to Colwyn Bay. The caravan. If you can't trace him, he's probably there. He won't have stayed with anyone for long. He never does.'

'If he's there, how could I get in touch with him?'

'You'll have to go there, basically.' She gave me rough directions; I wrote them down. 'If you've got a map, it's quite easy. But don't ask me to go. I've got a job to do, and a child to look after. I'm sorry I can't be more help, David.'

'I understand,' I said. 'Thanks for getting in touch.'

'It's nice to speak to you,' she said. 'Karl didn't say much about you, but I got the impression you were all right.'

'I got the same impression about you,' I said unhappily. 'Take care.' Then I phoned Ian to let him know I was going to look for Karl. If I was lucky with trains, I should be there before it got dark. It was ridiculous: no address, no telephone. I couldn't believe that one person could be so hard to reach.

———

Colwyn Bay was brighter and colder than Birmingham. It had rained that morning; the pale rock of the hilltops gleamed from miles away, as though you could reach out and touch. Sheep were grazing on the waterlogged slopes. From the bus, I caught glimpses of the Irish Sea, dark and ridged like a vinyl disc. On a roadside wall just outside Abergele, a message was sprayed in white: WALES IS NOT FOR SALE. It was more a village than a town; a few small shops were open, and no one much was about. I noticed a phone box outside the post office. From here, Elaine had said, it was about two miles on foot.

The sheer absurdity of chasing after Karl like this made me feel disorientated. It reminded me of 'Fugue', the lines he'd written in a haze of whiskey and cheap hash: *Were you there ahead of me? / Are you here behind me?* Was I the only person too stupid to let him go? Out here, away from buildings and schedules, it was harder to believe that I was only after him because of the recording session he'd missed. I didn't want him back. So what was I hoping to achieve? The clouds were thickening overhead, wiping traces of sunlight from the rocky hillsides. This would not be a good place to get caught in a storm, I realised.

Elaine had said: 'There are two caravan parks along that road. Our caravan is in the second one from the village. It's painted black. If Karl's there, his car should be somewhere around. It's a really battered old blue Metro he picked up second-hand in Dudley, just after he came out of hospital.' I remembered now that I'd seen it outside his flat in Erdington, and hadn't realised it was his. I suspected he'd bought it to try and make himself stop drinking, then realised it was easier not to drive. As I passed the first caravan site, it began to rain. The sun was still glowing in the west; it filled the air with splinters of broken glass.

The second field had a dozen or so caravans, perched on metal supports or layers of bricks. In the near left corner, I could see a black caravan next to a rusty navy blue Metro. Neither looked like it had been used for travel in a long time. The caravan's greyish net curtains were drawn; a faint, wavering light showed through. I knocked on the metal door. After a few seconds' pause, it opened. 'Come in,' Karl said.

Behind him was a fabric curtain, half pulled aside to expose a small room. Two candles had burned down to stubs on a plywood table. A light glowed from the floor. Karl was wearing a denim jacket over a large pullover, rather like a guy for a bonfire. He was unshaven, but his hair and beard had been cropped ineptly with scissors. We embraced; his clothes smelt of cigarette smoke. His breathing was jerky, as if it was an effort. He muttered something, but I couldn't hear. The rain was coming down hard on the metal roof, like nails being hammered through.

I could stand up straight inside the caravan, but Karl couldn't. The walls of the room beyond the curtain were covered with photographs; most of them were people I'd never seen before, but I recognised one of Diane and one of Triangle on stage. Some were of Birmingham landscapes, including parts of Erdington. There were several photos of a small child, presumably Theresa. They were just ordinary photographs; but their concentration in this space, in this light, was a bit disturbing. On the table, between the two candle-stubs which stood on plates, were a pile of books and magazines and a few racks of cassettes. There were more cassette racks beside the table, stacked up against the wall, and a small ghetto blaster in the corner. A calor-gas heater on the floor held a tiny blue flame, whose light reflected in a row of empty bottles.

The hammering of the rain prevented us from talking at first. Which was lucky, as the words in my head would not have been helpful. Karl stood with his shoulders hunched, immobile, while I stared at his self-made prison cell. It felt much worse than visiting him at the clinic. The rain faded to a light, rapid tapping like amplified static. 'What have you been doing?' I said.

He looked at me; candles flickered in his eyes. 'Thinking. Trying to write songs. Listening to nature.' He lit a cigarette nervously, the match exploding his shadow on the dark wall. The photographs and bottles reflected light, but not images. 'This caravan's been here since the fifties,' he said. 'Elaine and I bought it from friends of her parents. We used to come here before Theresa was born. It was good in the summer, the black absorbed all the heat. We'd walk around naked, make love on a heap of blankets.'

'How nice for you,' I said. 'But why are you here now?'

'It feels safe.' He paused. 'David, I… I don't know if you can understand this. Nothing you hear in the city is real. It's all, like… echoed, overdubbed, fucked up. Artificial sound coming at you from everywhere. You can never really hear anything.'

'Maybe. Is that so dangerous?'

'Worst at Christmas. It always drove me mad, the same music playing in all the shops. It was so… lifeless. But it *was* Christmas. A manufactured spirit. We can't even live our own lives.' He stared at me, as if waiting for a sign that I understood. I hoped there was nothing sharp within his reach. 'Do you remember the Gulf War? Those images of bombers raining fire across the sky? Did anyone really see it? The way everyone talked, it was a firework display. Show people death and ruin, and they press the pause button, freeze the frame. Do you understand?'

'Yes,' I said, not entirely honestly. 'But how does coming out here help?'

'It's getting back to reality. To the truth. And I came here to stop taking heroin. It was the only way. Elaine threw me out. Whenever I came into Birmingham, I was scoring. Usually off Diane.' He laughed at my expression. 'You see? Nothing's real in the city. People hear what they want to hear. None of it means anything.'

'You should have got treatment,' I said. 'I would have helped you. Ian and Rachel would have helped you. We're your friends, Karl, for fuck's sake.'

'I don't know what that means.'

'It's a slang expression used for emphasis. It doesn't mean anything.' Karl stared at the net curtain across the barred window. I could hear sheep bleating from a field close by. 'The point is, you should have got help.'

'You don't know what you're talking about.' Karl sat down and gripped one of the cassette racks on the table. All the tapes in it had handwritten labels, in his scrappy handwriting; I couldn't read them in this light. 'Why are you here, David?'

Because I love you, I thought. The words sounded cold and false in my head. 'Because you missed our first recording session for the new album. It was yesterday.'

Bizarrely, Karl looked at his watch. 'I'm sorry. Tell them I'm sorry. But that's all finished. You've had a wasted journey.'

'You stupid fuck,' I said, my voice rising to a shout. 'Martin was right about you. You hide in your own little world like a fucking child, talking to the voices in your head...' The candles were nearly gone, pinpricks of light floating on lakes of wax. Karl's face was little more than a silhouette. We looked at what we could see of each other for a few minutes. Outside, the sheep were crying like scared children. *Fuck it.*

Fuck it. Karl raised his hand in the half-light. I pressed my palm against his. Very slowly, our faces moved together. We kissed deeply, hungrily, our tongues searching for a common language. Karl's hand rested on my chest, unzipping the jacket and unbuttoning the shirt. My fingers brushed his crotch and he gasped.

We undressed each other and made love slowly, tracing with hands and mouths. Karl was thinner than before; close up, his face was a charcoal sketch. His sperm tasted acrid. From the way he came, I suspected it had been a while.

By the time we'd finished, it was dark outside. The only light in the caravan was the blue flame of the heater. At floor level, I could smell the calor gas: a thin, sweetish odour, like the sensation of catarrh. Karl's beard and sideburns tasted of sweat and cigarette smoke; his mouth tasted of loneliness. 'Please come back with me,' I said. 'Ian wants to see you. If you can't make the album, that's okay. Tell them you're not well. See your doctor. Get some medication if that will help. Please try, Karl. Don't just sit here and rot. Will you come back with me?'

I waited minutes for a reply. Karl lay still in my arms, awake but passive, breathing unevenly. Then he said: 'In the morning. The car's fucked. I'll get the train with you tomorrow.'

We fumbled for our clothes. Karl lit four tiny night lights and put one at each corner of the table. 'I'm afraid there's nothing much to eat,' he said. 'Sardines, bread, coffee. And some vodka.' He showed me the caravan's facilities: a plastic box for food, a sink and a chemical toilet, but no ice-box and no electricity. This was Karl Austin unplugged.

It took fifteen minutes to boil a kettle on the tiny gas ring. I felt drained, not so much hungry as empty. While Karl made up a few sandwiches, I sat and looked at his collection of tapes. He seemed to have copied dozens of albums onto D90 or D60 blank tapes, each one faithfully labelled with the little COPY sticker that TDK provide. The tapes in one box were labelled with the MASTER stickers, but had nothing written on them. I looked for copies of the Triangle stuff: the album was there, plus the studio outtakes, the early demo, the new demo and the singles. Two years' work. How could he just let it go?

We ate by a candlelight that seemed pale and clinical rather than romantic. Karl put a tape in the ghetto blaster: a Velvet Underground album, violence and tenderness side by side. We drank black coffee from mugs and neat vodka from narrow shot glasses engraved with the logos of whiskey distillers: Jameson and Black Bush. I told him about the planned recording sessions, the work we'd done on Friday, the other musicians who might get involved. 'It's all waiting to happen,' I said. A familiar glow was building in my gut, overcoming the sense of strangeness. 'We need your voice. And your lyrics.'

Karl was drinking faster than me, but it wasn't having the same effect. 'What's the point?' he said. 'It's finished, the music's out of date. The industry's moved on.'

'What's the industry got to do with it?' Karl didn't answer. We carried on drinking, while 'European Son' raged quietly in the corner. The trouble with shot glasses is that you can always manage another shot.

'You're right,' Karl said when the tape ended. 'The music can't die. But that's the really terrible thing. No sound ever dies. It echoes through the universe, breaking up. All the shitty things you've said, all the shitty things you've heard, they're all floating around us. In a mindless orbit. Some day, you'll hear them all again.'

'You'm pissed,' I said. 'That's the kind of thing Ian comes out with after too many bottles of Diamond White.'

'Yo can never have too many bottles of Dimond White,' Karl said in an unnervingly perfect echo of Ian's 'drunken Brummie' voice. Our drummer's serious face flashed in the back of my mind like a glossy photograph. I shivered. 'You see? They call it "sampling" now, but it's been going on for ever. What the industry's got to do with it is...

like Christmas records or plastic Hallowe'en masks. A manufactured ghost. It's adding insult to injury.'

'What do you mean?'

Karl looked at me. All I could see in his eyes were the tiny reflections of candles. His face was very still, the jaw clenched hard. 'You can get used to injury,' he said, very quietly. 'You can live with it. But you can't get used to insult. I couldn't. I got just so far into that… into being degraded… that I couldn't go any further and I couldn't get away. And I haven't moved since.'

The flames in his eyes had melted into blank light. He was crying. I took his hand, the one without the glass, and squeezed it. The fingers were cold. His other hand lifted a full shot glass and poured its contents into his mouth. He swallowed with a shudder, then leaned across slowly and pressed his lips against mine. 'Come outside,' he said.

Opening the caravan door was like that film where the people get off the train and there's nothing there. Only a faint strip of moonlight, like a sleeve, was visible through the clouds overhead. I thought I could just see the outlines of hills in the distance; but I couldn't see the other caravans, or the stone wall around the field. The ground felt soft and sticky underfoot. Then Karl switched on a torch, illuminating a few yards of muddy grass. We walked on to the wall and the empty road. Ahead of us, I could just make out some bare trees and the glitter of the North Star. A strange neighbour in Moseley had once told me it was a UFO.

We continued uphill for a while, our route half electricity and half trust. Though I could hardly see him, I could sense Karl's tension from the deliberateness of his steps and the way he held the torch. 'I was out here last night,' he said.

'Walking for hours. The moon was bright. I felt like the last man on Earth.'

'Is that why you feel safe here?' I thought I was beginning to understand. Karl gripped my arm; his hand was rigid.

'I always feel like Dean's going to find me again some day,' he said quietly. 'Maybe he never really lost touch, and he's been stalking me all these years. Waiting for me to get somewhere, to be someone. Then he'll come back and start all over again. That's the real reason I've come here. He'd expect me to be in the Black Country or Ireland, but not here. It's a place to hide.'

My patience finally snapped. 'Fabulous. That's a great idea, Karl. Forget Triangle, forget your wife and daughter, forget everything. While you hide in a fixed caravan with your head up your arse, looking for the scars left by someone's cock fifteen years ago. What is this? I think there's been a medical error. Your doctor thought you were suffering from depression. You're not. You're suffering from being a fucking mad psycho lunatic.' I paused for breath. Karl didn't say anything. 'It's no wonder you were convinced you were HIV positive. You think the first time you took it up the arse, the world should have ended.'

Karl stopped and flicked off the torch. In the pale moonlight, his face was blank. I wondered if I'd gone too far. The words had poured out of me involuntarily, released by vodka. He turned and walked back towards the caravan site. I followed him, too drunk and tired to keep pace. The moon was clouding over; I could only just see the back of his head. Suddenly I had an overwhelming sense that we were going backwards, and he was chasing me. At the stone wall, I paused to take a piss. When I turned around, Karl had vanished. I had to feel my way past the car to the unlit caravan, where I knocked at the door before realising that Karl was standing outside by the window. 'What did you do that for?' I said.

No answer. Karl unlocked the door and drew aside the curtain. The torchlight ringed individual photographs. I saw the vodka bottle was empty. 'If you're not going to talk, we might as well go to sleep,' I said. Karl switched off the calor-gas heater, folded up the table and spread a few blankets across the floor. I reached out and touched his arm. 'Are you coming back with me tomorrow, or not?'

'All right,' he said. 'I'll come back with you, and we'll record the album. Are you happy now?' He sounded worn out and somehow relieved. My mouth was dry from the vodka, but drinking water might make me sick. We stripped to our underpants and lay down together, pulling the layers of blanket around until we were both sealed in. I think we kissed, but we didn't try to make love.

During the night, I woke for a few minutes. I'd dreamt something, but I couldn't remember what. Some moonlight filtered through the net curtains and a narrow glass hatch in the roof. I could hear Karl's steady breathing, feel his warmth close beside me, but I couldn't see his face. Whatever I couldn't see felt like Karl.

The next time I awoke, it was light outside. Rain was scratching at the caravan like a needle trapped in a groove. Beside me, the shape under the blankets was hollow. The heater was still off; my breath made little clouds above my face. Karl was somewhere beyond the curtain. I stood up, wrapping a manky green blanket around my chest. The light through the net curtain caught a flicker of dull red: something on the table. Karl had pulled all the tape out of a cassette and spread it over the wooden surface, like dried blood on a sleeve. Something gave way under my feet, scratching: another tape. The floor around the table was covered with them.

'Karl!' There was no response. I pulled my clothes on; they felt stiff and tight, as if they'd just been washed. Beyond the curtain, there was no sign of him. I unlocked the metal door; the wind blew tiny, sharp raindrops and the smell of sheepshit into my face. More tapes were scattered over the bricks supporting the caravan. Brown ribbons stirring in the wind, spelling out an unreadable message. In the distance, sheep grazed on a blackened slope. There was no human figure in sight. The cold air gave me a sudden, painful cramp; I spent the next ten minutes perched on the chemical toilet, adding my shit to Karl's.

Wherever he'd gone, he hadn't taken the car. It wasn't just battered and rusty, I saw: its windscreen was cracked across, and the bonnet was slightly crumpled. I imagined him driving up here, perhaps at night, bitter and obsessed. Maybe he'd swerved to avoid a sheep, and crashed into a tree or a dry- stone wall. He couldn't drive as fast as whatever was driving him. And he'd been out of practice.

Maybe he'd gone into Abergele to buy something for breakfast. I'd hoped to get an early start, but that was an old story. Besides, when I got him back to Birmingham, where was he going to stay? I kicked the Metro, adding a fresh scratch to its mottled blue paintwork. Then I went back inside the caravan. There was no note, no calendar, no diary: nothing that could have contained a message. By the light of a spring morning, the photographs looked faded and pointless. The disembowelled cassettes worried me. I left them where they were.

The books on the table were a mixture of second-hand crime novels and technical handbooks on sound recording and transmission. Among the tapes Karl had copied from his record collection, there were albums by The Fall, Joy Division, Felt, the Kitchens, Primal Scream, My Bloody Valentine, Iggy Pop, Sinéad O'Connor, Hüsker Dü, Van Morrison, Nick Cave, The Pogues, Scott Walker. If he'd been running away from his past, he seemed to have brought a lot of it with him. The box of tapes labelled MASTER was right at the bottom, facing the wall. I took out a cassette and examined its sleeve: no handwriting anywhere. I put the tape in Karl's ghetto blaster. There was nothing but a faint hissing or crackling sound. I couldn't tell if it was a new blank tape, or if something had been erased. I tried another of the MASTER tapes, with the same result.

Perhaps the batteries were flat. I pulled out a COPY tape at random and played it. After a few seconds of static, I heard the opening of a track that sounded familiar, though I didn't recognise it. Thudding bass chords, a rapid drum beat. A harsh guitar riff, played twice. *They brought me here when I had nowhere to run / This is the place where they kill you for fun.* Triangle. I switched off the cassette player, stood up and walked out of the caravan, leaving the door unlocked. It was ten o'clock. The sun was bright; the wet grass was littered with tiny crystals. I walked into Abergele, where the church bells were ringing. Nowhere was open except a garage. I asked the attendant where the nearest police station was.

The officer I spoke to there looked at me in a way that suggested he had little time for tourist drama queens. I told him that Karl was mentally disturbed and potentially violent; I described the torn-out cassette tapes, but didn't tell him my own suspicion that they were intended as a message or note to me. He drove me back to the caravan, where there was no sign of Karl's return. 'We'll ask around locally,' he said. 'If he doesn't turn up, we'll try a search. Are you going back home?' I said I'd better stay in Abergele until something happened. 'Okay. Keep in touch, then.'

That afternoon, I walked a few miles inland. The landscape changed rapidly: grassy fields patrolled by sheep with red or blue spots on their wool; undivided miles of boggy moorland; heaps of black slate, taller than houses, around a quarry.

From a distance, I saw the outline of a ruined building: a jagged black crown on a hilltop. Closer up, I could see it was a partially demolished hunting lodge. The timbers and slates of the roof had collapsed, leaving a shell with walls a foot or so thick. Chunks of masonry bit deep into the hilltop; sheep browsed among the fragments.

I couldn't face sleeping at the caravan, or even being alone there after dark. The afternoon I'd spent with Karl in Stourbridge kept coming back to me. I shuffled its elements like a pack of Tarot cards: train, factory, canal, house, river, tree. As banal as an infant reading primer. The things he'd talked about: Enoch Powell, the Birmingham pub bombings, Dean. I found a bed and breakfast in Abergele, phoned Ian in Birmingham and Elaine in Stourbridge. Nothing. I phoned the police station; they told me that DS Heyward had gone out to the caravan site. Half an hour later, he phoned me back: Karl wasn't there. He said the local bus driver had no memory of anyone matching Karl's description. 'I think we'll look for him in the morning. Can you stay where you are for another day?' I knew I wouldn't be able to sleep without alcohol, so I sloped off to the pub and drank three pints in the last hour before closing time.

At eight the next morning, DS Heyward phoned again. 'I think we've found him,' he said. They picked me up twenty minutes later and drove me to the edge of a patch of woodland, where a stream whispered between the bare trees. Last year's dead leaves were a thick crust underfoot. I'd slept badly, and part of me just wanted to lie down and forget about everything. *Perhaps it's not Karl,* I thought. *Perhaps it's not me walking through these woods.* I desperately wanted this to be an outtake.

The body was lying in a patch of shrubbery between three birch trees. It was off the path. Two of the policemen at the scene had dogs. He was lying face down, with his hands under his chest. There was dried blood in his hair. A policeman turned him over, and I saw his face in the sudden glare of a flashbulb. He didn't look peaceful. He looked the way he sometimes did on stage: tense, coiled, ready to explode into the cold rage of a song. His face was coated with a skin of dried blood. Something had eaten part of his left ear. 'Yes,' I said. 'That's Karl.'

I watched as they zipped up the body. It was cold in the forest; I could see the white sky framed by darker twigs, like a broken window. *Don't wrap him up,* I thought. *Just shake him, he'll come round. Let me take care of him.* I almost asked them to let me try and revive him. The long canvas bag irritated me. It was pure Army surplus. Karl wouldn't have been seen dead in it. As we walked back to the car, DS Heyward put his hand on my arm. I wasn't sure whether he intended it as comfort or restraint. An image haunted me for a long time afterwards: Karl's shadow remaining in place when his body was moved, as if he'd been lying there for weeks and the grass underneath was dead. I know I can't really have seen that.

They kept me at the station for a day and a half, going over my account of the last few days. Three people interviewed me. I was told that I wasn't under arrest, but they would appreciate my full cooperation. Nobody would tell me anything about how Karl had died. In between sessions of questioning, I caught a few hours of stunned, apathetic sleep in the cell they'd given me. I told them everything I could, even mentioning private things – like the last time Karl and I had made love – in case they thought I had something to hide. Late the following afternoon, they said I could go home. By then, they had spoken to Ian, Martin, Elaine and Karl's parents. So I had no one much to tell, except Diane.

The inquest stated that Karl's death was caused by 'misadventure'. He'd left the caravan in the dark, without his torch, and walked or run for several miles. In the forest, he'd undergone some kind of seizure – perhaps related to drug use in the recent past. Blood on the trees close to where he'd been found indicated that he'd run into them frequently, in some terrible frenzy. DS Heyward told me:

'His skull was broken in several places, and so were some of the bones in his face.' They'd found no evidence of an assault. What the verdict amounted to was that Karl had been killed by the voices in his head. The silence he'd wrapped himself in had split like a torn condom, leaving him naked all the way through.

CHAPTER 14

playback

And when you kill
Would you really kill
Because the news never changes?
— Kingmaker

Karl's funeral was in Tile Hill on the edge of Coventry, where his parents lived. They wanted him to have a church funeral; since he'd left no instructions for his burial, their wishes had to be respected. I suspect that many of Karl's friends didn't know he was dead until later. His life was so compartmentalised that nobody knew who to tell. The music papers reported his death; Mike wrote a short obituary for the *NME*. I told the people at the TV and video shop where Karl had worked in Triangle's early days. His parents took the contents of the flat in Erdington. Later, they gave his records to Elaine; later still, she gave them to me.

The morning of the funeral – I think it was February 27th – was bright and cold. Alan drove me, Ian and Diane to Tile Hill in his car. I'd never seen Ian in a suit before; he looked deeply uncomfortable. I assume I did too. Diane, who normally wore black, had put on a navy blue dress that made her look much older. A fierce wind was blowing across the M6, rattling the car and making turns dangerous. Diane gripped my hand on the back seat, both giving comfort and needing it. It didn't seem to help that we'd all seen his death coming. Sometimes it's easier to live with chaos than with patterns that destroy hope. For Alan, I think, part of the grief was the memory of his ex-lover. I'd never known him to drive so carefully, or be so quiet.

The service was held at a small Catholic church in a heavily built-up area. There were about twenty people. Karl's parents, a dignified couple in late middle age, shook hands with me and Ian. 'We liked your group,' his mother said. 'It was very powerful music. Sad and angry, like you hated the past as well as the future.' Her voice sounded more Irish than Karl's had. His father said nothing.

Behind me, I heard a child say, 'Who are these people?' At once, I knew who it was. I turned slowly to see a woman in her thirties and a young girl with frightened eyes. The woman had short black hair and shadows under her eyes so dark I mistook them for make-up. She reached out a calm hand. 'David, isn't it? I'm Elaine. This is Theresa. I'm sorry we have to meet under such bad circumstances.' Theresa looked at me angrily, as if I might be to blame for all this. I don't think it was personal.

The only other person I recognised in the church was Mike, who was sitting alone at the back. I went over and talked to him for a few minutes, though his stammer blocked nearly everything he tried to say. It all seemed unreal, like a soundcheck with the PA disconnected. Stefan and James hadn't come. I hadn't really expected them to.

The priest said something about Karl's technical skills in the field of electronics. 'And then he went from working on the machines people listened to to making the music they heard. This was a young man who cared very deeply about communication.' I reflected bitterly that it hadn't always seemed that way. My sense of grief was turning into a confused, blank depression that seemed utterly wrong. We knelt to pray – or at least, to say 'Amen' where appropriate. And then the hymn started, except it didn't. The organist played an instrumental version of 'Road Into Fire'. Ian laughed quietly on my left; Diane wept on my right. I couldn't do either.

Then came the slow drive to the cemetery, and the burial. The wind pushed against us like an invisible hedge, blurring the priest's quiet words. The freshly dug grave, surrounded by green canvas, was an ugly mark on the landscape. As always at funerals, I had a sense of the people's energy draining into the ground. If Ian and Diane hadn't been with me, it would have been like the burial of someone I didn't know. I had no feeling of Karl's presence at all. A ghost, an echo, a shadow of some kind would have been welcome. But there was nothing.

Afterwards, we went to the Austins' house. The front room, where they held the reception, was immaculately clean. Among the pictures, I noticed two framed photographs of Karl. One as a boy, wearing a school uniform and looking angry; the other as a young man, together with Elaine and smiling at the camera. Perhaps that was at their wedding. After the jarring strangeness of the funeral, the reception seemed to restore a normal scale to things. We ate triangular sandwiches and drank small glasses of Irish whiskey. Ian, always the most stable member of Triangle, took me aside and asked 'Are you okay?' I said I was a bit shaken up. He put his arm round me, a brotherly gesture that had the unexpected effect of making me cry briefly. 'I liked the organ version of "Road Into Fire",' he said. 'Didn't you?'

I said I'd always thought Triangle could do with a keyboard player. 'Maybe we should release it.'

'How about an orchestral version? Fugue in D Minor.'

'Or a dance version? Nowhere To Go-Go.'

'Or a soul version? Songs in the Stranger Key of life.'

'Or a Satanic metal version? Rodent Into the Fire.' Neither of us needed to say that Triangle was finished without Karl. We'd been more than backing musicians, but not that much more. We didn't stay very long at the reception. There were too many different kinds of grief, too many different Karls being missed, too little being said. His whole life was unfinished business.

That weekend, we had a wake for Karl upstairs at the Jug of Ale. His parents didn't come, but they sent their best wishes. All the Furnace Records people were there, as well as various local bands. We played and drank until the early hours, sharing equipment and amps. The Vacant Lot played Diane's love song 'Fingerprint'. Webbing played a long, woozy instrumental that Karl would have loved, and

I would have told him was pants. Box 'Em Domies, the Brummie Pogues, played their song 'Gravy Beat'; then most of The Great Outdoors blasted out a raging performance of 'You Do Lose Hope'.

Finally, Ian and I took the stage with Diane on vocals and lead guitar. We played 'Stranger Key', 'His Mouth' and 'For the Distance'. Then Diane played a solo version of 'Blue Glass', based on the demo I'd sent her; and the three of us thrashed our way through a maudlin version of The Charlottes' 'Love In the Emptiness'. It was Triangle's final gig. Nobody taped it: we didn't want to dilute the memory with a record. It was a good night. But somehow, it failed as a wake. It didn't bring back the memory of Karl, because he'd died inside himself a long time before he went missing in Wales.

At the end, we all packed away the equipment and cleared up the empty bottles. Ian went home with Rachel. Diane, who was even more drunk than me, asked me to stay with her. 'I don't want to be alone in the morning.' As we left together, the wind blew pale scraps of cloud across a half-moon. There was a complete silence in the empty streets: no cars, no dogs.

The day after next, I was at home when the bell rang. It was James or Stefan, I couldn't remember which. 'Come in,' I said. He looked dazed, as if he'd just woken up. 'Stefan, isn't it?' He shook his head. 'Sorry, James. You've heard about Karl?'

'It was in the local paper.' He sat down without taking off his jacket. Rain glittered in his cropped hair. I offered him a drink; he knocked back a Scotch easily. He was a solid man, too much flesh around the jaw, fingers heavily stained from roll-ups. 'He gave me your address, you know. Karl. He stayed with me a few nights in September. Not the days, just the nights.'

'So he wanted you to get in touch with me?'

'No,' James said uneasily. 'I wanted to. He told me he'd taken you to Stourbridge. That place where... Between the canal and the river.' His gaze was fixed just to one side of my face, as if he were talking to my shadow. 'Would you like to go back there?'

'What do you mean, would I like to? What's this about?'

'I want to show you something.' He put the empty shot glass down on the floor. 'All right?' He said it as if he were asking me whether everything was all right. I shrugged. Outside, rain was darkening the sky.

Stourbridge is exactly west of South Birmingham. The direct route takes you through a chain of built-up districts that merge into Black Country towns: Bearwood, Quinton, Cradley, Lye. It's like going back through a family album. Rain scratched at the windows of the car. New roads cut through the blackened factory landscape. 'Why did Karl go to stay with you?' I asked.

James glanced at me, then stared at the road ahead. 'For old times' sake, I suppose. Stefan got married, but I never did. What did Karl tell you about us?'

'He said you were friends of his at school. The only people he told about Dean.'

'Did you believe that?'

'No.' James drove on in silence. Lights shone through factory windows. The expressway was packed with cars, but the streets were empty. I recognised the high windows of the glassware museum in Stourbridge. Then James drew into a small, almost vacant car park framed by two brick walls and the back of a factory. An extractor fan turned slowly just above our heads.

We walked through an alley that connected the backs of houses and ended at a canal bridge. A few stone steps brought us onto a towpath that I recognised at once. It didn't look the same from above. Overhanging trees rained on us more heavily than the sky had done. A few statues in plastic raincoats sat holding rods that arced into the murky water. To our right, I could hear the whispering of the river across the strip of overgrown woodland. It was only a little earlier in the year than the last time: a little colder, more decay and less green.

'There's no such thing as the whole story,' James said. 'Everyone's got their own angle. And when you're a kid… you never see anything affecting the future. It's like a film, you're waiting for the end credits. But they don't come. Did you love Karl?'

'Yes,' I said. 'I did, yes. But it wasn't enough.'

'I'm sorry.' We'd reached the metal grid across the overflow conduit, where the ground was marshy and stank of rot. James paused, staring into the dense foliage. 'I was at junior school with Dean,' he said. 'We were mates even then. He was always hard. Into Paki-bashing and stuff. Whenever he got wound up, he'd need to batter someone. But he was a strange kid. Very quiet.

'We came to Redhill Comprehensive, and I think Dean was a bit out of his depth. All these older kids who could spread his face all over the playground. He took a few beatings at first, like. Him and me started hanging out with this German kid called Stefan. We got this camo gear, went to cadets a while but got bored with all the marching up and down. Then there was this weird Irish kid, Karl Austin. He was a sarky little prick, to be honest with you. Had this way of looking at you that made you want to break his face.

'Everyone was anti-Irish in those days. Know what I mean? It wasn't long after the pub bombings in Birmingham. After they jailed those six bastards, people were saying they'd been fit up for it. I thought, so what? They could have jailed every fucking Paddy and I'd have been happy. So we did that Karl a few times, tore his nice white shirt, threw him in the canal. That was enough for me and Stefan. But not for Dean. He had an obsession. We thought he'd kill the fucker. I said to Stefan, "What'll we do if he kills that Mick, and we're like accessories?"

'But it didn't happen. We got a bit older, started seeing girls. All of us, Dean included. Redhill was fuck city. Dean got into politics as well. Hung around with some of the National Front lads. But I think they were a bit scary for him. He liked to keep his enemies where he could see them. He had this thing about Enoch Powell, used to collect newspaper cuttings about him. Kind of hero-worship. That was when I first suspected he might be a bit the other way.'

James stopped talking and walked on, then stepped through the trees. The ground beneath our feet was yielding, slimy. He led me to the edge of the clearing with the derelict house and the half-demolished workshop. I couldn't hear the river, or any other sound. The air in front of me was webbed with fine cracks.

'It was about this time of year,' he said quietly. 1978. Me and Stefan were walking along the canal towpath. It was nearly dark. And we heard these sounds. A courting couple, like. Through the trees. So we crept towards the noises. Stefan was in front of me. Then he stopped dead. I looked past him and saw these two queers. One was fucking the other up the arse, against a tree. I couldn't help myself, I laughed. The one who was giving it turned round. It was Dean. Then I saw the other guy was Karl. I couldn't believe it. I went on laughing, though I didn't find it funny at all. It was just a reaction. Stefan started laughing too.

'Dean went bright red. He wouldn't look at us. He just stood there, trying to zip his jeans over his hard-on. Then he picked up this stick and ran at Karl with it, tried to stab him in the gut. It grazed him, drew blood, but it didn't go right in. Dean kicked Karl on the leg, punched him in the face, got him against the tree, kicking and punching in a frenzy. We just stood there, watching. Once he got Karl on the ground, that'd be it. Dean would kill him. A few kicks to the head, end of story. We saw Karl go down. I shut my eyes... then heard a scream. The most terrible sound I've ever heard.

'When I looked, Karl was standing there with half a brick in his hand. Dean was on his knees. His skull was split like an eggshell. He was twitching. I could see one side of his face, covered with blood. Then he curled up, like he was going to sleep, and just lay there. For a while, none of us could move. Then I went up to Dean and turned him face up. He wasn't breathing.

'In a few minutes, it would be too dark to see anything. What happened next, I can't really explain. It was my idea. We'd leave Dean there, come back with torches and spades and bury him among the trees. I remember Karl dropping the half-brick in the canal, then washing his hands slowly. He hardly said a word all night. Three hours later, we came back and dug the hole. Filled it, covered it with dead leaves. They never found him. Funny thing was, he'd been talking about running away. His dad used to get pissed and hammer him. His mum had moved out. So when he went missing, they didn't really think to look for a dead body.

'So that was it. The three of us … well, you couldn't call it friends. Wasn't friendship, wasn't love, wasn't hate. It was different. We kept in touch. But we never went to his wedding, and he never went to Stefan's wedding. Wasn't that kind of thing. But it mattered. Now he's dead, I had to contact you. To make up the triangle.' In the silence that followed, I could hear his breathing; it sounded ragged, as if something had torn in his chest. He turned around and walked back into the trees, where it was still raining. At a point quite near the river, heavily overgrown with bushes and pale grass, he stopped. 'Here.'

He was standing at the midpoint between three quite similar trees, whose leaves blocked the view in any direction. 'Do you believe me?' he asked.

'I don't know.'

'There's a spade in the car. After fifteen years, there'll be nothing left but bones. It's up to you, David. If you want proof, you can dig for it.'

I stared at the ground. The stringy grass and brambles wouldn't be hard to dislodge. But how hard would the ground be, a few feet down? Was it worth it? I tried to imagine a buried skull with a broken crown, and could only think of Karl as I'd last seen him, face up on the muddy ground in Wales. 'No,' I said.

James turned away and headed back towards the canal towpath. 'I'll give you a lift to the station.' Overhead, it was beginning to get dark; stars were just visible in between the streaks of cloud.

There were several cars in the small car park, but no people. As James switched off his alarm with a hand-held device, I asked him: 'So what happened when Karl stayed with you? In December.'

He laughed bleakly. 'What do you think happened? I fucked him. And while I was fucking him, I punched and bit him. He liked it. And then I smacked his face until his nose and lips were bleeding, then fucked him in the mouth.'

His face was a shadow. 'I don't believe you,' I said.

He shrugged. 'Please yourself.'

We got into his car. As soon as I'd fastened my seat-belt, I felt his hands on me, his open mouth pressed against mine. It seemed pointless to fight him off. My passivity seemed to excite him; he trapped my tongue between his teeth and sucked. Eventually he had to stop for breath. When his hand began to pull down the zipper of my jeans, I stopped him. 'Forget it.' He started the car angrily and drove the short distance to the railway station without speaking. I opened the car door. 'Cheers.' He was driving away before I'd entered the station.

There was a young woman on the platform, with a child who kept singing the same words over and over. It sounded like *Aba, aba, aba cola ba*. He was almost shouting. When the train came, I got into a different carriage from them. The steady rhythm of the wheels helped me to calm down. I looked out the window, seeing the security lights in empty factories and warehouses. And then, like a silent awakening of the landscape, the streetlamps came on.

CHAPTER 15

noise

I am a message
— Idlewild

There was one more Triangle release. Alan persuaded me and Ian to help put together a compilation of unreleased material and B-sides. We were both unhappy about putting out sub-standard material, but Alan said the demo tapes had aroused too much interest to be left in a box. Besides, Furnace wouldn't pretend it was a studio album. With Pete's help, we made up an album from the four demo tracks, the two B-sides and some bits and pieces, including live versions of two songs that Alex had taped. In a fit of maudlin gloom, we gave it the title *Nothing But A Sound* – which was a slightly altered version of a line from 'Broken Strings'. The overall result was harsh and uneven; but it sold much better than *Hard Shadows*, and a lot of people said it had Karl's best songs on it. Nobody called it a ripoff, which made me feel better.

'Blue Glass' was used as the title music for a Channel 4 film called *Down In One*, about alcoholism and domestic violence on a North London housing estate. They used bits of 'Third Flight' and 'Curfew Town' as well. Furnace have kept both of the Triangle albums available for the last six years. Which is a scam, because Alan sold Furnace Records to Warner Brothers during a financial crisis in 1994. All of Furnace's bands were immediately dropped and the label was closed down, but they kept the Furnace logo for Triangle records.

I toured with Frozen Gin for a while in 1993, but found the ghosts and the alcohol were crowding the music out of my head. By mutual agreement, I left the band and took a break from playing. Then I got a technical job in a paint factory, which led to an NVQ and a career in the chemicals industry. I always thought I'd get back into music, but there was too much I needed to leave behind. Now, when I look back, it's not to check that the ghosts are following me: it's to make sure that they stay underground.

Diane and I went out together for a while in the summer of 1993, but it wasn't serious. We both found the relationship a kind of escape, something peaceful and unthreatening. We got drunk together a lot and clung to each other like children. But there was always Karl between us, a link and a barrier. One night Diane said, 'I think we should stop,' and I said, 'So do I.' It was quite amicable. We told our friends the split was due to musical differences. The Vacant Lot broke up a few months later, without ever having got a recording contract. Diane went to college and became a journalist, working at Pebble Mill. The last time we spoke, she was writing a novel about Goths, serial killers and bisexual vampires.

The only one of us to stay in music and actually do well was Ian. He teamed up with an electric violin player called Erik Zan, who wanted to be a new John Cale. With the help of a keyboard player and a rhythm guitarist, they formed the voiceless rock band The Unknown. One of the casualties of the Furnace sell-off, they got nowhere for years. Then, in the Britpop-backlash period of 1997, they recorded a critically acclaimed album: *Ninth Planet*. Their single 'Abductee' was remixed by Goldie and became an underground hit. They were never a dance band; but by that time, dance musicians and rock musicians were trying to be big mates instead of mortal enemies. I always thought Ian had held onto a lot of Karl's musical ideas. The track 'Scream of A Mask' even used distorted samples from 'Still and Moving Water'. Warner Brothers wanted to charge The Unknown a massive copyright fee, but I threatened to block all Triangle re-releases unless they let Ian use the samples for free. He'd earned the right.

Ian and Rachel got married in 1996, a church wedding that brought a lot of the old crowd back together. Alan came up from London with his partner Conrad. Diane brought a new, very good-looking boyfriend who painted cover illustrations for *Doctor Who* books. Some of Ian's former colleagues from the Triangle cinema were there, though the cinema had been closed down by the breadheads at Aston University. Erik played his violin at the reception: a chilling atonal performance that was impossible to dance to, no matter how drunk you were.

I avoided reading the music papers for a while after Karl's death. But the release of *Nothing But A Sound* led to a revival of interest in Triangle. You could hear our influence in various bands: Marion, Arab Strap, Puressence, maybe Radiohead. The Kitchens' third album, *The Death of Cool* sounded like it might have been influenced by Triangle. If so, it was only fair, considering how much Karl listened to *Love Is Hell*.

But the whole indie scene was falling apart. Bands like Blur and Oasis, with major-label backing, peddled a mainstream rock lifted wholesale from the past, while minor labels no longer had the means to back less commercial acts. The music became pale and frothy like cheap beer, obsessed with 'entertainment value'. The momentum of seriousness passed to dance-based artists like Tricky and Massive Attack. That may have prompted an *NME* journalist's comment in 1996 that 'Triangle's music expresses a nostalgic and implicitly white-supremacist desire for a world in which hip-hop, house and jungle have never existed'. Karl would have gone ballistic at that. I couldn't make the effort.

Maybe Karl was right, and the music's out of date. Or maybe it's just the scene that's gone, not the music. I felt like that about the gay scene, when I started exploring the new clubs and bars after breaking up with Diane. They seemed just like straight venues, except that the foreplay was less obvious. I was more likely to come across my gay friends from the old days in the Moseley and Kings Heath pubs. The lads in the new, three-storey Nightingale were *clubbers*. I wondered where, if anywhere, the old queens went now: the furtive civil servants and Church types who sat in corners, talking about how they were *bound* to make it illegal again – and have you *heard* that new Tory councillor is a friend of Dorothy? In the new world, everything was brighter and there was nowhere to hide.

These days, older queens always say the gay scene is too youth-orientated. What they usually mean is that the youngsters are no longer available to them. The romantic appeal of the *older man* has gone with the films that created it. Now, if you're an inexperienced teenager, you find yourself an experienced teenager. Or if you *really* want an older lover, you find yourself a twenty-five-year-old with a good job, a car and a flat. Middle-aged farts don't cut it with the young. Which is, frankly, the way it should be.

Karl always had a big problem with the gay world's hatred of rock music. He saw it as part of the gay culture's obsession with image. But again, the boundaries are shifting. Last year, I went to see Pansy Division at the Foundry in Birmingham. They played hard-edged, abrasive guitar rock with blatantly gay lyrics – sometimes funny, sometimes angry. The young fans at the front of the audience were totally into the band: shouting requests, singing along with the lyrics. After the encore, a fan and the band's vocalist got into a clinch at the edge of the stage. I'd never seen two men kissing like that in a non-gay venue. I went home with tears in my eyes and a painful hard-on.

For whatever reason, I've found relationships difficult since Karl died. Sex helped to fill the gap for a while. But these days, I find it hard to make love to anyone without sensing a horrible mimicry of affection behind my shoulder, like a bully in the playground imitating the way you move. I never quite believe what a lover says to me, or what I say to him. There's a common ground, a layer of memory and pain, that I'm not willing to touch. Instead, I treat boyfriends like pets, fuss them with cuddles and gifts. It adds insult to injury.

Karl and I belonged to that generation who were just spared the first terrible wave of the AIDS epidemic. If I'd been born five years earlier, I might well have died before I met Karl. We both had an odd sense of unearned luck, like survivors of a bombing raid. There's a certain coldness that comes with that, a reserve I see in a lot of my friends. We learned to put our trust in barriers. Have you noticed how many people's sex lives include technology: phone sex, websites, computer dating? From male and female to e-mail and voicemail. We're all hiding behind walls. But perhaps machines communicate more of us than we realise.

———

After Karl's death, I had a recurrent dream that bothered me on and off for years. I was trapped in some huge, unlit building with gaps in the roof that let in some moonlight, but also let through strands of mist. The floor was covered with rubble and empty boxes. I could hear several men calling to each other: *Help me.* Eventually I found one of them walking through the mist and the shadows. He looked like Karl, but he didn't recognise me. Then I found another, and he was the same. They all seemed to be in a trance. All of them were Karl, or somehow copies of him. They never reached each other. Their lonely cries overlapped like echoes in the dark. At the end of the dream, I always realised that I, too, was one of the Karls.

Maybe there's a life after this one that isn't necessarily better or worse. It's just a kind of hangover. Or maybe it's the other way round. Not a life after death but a death before it, like a recorded sample. I once read a quote from a biologist called Bruce Cummings who died in his thirties. He said: 'Death can do no more than kill you.' For Karl, I think it did a lot more. But I don't want ghosts, spirits or an afterlife. There's something sick in all that. I want death only to kill me.

I really don't know if Karl committed suicide, or if it was something else. A seizure, a blind rage, or a part of himself that wasn't really him. I'm tired of reading articles by journalists who say he was killed by the rock 'n' roll lifestyle. When a spot-welder commits suicide, nobody blames it on the welding lifestyle. I'm even more tired of Triangle obsessives who say I let Karl down. Whether I did or not, how could they possibly know? They think the only real Karl is the one they hear on the records.

But there wasn't any 'real' Karl, except Karl himself. Even his secrets don't explain anything. Karl's confusion about his identity, national and sexual, was a smokescreen. I used to wonder why he made so much of being Irish when he'd seen so little of Ireland, and was so cut off from it. But Dean and his mates had stamped MICK on Karl's forehead, given him a rage he couldn't understand. All he could do was keep spinning round, trying to catch whoever was hiding behind his back.

Last year, when Enoch Powell died, they showed a retrospective of his career on TV. Suddenly I could see why Karl hated him so much. It wasn't just that Powell was Dean's hero: he was Dean's shadow. His racist speeches were a calculated, empty performance of hatred. Like Karl said, there's nothing natural about prejudice. And Karl had a deep fear of mimicry, of fakes. I began to see, as well, how Powell had cast a shadow over the Thatcher years. He wanted to turn all of Britain's ethnic minorities – including the Irish – into subject peoples, internal colonies. And the key phrase of the Thatcher government was 'internal security'. If you want a key to Karl's lyrics, that's a good place to start.

But in the end, I can't give you any inside knowledge. All I have is tapes. Some clear, some faded or distorted as if they'd been through many generations of copies. I can't extract the meaning and write it down. The music isn't just in the tune. It's in the beat, the feedback, the background noise, and the silence afterwards. It's different every time you listen. These days, I don't remember Karl's music unless I play it; but I can always hear his voice.

TRIANGLE
The Answer b/w Empty Stations (Relent Records, 1991)

Road Into Fire b/w Silence Broken Down (Furnace Records, 1992)

Hard Shadows (Furnace Records, 1992): Third Flight / Road Into Fire / Stranger Key / Nowhere To Go / His Mouth / Fugue / Curfew Town / Still and Moving Water / The Answer / For the Distance

Stranger Key b/w Rise and Walk (Furnace Records, 1992)

Nothing But A Sound (Furnace Records, 1993): Blue Glass / Oubliette / The Ruins / Punishment / Rise and Walk / Broken Strings (live) / Made Of Clay (live) / Silence Broken Down / A Yard of Skin / The Lost View

BLUE AWAY
Midnight Beat (A-Z Records, 1990): Edge Of the City / Hiding Place / Lovechild / Blue Label / The Small Hours / Skin Like Milk / Midnight Beat / Four Letters / No Second Chance / Speed Trap

FROZEN GIN

Slipping Down EP (Private Music, 1992): Roadblock / Black Ice / No Witnesses / Knocking It Back

THE UNKNOWN

The Echoing Void b/w In the Walls (Furnace Records, 1994)

Abductee b/w Voice Of Chaos (No-Mark Records, 1995)

The Crystal Spheres b/w Greys / Easter Island Men (Destruction Records, 1995)

Ninth Planet (Virtual Records, 1997): Ninth Planet / Abductee / Bitter Limbo / Out Of Focus / The Crystal Spheres / Remember Tomorrow / Scream Of A Mask / Blue Ice / Silent

Abductee *(Goldie remix)* b/w Implant (Virtual Records, 1997)

ACKNOWLEDGEMENTS

Thanks are due to Nick Royle for help, support and encouragement; to Graham Joyce and Michael Marshall Smith for repeatedly asking 'Where's the novel?'; to the Tindal Street Fiction Group for valued criticism, support and setting a great example; to Stuart Crees and Steve Bishop for musical advice; to Gul Davis for a very helpful suggestion; to Ian Peacock and Peter Coleborn for sharing their music with me; to Kate Pearce for help, advice and moral support; to Jo Saxelby (RC) for invaluable advice on venues; to Dad for practical help, advice and moral support; to Greg Mumford for technical assistance; to Simon MacCulloch and Jane Wright for thoughts on music; to Chris Morgan for long-term advice and support; to Mum for ideas and encouragement; to Gina Standring, Dorothy Hunt, Clare Morrall and Pauline Morgan for useful feedback; to Laurence O'Toole for helpful and perceptive editing; to Chris Kenworthy, Conrad Williams, Paul Drohan, Helen Kitson, Simon Avery, John Howard, Deborah Fields, Jonathan Oliver and Sarah Crowther for encouragement; and to Kitchens of Distinction, The Family Cat, Bob Mould and Marion for inspiration.

Grateful acknowledgement is made for permission to reproduce excerpts from the following material:

'In the Long Still Night' by Gallon Drunk, reproduced by kind permission of Clawfist and Schnozza Music.

'Happy When It Rains' by The Jesus and Mary Chain, reproduced by kind permission of Blanco Y Negro/Warner Music.

'Prize' and 'Quick As Rainbows' by Kitchens of Distinction, words and music by Julian Swales, Patrick Fitzgerald and Daniel Goodwin, © copyright 1994 Chrysalis Music Ltd, The Chrysalis Building, Bramley Road, London W10. Used by kind permission of Music Sales Ltd. All rights reserved. International copyright secured.

'Marbles5 and 'Drunk Tank' by Tindersticks, written by Stuart Staples, Dickon Hinchliffe, David Boulter, Neil Fraser, Mark Colwill and Alistair Macaulay, reproduced by kind permission of Rough Trade Publishing Ltd.

'Hours of Darkness Have Changed My Mind' and 'Down But Not Yet Out' by Felt, reproduced by kind permission of Complete Music Ltd.

'Under Clery's Clock' by The Radiators, words and music by Philip Chevron, reproduced by kind permission of Perfect Songs Ltd.

'Quiet Day' by Strangelove, words and music by Alex Lee, John Langley, Patrick Duff, Joe Allen and Julian Poole, © 1993,

Joel Lane was the author of two novels, *From Blue to Black* and *The Blue Mask*; several short story collections, *The Earth Wire*, *The Lost District*, *The Terrible Changes*, *Do Not Pass Go*, *Where Furnaces Burn*, *The Anniversary of Never* and *Scar City*; a novella, *The Witnesses Are Gone*; and four volumes of poetry, *The Edge of the Screen*, *Trouble in the Heartland*, *The Autumn Myth* and *Instinct*. He edited three anthologies of short stories, *Birmingham Noir* (with Steve Bishop), *Beneath the Ground* and *Never Again* (with Allyson Bird). He won an Eric Gregory Award, two British Fantasy Awards and a World Fantasy Award. Born in Exeter in 1963, he lived most of his life in Birmingham, where he died in 2013.

INFLUX PRESS

Influx Press is an independent publisher based in London, committed to publishing innovative and challenging literature from across the UK and beyond.

Lifetime supporters: Bob West and Barbara Richards

www.influxpress.com
@Influxpress